VICTORIOUS TROY

VICTORIOUS TROY

OR

THE *HURRYING ANGEL*

BY

JOHN MASEFIELD

NEW YORK

THE MACMILLAN COMPANY

1935

PRINTED IN THE UNITED STATES OF AMERICA
BY THE STRATFORD PRESS, INC., NEW YORK

TO
MY WIFE

NOTE

MANY seamen now living will remember cases in which sailing-ships dismasted, or left without officers, were brought to port by boys. I have talked with one of these boys, and have seen the portrait of another. Their deeds are among the glories of their profession.

The *Hurrying Angel* and her crew are entirely imaginary. No reference is made in this book to any existing ship or living seaman. I have tried only to make an image of what seamen have done, when there was "Hell to pay and no pitch hot."

JOHN MASEFIELD.

VICTORIOUS TROY

IT WAS a wild afternoon in the South Pacific in the late summer (late February there) of 1922. The full-rigged ship, the *Hurrying Angel,* was running uneasily, under reduced canvas, homeward-bound with grain from Melbourne. Away astern and on her starboard quarter, to the north and east, the sky was dirty and dark, livid above the darkness, and plumey above the glare, with angry, whitish manes and smudges swiftly changing. The wind was freshening with squalls of rain; the sea was rising, somewhat confusedly; the sun, such as he was, now about to die in an evil heaven, was a sightless eye of paleness surrounded by a halo. In the air there was some quality beside that of menace which warred upon the body and the soul, giving to the one an irritable touchiness and to the other a sense of dread.

To Dick Pomfret, the senior apprentice, who was at the wheel, this sense of dread had come before, more than once, as a storm-signal. He put it down to some effect of changing atmospheric pressure on the skin and took it to be a useful warning. Certainly, ugly weather was coming up, with a nasty lumping following sea which made her steer wild. Throughout his trick it had been worsening.

He was a lad in his third year at sea. He was of the middle height, five feet eight inches, strongly built, nearly eighteen years old, with black hair and eyebrows, a broad, smiling mouth, and a face always pale, even under its tan.

His lips moved a little as he steered, and sometimes wried as a kick of the wheel gave him as much as he could manage. His eye roved aloft to the straining topsails above him, then along the poop to the rail, where the Old Man, Captain Robin Battler Cobb, was sucking a cigar, with an eye now upon the sails, now upon the sky astern. The Mate, whose watch it was, had gone forward with the watch to get a small pull on the foretack, and similar matters.

To Dick Pomfret steering there, the scene was familiar enough. He had been nearly two years in the *Hurrying Angel;* he had steered her throughout that time, taking his regular trick, in fair weather and foul. He had often seen her like this, running rather wild before a lumping, following sea, snarling, whining and complaining, putting her snout down into it, then rising, dripping, and shearing on again, with the sea white from her passing. She was at her best point of sailing with the wind on her quarter. She was now doing nine; she had done eleven and twelve earlier in the day, but they had shortened her down when the Mate's watch came on deck at noon. Now she had a reef in each of her three upper topsails, and the thin, dark, wet ribbon of the main lower topgallant, bellied stiff on long sheets, above the main topsail yard; her foresail was still set; her mainsail had been stowed to ease her.

It was plain to all hands that she had too much on her, but they understood her Captain's wish to drive her. It was the first plentiful fair wind after weeks of failing Trades, calms and light airs. They were in what the newspapers called the Grain Race; now that the chance came her Captain took it. She had a lot too much after sail upon her, she was burying her bow and would be all the better with the two mizen topsails and the main topgallant-sail away, but Dick knew that the Old Man would hang on to them till one of them went to glory.

When she lurched down at a descend, just before the spray went in a sheet over her fo'c's'le-head, Dick would have a fair view of the weather main deck as far as the straining foresail. She gave a great impression of power, and had still some glimpses of grace, though like all the ships of her time she had come down in the world since cheapness had become the word. When she had been built at Liverpool in the late eighteen-nineties, she had been a fine clipper-ship, with painted ports, a main skysail yard, and the look of a queen. She had made some good passages, to Australia, with passengers and general cargo, before coming down in the world.

Like many other ships, she had suffered from the competition: there were too many ships, and not enough prosperity, too many nations trading and only the moment's penny to buy with: she was presently sold to plain businessmen who considered themselves efficient. Her painted ports were the first things sacrificed: then her masts were standardized, and her royal and skysail poles struck. She was now what sailors called "bald-headed," with double topgallants on each mast, nothing above them; at the same time, her ratlines had been scrapped and tarred battens shipped instead.

Dick, who had not seen sailing ships in the days of their glory, did not know how much beauty had been rent from her. Old sailors at Melbourne had looked at her, spat, and muttered "parish-rigged." He thought of this as he steered, and muttered that with a small crew you *had* to be parish-rigged. Of course, she was not now at her best; she was homeward-bound, and had not yet been smartened for home: she was dingy; her black hull was all raddled and rotched with rust; her dull yellow masts and yards looked dirty, her bulwarks, deckhouses and boats, now painted pale green, picked out in white, needed sand and canvas and a new coat.

"Still," Dick thought, "there's something about her. Her bold, flaring sheer gives her a real clipper look."

He took in all her deck as she dived, the long, full poop, the half-deck for the boys just abaft the main-mast, with the boats on skids one to each side of it, the big fo'c's'le abaft the foremast, with more boats on chocks, and the galley-funnel trailing sparks; the little donkey-house beyond it, and the short topgallant fo'c's'le just beyond that. He had a glimpse of old Mr. Duckswich, the Mate, straddled forward, in the opening of the topgallant fo'c's'le; he was staring aloft while his watch took a pull of something. "Poor old chap," Dick thought.

The Captain did not approve of old Mr. Duckswich, and made his disapproval known. From the Captain's look, Dick judged that even now he was watching for some chance to interfere.

"Savage devil," Dick thought. "Why can't he leave the poor old chap alone? He's as good a seaman as himself any day."

However, that in itself was sufficient cause of war.

The Captain was usually known as the Battler or Battler Bill. He was a man of rude energy, with much ignorance and intolerance. He was sanguine-faced, with a grizzled hair and beard. He had a malignant look in the eye when displeased; he could be cutting in sarcasm; he could be a devil. Even when not displeased, he was rude, imperious and overbearing to most people. He was unforgiving. "All bunk," he would say, "all this forgiving your enemies. Who began it? Answer me that. I say, rub their noses in the mud, then wring their necks." He had served all through the War in the Narrow Seas, in drifters and transports, and had had the chance he had longed for towards the end, when he sank a U-boat by gunfire. After the War, he got back into sail, not because he preferred it, but because the chance was given to him.

The War had taken toll of him. The long strain of nights in mined areas watching for submarines had given him the habit of taking nips to freshen his hawse. He now took a good many nips. For some days together, he might hold off and take none, "so that he would enjoy it more," then he would open up a couple of new bottles and start to go over the Bay.

From the manner in which he hung on to his sail, Dick judged that he was well over the Bay at this moment, and that he, as helmsman, had better watch his tip or he would get it in the neck. Somebody always got it on these occasions, never justly, which made the *Hurrying Angel* a less happy ship than she might have been.

A gust of greater venom than usual caught the Captain's cigar and whisked the sparks from it; he turned, sucking and chewing the stub, to look at Dick's steering. Something in the lad's moving mouth and flying hair made him step from the poop-rail to him.

"How is she?" he asked.

"Jumping about a bit, sir."

"Is she griping?"

"She is a bit, sir."

"You young devil," the Captain said, "you are chewing tobacco again."

"No, sir."

"The hell with 'no, sir.' I have been watching you the last five minutes. Now don't swallow it: open your mouth."

The helmsman opened his mouth and showed a very good set of teeth; there was no quid of tobacco among them.

"Swallowed it, have you, hey? No. What's that in your mouth there?" the Captain said. "I will hold her while you take it out."

The boy produced from his mouth a single clove, rather the worse for wear.

"You young devil," the Captain said. "Where did you get the clove? You've been robbing my pantry."

"No, sir," the boy said. "The Steward gave me a few cloves for helping him stone his raisins."

"Ah," said the Captain, "and you chewed and chewed, meaning to fool me. You knew I should think that you were chewing tobacco, didn't you, you young limb? Why don't you wear a hat when you're steering?"

"I lost my last overboard this afternoon, sir. I was going to come aft to ask for one this evening."

"You see what it is," the Captain said, "that's lumping up astern there?"

"Yes, sir."

"What is it, then?"

"Bad weather, sir."

"Bad weather be damned. It's the first fair slant since Melbourne. What would you do if you were in command of her?"

"Look at the barometer, sir."

"Barometer be damned."

"Yes, sir."

"What's that you say?"

"No, sir."

"Don't you try to come the old soldier over me, boy."

"No, sir."

"Then I suppose you'd look in your book, after looking at the barometer, and call all hands, and say, 'My lads, we're in for some blowy weather by the look of things, but you stick by me, my lads, and they'll drink our healths at Lloyd's when we reach England.' You and your barometer and your book. I knew the author of your book. He knew no more about the sea than my maiden aunt; no, less."

The Old Man snorted and moved away.

He had been dead to windward of Dick during their talk, so that Dick had caught a warm whiff of spirits, and knew that the Captain "had a drop taken." "You could tell he'd been lunching," was the crew's phrase.

His bitterness about Dick's book was a continual puzzle to the boys, who put it down to a general loathing for any work of intelligence. It had begun thus. Once in the passage out he had visited the half-deck to see if the boys had any indecent books or photographs. "I'll skelp the life out of any of you that has as much as one," he had said, though the chances are that he would not have destroyed any had he found them. He had found nothing of the sort, of course, the boys were much too cautious, but in his search he had found among Dick's books a copy of Gilbert Topsell's *Laws of Storms*.

"Ha, see," he had said, "Topsell's *Laws of Storms,* the damnedest, silliest stuff that ever was put together. I knew that Topsell. He was the damnedest, silliest thing that ever got a certificate. Look at the stuff. All this about D.Q. and S.Q. He knew no more about storms than I do about McGinty's tart. That's the way they teach sailors nowadays, all out of a book. I wish you'd seen what sailorizing was in my young days. Sailors were men, then, let me tell you. They learned about storms from God Almighty, not out of a damned book, let me tell you. Did you ever see a storm, a real storm, a Western Ocean Hurricane?"

"No, sir," Dick had said.

" 'No, sir'," he had mimicked. "Well, when you do, you'll be hit so hard you'll think you've been shot by a buzz-saw. You won't turn to page thirty to find which way the wind blows. No. You'll be on deck with all hands trying to save masts and ship. *Laws* of storms, I'd like to

have Gilbert Topsell with me in one of those. Any Law
he could find in it he could have for his tea," etc., etc.

He had talked of the book at intervals in this strain ever
since.

Old Duckswich, the Mate, came aft from his job forward.

Dick thought, "Now, probably, there'll be a row. The
Old Man will swear at him for something."

However, the time was not yet ripe seemingly. The
Old Man glared at his Mate, with contempt and bitter dis-
like, but did not speak.

The Mate came up to the wheel, and said kindly, "Ha,
Pomfret, boy; got your hands full?"

"Yes, sir," Dick said.

"Well, keep hold of her. You'll soon be relieved."

He watched the steering, eyeing now the compass, then
the sails. He stared very hard astern at the darkness to
windward, moved over to the Captain, who was now by
the mizen rigging, jerked his thumb over his shoulder and
said:

"Looks like a bit of dirt, sir."

"It'll be nothing, Mister; not even a flick," the Old Man
answered.

"She's griping a bit, sir."

"It don't hurt her any," the Old Man said. "Let's use
wind when we've got it, for God's sake."

The Mate knew very well that he was near an explosion, however, he risked another match.

"The glass is down again, sir," he said.

"It's all the damned thing does," the Captain answered, "to go up and down."

The Mate edged away, walked to the poop-rail, and called:

"Heave the log, there."

The two other boys of Dick's watch, Bill Guller and Christopher Pillows, came hurriedly up the lee ladder, brought out reel and glass, and hove the log from Dick's side.

"What's she doing, Mister?" the Captain asked.

"Nine, sir."

"She ought to be doing more."

"There's a bit of swell lumping up, sir," the Mate said, "and she's griping a bit."

The Old Man didn't answer this, but looked to windward, looked again at the upper sails and went into his charthouse, which stood on the poop directly abaft the mizen-mast. The Mate stood by Dick for a moment, watching his steering.

"She gives you all you can do, boy?"

"Yes, sir." As helmsman, he was keeping the time by watching the clock through the cabin skylight. "It is One Bell, sir," he reported.

"Make One Bell, there," the Mate called.

Christopher Pillows struck the poop-bell: the fo'c's'le bell repeated it: Dick as he steered presently heard Pillows' voice rousing the Second Mate in the cabin-alley, then calling the other two boys in the half-deck. Someone with a bellowing voice called the watch below in the fo'c's'le.

"Thank the Lord," he muttered, "only another ten minutes before I'm relieved."

He was hot and aching from the hard work of the trick. What was worse, he felt queer and rather frightened, he could not say why. He told himself that he was not feeling well, yet it was not illness, it was a foreboding.

He began to say to himself, "I do wish they'd take this after sail off her. I do wish they'd take this after sail off her. Why is he running her like this, shoving her bows down?"

He repeated this over and over again, with the thought, "Of course, what is really the matter with me is that I've got a touch of fever. I'm just a scrap lightheaded. I was bareheaded aloft there in the sun when we shortened down: it was very hot then. Perhaps I got a touch of sun; a little touch; nothing very much; just knocked out my clutch; its little way is such; it's made me rather Dutch; a little tiny touch, on head without a hutch. I wish he'd shorten her down; she's steering as wild as a cow in the bull-patch, she's burying her bow, as wild as a cow, he ought to furl them now."

Somehow, in the last half-hour, the air had changed its quality, so that the ship looked more real than she had ever looked before. He could not account for this. "It isn't really so," he muttered. And yet, when he looked again, he was sure that it was so. The great lurching, straining fabric had taken on intensity. "She *is* more real," he muttered. "She has become so important."

Perhaps it was the queer look of the heaven above her that made her strange: the sky was now overcast with a

haze which looked as though a sandstorm were coming.
In the darkness away to windward the colour was deeper
than in the zenith; away to leeward it was still pale; though
all was tinged with it. Under this sky, the sea had taken a
new colour, like claret in the hollows, like burnt clinker in
the hills. Against the sea and sky the ship moved with an
intensity that seemed terrible.

"She is how a Will looks," Dick muttered; "all selfish
and set and utterly regardless: but I must be batty to be
thinking this kind of thing."

Yet he continued to think that kind of thing, and to
mutter that the time was no longer passing, and that he
must have come into eternity, for the minutes stretched on,
though One Bell had gone long ago. Another thing which
struck him was that the ship was enormous. That great
sweeping sheer of hull bowing down and crashing into the
waters must be more than 1475 tons, as stamped on the
brass plate on her capstan.

"She must be 14,750 tons," he muttered, "and those great
yards and masts were put up by giants, and secured by
other giants, who put those great battens across the shrouds,
and stretched those sails of old iron."

Very soon he found himself saying, "Of course, she isn't
a ship at all: she never was a ship: she is really a Roc or
Sea-Bird, or else a Sea-Devil, and we are little impulses in
her will or mites in her feathers. Presently she will get up,
out of the sea, and scream, and fly away to some crag as big
as Aconcagua, and perch there with anchory talons that
could grip whales."

Christopher Pillows signalled to him at this point from

the lee side of the poop, to show that he wished to know if it were now Eight Bells. As it was within one minute of four o'clock, he nodded; Kit reported it to the Mate and at once made it. The four double strokes were repeated on the bell forward; Mr. Dudley MacLerrinnan, the Second Mate, swung himself up the poop ladder to take over from Mr. Duckswich. "Dudley MacPorridge," as the boys called him, was the biggest and strongest man on board.

Dick watched his great, slow, easy bulk lean over the poop-rail to survey his watch as they gathered to the muster. He liked Dudley Mac, as a very fine man and sailor. This time, he found himself saying:

"He isn't a man at all, really, but a giant from the old time. It would be terrible, if he started to break things."

Somehow, there was an instant's delay in the calling of the port watch muster by Mr. Duckswich. The delay was almost more than Dick could bear.

"Why can't they begin?" he muttered. "It is so frightfully important. It is almost more important than the roll call on the last day."

He watched the two officers standing there together. They were talking about the weather, that was plain. He noted specially the Mate, Mr. Duckswich, generally called "the Duck," a slow, broken, kind old sailor, whose sad face was very white, seamed and resigned, as he wearily watched the scene. He was famed to have been a merchant in a small way before the War, with all his savings in a small coasting steamer, which had come to grief while improperly insured. Early in the War, he had gone back to sea in a collier, which broke down and went ashore in severe, blind weather near the Lizard. He himself came ashore with a broken thigh, which had left him permanently lame.

"Poor old chap," Dick thought. "He has nothing but the workhouse to look forward to: and it can't be long before it comes."

The names of the Mate's watch began to sound. As each was called, Dick's mind made a kind of image of the man with comment, thus:

Barty Berrow. "Here, sir." A short, slow, powerful man, without many brains, but a good seaman.

Will Aylton. "Here, sir." A very fine seaman, as strong as Barty, and much cleverer.

Evesbatch (Kruger Evesbatch). "Here, sir." A dangerous sort of man, old pugilist, crook and chucker, under suspicion of a man-killing.

Staplow (Sock Staplow). "Here, sir." A good seaman, strong, quick, active, in the line in the War and wanting never to see mud again. Thought by some, from his manner, to be a gentleman's son, i.e. a bastard; supposed by the half-deck to have been in the sock department in a haberdashery; hence the nickname Sock, or Socks Forward.

Wallers (Nab Wallers). "Here, sir." An elderly man, who had dyed his hair before going to the shipping office to try for a ship, and was now snowy like a patriarch. A fair seaman, with much skill as a sailmaker, but old.

Cradley (Nick Cradley). "Here, sir." A good-humoured,
pleasant, smiling, red-faced man, with blue eyes, and a
very small nose, which looked as if it had been flat-
tened-in by a blow: one of the most agreeable men on
board: he sang, and played a whistle.

Pencome (Mat, or Harry, or Penk). "Here, sir." A dark,
melancholy-looking, handsome man, aged about 23,
who was supposed to have come to sea owing to a love-
affair.

These seven were the watch; after their names came the
names of the boys.

Pomfret. "At the wheel, sir," this in Christopher Pillows'
voice.

Guller (Bill). "Here, sir." A lad of seventeen, who
looked like a foreigner's caricature of an Englishman,
being hatchet-faced and pale, with prominent front
teeth and a wide mouth. As he had been growing
since he left home, he had grown himself out of his
clothes at knees and ankles. He was a somewhat lawless customer ashore, but a good seaman, eager to do
all things smartly. He was a very smart hand aloft,
though he growled a good deal. Like Dick and some
of the other lads, he was a *Conway* boy.

Pillows (Christopher, or Kit Pillow-Slip). "Here, sir."
An alert-looking, yet really foolish lad, with bright
blue eyes and flaming red hair. He was a creature of
great good nature, who took what came and did what

he was told. He neither liked nor disliked the sea: there he was at it, because someone had suggested it; there he would stay till someone suggested something else. He had a little, faint gift of mimicry, with which he would sometimes slyly take off the Old Man, or old Duckswich. He also played on a whistle a part of a tune, which he said was called "I sat by my fireside a-sighing." In this, though he would begin with much confidence, he always broke down between the fourteenth and seventeenth notes.

This ended the list of the Port Watch: Dick heard the old Boatswain, William Purple, clear his throat, spit, and begin upon the Starboard Watch. Old Purple was a truculent-looking ruffian, a good seaman, slow from age, who was savage with the worse members of the crew, because the better ones were better seamen than himself. He had been in the Navy in his youth (in the 'seventies), had deserted in a Pacific port, and had lived for a time as a crimp's slugger in San Francisco, till the crimp, wearying of his jaw, had drugged him and shipped him foreign. Since then, he had been at sea in sail, usually as boatswain in four-masted barques, to the West Coast, or the round voyage, ballast to New York, oil to Japan, ballast to Portland, and grain, or timber, home. He was a man of great strength, rough as a bear, surly, sour, and apt to bully, very vain of his seamanship, which had been well taught to him in the best school, and intolerant of the methods of the service to which life had brought him. In port, he used to hire a room, into which he would lock himself, with half a dozen bottles of gin, and out of which he would totter an hour before his leave was up.

"Alfrick," his querulous, husky voice called, and Jim Alfrick answered.

Jim was the best man on board, the only good man in Dudley Mac's watch. He was of the very pick of the prime seamen of his time, a big, spare, quiet, civil-spoken man, from a village in the Southern Cotswolds, where his father had been, and still was, a shepherd. Jim was about fifty years old. He had never had any ambition to rise in his profession. Having no learning more than the elements of reading and writing, he had never "gone to school" to try to pass for second mate. He had sometimes been a boatswain in a ship for three or four years together, till a change of captains sent him back to the fo'c's'le. In the War, he had been mainly in steamers in the Atlantic trade, where he had had some close calls. He had gone back to sailing ships after the War because he understood their ways and liked them. As a helmsman and a practical seaman he had no peer anywhere. Dick had often thought that if the ship were ever in danger, Alfrick would be the one certain help. Jim was always a clean-shaven man. He had a sailor's sallow face, and look of quiet power; brown hair that seemed to have been bleached by the sun and salt water to a lustreless grizzle; and bushy eyebrows. There was something in his walk, voice and bearing which made all feel that here was somebody vital.

"Torrent," the Boatswain called.

"Here, sir," a pleasant voice answered.

This was "Niagara," or "Zambesi," or "Lodore" Torrent,

who, as Dick knew, would presently relieve him at the wheel. Niagara was a quiet, hard-working man, still young, though prematurely grey and wrinkled. His grizzled hair was thick, coarse and curling. His face was yellow, like old bone, and seamed all over with deep lines. He came from a horsey stock; his father had been a groom. He had been in the cavalry in the War, sometimes dismounted in the trenches, sometimes going up with stores after dark. He had kept of the War a horror of darkness with the star shells going up and down; a memory of two officers, one good, the other bad; a memory of several horses and mules; and a repertory of the choruses of songs, which he often sang to himself. He had married in 1916 in the one leave he had had from the front, and had come to sea soon after leaving the Army because his wife was a terror. Horses were the things he most loved; he thought that some day he would come ashore somewhere, to see if he could get a job with horses, though he was much afraid that his wife would come to know wherever he got to. He liked the sea, because there he was free from her. He did not know why men married, when they could be so happy working with horses. He had had a horse called Tony-Anna at Netheravon, which would do anything for him, kneel down, roll over, and take a lump of sugar from his lips. Often he thought of Tony-Anna till the tears ran down his cheeks. He was always very neat and spruce in his dress. He wore a pair of mutton-chop whiskers always neatly trimmed. He was a very neat hand with paints and brushes; he was always put on to do the fancy work on the ship's boats and life-belts. He was now in his fourth year at sea.

"Suckley," the Boatswain called, (Peter). "Here, sir." An active, dare-devil man, all wire and whipcord, ever forward and quick on his feet. His eyes were small, dark, quick, and very bright. He was still only twenty-two, but had contrived to see something of the War in North Sea drifters. He had a green flannel coat (a blazer), which he wore in the tropics on Sundays. Some people called him "Paddy," because of this.

"Botloe" (Ed Botloe). "Here, sir." A chubby little chap, pretty strong and stuggy, with a head quite square in front, quite round at the back. He was wilful and not very intelligent. He believed that if a man stood in a boat and pulled the painter the boat would move, and that, therefore, ships should be fitted with hawsers secured to their sterns, so that the crews standing on deck and heaving on these would force the ship forward. He had been a fruiterer's lad until the War; the War had given him a taste for wider spaces; he knew no seamanship, but did his jobs and saw something of the world.

"Loach" (Ob or Obbie Loach). "Here, sir." A spare, short, silent, sinister man, who looked sideways at those who spoke to him, and answered out of the corners of his mouth. As he also seemed to breathe out of the corners of his nostrils, he gave a very sideways effect generally. What went on in the frontways parts of him meanwhile was not so clear. Dick thought that the man had been knocked or blown sideways by something terrible in the War; and that all the rest of him was a silent, brooding anger against the powers which had made such blowing possible. He gave an impression of nursing a strength within him for some chance of striking back at something which might be taken as the enemy. He did not talk of his past. He had been a soldier during the War, and had come to sea as a sailor for the first time after the peace.

"Kempley" (Bert, or Kempenfelt). "Here, sir." A big, burly, powerful, slow-witted, patient and very likeable man, useful because of his strength to any watch, but of exasperating stupidity. Orders had to be repeated to him three times; he would then usually do the wrong thing if the officer took his eyes off him. He had a charming, wistful, smiling face, with blue, wandering eyes, which made one feel that he was not quite sane. He had been at sea all his life and was now well over sixty. He had been torpedoed twice during the War. He was a remarkable man, with a natural skill in music and the use of tools. He used to make and play stringed instruments of his own invention, some of them like banjos, others like fiddles. He played the whistle by ear, and sang a sweet tenor; he knew only one song, about a wood-dove and a peacock, (a very moral song).

"Morritz" (Harry, or Lefty Morrissey). "Here, sir." A bad specimen from some unknown part of Central Europe, who had passed some years with a lawless company in Chicago, and had then returned to Europe with the American Army, which he had contrived to desert somewhere after the peace. He had been found, stowed-away, in the 'tween-decks, two days after leaving Melbourne, and had been signed-on, as O.S. at no wages. He was a crook by instinct and by training; he loved evil. He diffused about him a flavour of secret vindictive murder that was very terrible. Dudley Mac had thrashed him once for lip, and had never since allowed the man to get behind him. "He might be handy with a knife, yon wee buckshot," he had said. Lefty was a small man, with a slobbery, wide mouth, big ears, and little snake's eyes. The Old Man had been furious at finding him on board, for it had been his boast that the ship carried an all-British crew.

This ended the list of the men of the Starboard Watch; the Boatswain called the two boys, Rue and Newbarn.

Aloysius Rue was the oldest lad in the half-deck; he was six months older than Dick, but had not been quite so long at sea. He was a Roman Catholic. He was of a robust build, with black hair and eyes and very red cheeks. He was a cheery, merry-hearted, high-spirited lad, the best of good shipmates, but not much of a sailor. He had been sent to sea to cure some supposed, or feared, frailty in his chest. As this was now held to be cured, he was about to leave the sea and settle ashore, on his father's small estate in Sussex. He was a lad of more breeding and reading than the others. He was liked, because of his merry good-temper. Once, at dinner in the cabin, when the Captain had been laying down the law about Roman Catholics, he had answered back with such wit and knowledge that the Captain had ordered him out on deck; "no Popish hell-work here, my lad. You've come to the wrong shop, you'll find."

Ed Newbarn was a very different type of boy. He had come to sea because he would have been miserable any-where else; he had been salted and signed to the sea from earliest infancy. He had begun as a pirate (stealing boats for a row or sail) at a very early age; and had gone to the *Conway* at thirteen. Here, in a few weeks, he had become salter than the sea. He had learned to chew tobacco in his first term: in his second, he had been tattooed on hands, arms and chest. He always said that he was a damned ass to mark himself thus, but he was very proud of the tat-tooings, crude as they were. His marks were: big blue rings round three fingers of each hand, done by himself in gunpowder; on the back of his right hand, a foul anchor; on the back of his left hand, the Union Jack, both done at the same time, in India ink, at a shilling a hand, by an artist in a pub in Paradise Street; on his forearms, he had designs of crossed flags, done for a plug of tobacco an arm by a fellow foretopman. In Melbourne, an artist had worked a big heart transfixed with an arrow, in blue, across his chest. Drops of blood and the motto "For Polly" had been added, in red, with a very chaste effect, of which he was more than proud, though the artist had been expensive, and the red in "taking" had given him days and nights of agony. His pride was to strip for a wash on the

open deck so that the Mate or Captain might see these
things and perhaps ask:

"Who the hell is Polly?"

He would answer, "My best girl, sir."

Then perhaps the answer would come, "Well, she's got
a young fool for her beau, if you ask me, marking yourself like that. You go straight, son, and watch your step,
for if you kick over the traces now, the police will soon put
salt on to your tail. No disguise will help you now."

His father was a sea-captain, whom he seldom saw; his
mother, who found him a handful, was glad to have him
away from home.

He could not work the simplest problem in navigation.
"I'll learn all that at a crammer's," he said, "when I have
to." He was a glutton for knowledge of practical seamanship. He was always begging the oldest seamen to show
him how to make fancy mats, knots and sennits; how to
work shackles, make fenders for boats, or put coach mat-
ting over staunchions. He had no particular friend in the
half-deck; he needed something much salter than the half-
deck; he wanted to be a man in a fo'c's'le, with the tough-
est old shellbacks gathered about him, exchanging oaths,
tales of the sea and methods of fitting gear. He had the
seaman's build, being short and broad. He was not yet
sixteen, but the sea had given him the face of a man of
thirty. He was as tough and pickled as the beef in the
harness-casks. His favourite companion was Barty Berrow, whose oaths he used when vexed. The chances
seemed to be, that when he was as old as Barty he would
be much such another, handling ropes on deck, using the

same oaths, spinning the same yarns, and having nothing to show for forty years at sea, but a dungaree-suit and a plug of tobacco bitten off at the end.

"Relieve the wheel," Mr. Duckswich called.

Niagara Torrent, in oilskins, came clattering up the lee ladder, and across to the wheel. He grinned at Dick and took the course and the spokes from him. Mr. MacLerrinnan moved up to the wheel.

"Stay at the lee wheel just a moment, Pomfret," he ordered, "till Torrent's got the hang of herr."

Dick slipped across the wheel to the lee spokes. Mr. MacLerrinnan stood by them.

"How is she?" he asked.

"Steering wild as a kite, sir," Dick answered.

"Ye'll want to mind yeir tip, Torrent," Mr. MacLerrinnan said in his very slow grave Scotch voice. "Don't let herr get away from ye."

"No, sir," Torrent answered.

Mr. MacLerrinnan stood beside them watching the steering and eyeing the sails; presently he moved forward a few steps. Dick cursed at not being relieved. Why the devil couldn't Dudley Mac put one of his own watch to the lee wheel?

"She's a handful," Torrent said; "she really is."

Dick noticed then, for the first time, that Torrent's left hand, on the next spoke to his own right hand, bore a wedding ring.

"Are you married, Torrent?" he asked.

"Oh yes," Torrent said. "I've been married six years;

but I don't live at home. I got married just before the
Somme . . . 1916. Are you married?"

"No such luck," Dick said.

"Sometimes it isn't such luck," Torrent said.

Mr. MacLerrinnan came up to the wheel.

"Ye've got herr, now, Torrent. Run away with ye, Pomfret. . . . And if ye'll nip into my cabin ye'll find a peppermint for yeir trouble."

That was like Mr. MacLerrinnan. He would sometimes
press a little hard on a fellow, as here, keeping him from
his relief, but then immediately afterwards, he would make
it up in some way, as here, with this peppermint. Dick
thanked him. He knew the peppermint tin of old.

As he moved away to go below, old Mr. Duckswich
called to the Second Mate and jerked his thumb to windward:

"There'll be a good big push, behind yonder packet, by
my way of it."

The words thrust into Dick's brain like something sharp
and shrill.

"A push behind the packet," he muttered to himself.
"A push behind the packet. Which is push and which is
packet? I wish he wouldn't try to scare a chap. . . . I've
got a touch of sun; there's no doubt of that."

Certainly, he did feel queer as he went down the lee ladder to the deck; apart from the feeling that he had been
in a fight his skin was all prickly and tickly as though he
had developed "prickly heat"; all about him, ship, sea and
sky seemed fraught with portent; and there was no doubt
that he was scared. He longed to run away and hide. A

couple of years before, he had had a nasty wound in the shoulder, from Kit Pillows dropping a marlinespike into him from just above him. It had been healed for the last twenty-one months, yet it was now so smarting that he had to feel the scar to make sure that it had not broken out again.

At the foot of the ladder at the lamp-room door he met Newbarn, who was bearing a hand with Kempley at the repair of one of the side-light lamps. They were about to solder some loosened metal, but were not talking about the job in hand. As their officer was on the poop, where he could not see them, and the Boatswain was forward on another job, paying no heed to them, Newbarn was discussing with the old A.B. the lead of the crojick and mizen-topsail braces. There they stood, each with a bit of oily brass, and a black rag, gossiping at the lamp-room door.

There had been a good deal of talk on board about the lead of the crojick and mizen-topsail braces. Usually, those braces had been led to the doublings just below the main-mast head, and thence down on deck to the main bitts. On the passage out to Melbourne, Dudley Mac, who was a scholar in his profession, and a student of ancient seamanship, had mentioned at dinner that the early lead had been to blocks on the mizen and mizen-topmast stays, or, in some cases, when the gaff was a standing-gaff, to blocks at the gaff's end. He had mentioned the matter as a thing of some professional interest, and roused a little discussion. Old Mr. Duckswich had said that the lead to the gaff could only have served for light yards of very small spread, and that the lead to the stays must have put an unwarranted

extra strain on them. Dudley Mac had answered (again as
a philosopher who had given a great deal of thought to
the problem) that he had always thought that the present
lead, to the main-mast head or just below it, put the wrong
kind of strain on the collar of the main stay, and that he
wanted to work out the exact strain they put upon it; because it seemed to him that the strain would come better
a good deal lower down, possibly below the futtock-bands.
Duckswich had pondered a moment, and had then said
that the mainmast head and its doublings were strong
enough to take any strain that the mizen braces could possibly put on them, and that they were certainly much
stronger than the place lower down, because the futtock-
bands took the strain of the topmast rigging, and something of the push of the mainsail. It had been a friendly
professional talk. Old Duckswich had enjoyed it, and had
had much pleasure later in looking at Dudley Mac's copy
of d'Arcy Lever's *Seamanship,* which showed the ancient
fitting in an engraving.

Unfortunately, the Captain had been present. He had
said nothing at the time, but had found in the talk a
chance of wounding his chief officer. In Melbourne, he
had had an iron hoop clamped to his mainmast, at the
futtock-band, with blocks hooked to it for the lower mizen
braces. On setting sail from Port Phillip Heads, he had
ordered Mr. Duckswich to lead his crojick and mizen-
topsail braces through these. It was a worse lead for the
upper yard; and perhaps a slightly better lead for the
lower yards. Mr. Duckswich knew that it was ordered because it countered his opinion. He shifted the lead with

an ill grace; but was ready to admit that the lower yard lead was an improvement. If he had been cleverer, he would have praised the lead as a vast improvement and blessed Dudley Mac in public for bringing it to be. Had he done this, the Captain would have shifted it within an hour. Instead, however, Mr. Duckswich took the line that the new lead made the upper topsail brace a downhaul, not a brace at all. The Captain would not answer immediately, but would presently say:

"Mr. MacLerrinnan, them new leads of yourn for the mizen braces, they'd ought to have been shipped years ago."

All hands knew about the dispute and took sides for or against the Captain. It was debated after each shifting of the trim. Now Newbarn was going into the matter with old, blue-eyed, wandering Kempley, who thought it a poor fitting, but had no reasons for his judgment. Nobody on board knew at that time how important the new lead was to be to them in a few short hours.

"At your leads again?" Dick said. "You can see with half an eye it's a bad lead for the upper yard. You've got one good fitting there: a second topmast stay."

He went into the cabin-alley, and turned to the right to Dudley Mac's cabin, where he helped himself to a peppermint.

It was a snug cabin, just to the port side of the after alleyway. It measured twelve feet by twelve feet. To Dick, it seemed like all that heart could desire; a cabin of one's own, not likely to be flooded, with an empty upper bunk in which to stow bags, a real chest of drawers, that made a settee or sofa, and a shelf high up, wedged tight with books. There was a photograph of Dudley Mac's girl just inside the bunk. She wasn't Dick's idea of a girl, but then, she was a girl, and there was rather a shortage of the article on board. The general verdict of the half-deck was that she was long in the lip and had a chest like a shilling rabbit, but Pillows, who had seen her, denied this.

Dick did not wait half a minute there, for old Duckswich had come down to his cabin, just opposite on the starboard side; he was calling Mince, the Steward, for a cup of hot shaving-water. But for this, Dick would have nipped aft, into the saloon, for a glimpse at the barometer. Instead, he went out on deck to look at the weather there.

"That's God Almighty's barometer," the Old Man used to say, "the weather sky. You fill your head with that, and you'll not need any mercury in a tube, unless you go running the girls."

He had had no chance of looking at God's barometer during the last hours. He had had enough to do to keep the ship on her course, and had had besides, strict orders not to look astern, for the *Hurrying Angel* had no wheelhouse, and the sight of the sea astern in a running ship may upset the bravest.

Dick was interested in weather. He was now feeling so scared, with the sense of something coming, that he wanted to work out the problem of what *was* coming. He had come on deck at noon to find a freshening gale and a big swell coming up on them. While they were shortening down, he had heard old Duckswich say that the glass had dropped a tenth, and Dudley Mac had answered that they could do with a flick after three weeks in a Prevalent High with not enough wind to air the bedding. All through his watch, and especially through his trick at the wheel, the wind had increased in gusts, though blowing true from about north-east, while the swell worsened. He was pretty sure that the swell was two points foul of the wind. All these things had told him much. Now he could look at God's barometer, see what that said, and then work out the sum.

A single glance to windward showed him that there was indeed a packet with a push within it. All the lower heaven was coloured a savage purple, burning, as it were, with an inner anger. From this darkness a redness rose to smear and cover heaven till it all glared. Away ahead, to leeward, a firework of cirrus pushed; the redness following fast upon it kept overtaking it and blotting it. The sea had on her all the menace of the heaven in colour, and a menace the more in the movement of her surface. It was big, ugly, and the colour of old blood. On the surface there was a play of gusts which took the tops off crests and flung them forward, angrily, capriciously, as though some little devil, swimming unseen there, had stricken them off with his hand. Dick watched this for a full minute; he had never seen this sudden, jerky, scattered devilry at play before. After, trying to decide how to describe it and account for it, Dick decided that it looked as though someone far aft were spraying the sea with grape-shot, and that it was caused by violent, sudden down-draughts of upper air. All over the near sea these sudden little savage scutterings came, lifting in each case what seemed like a gallon or so of spray, cutting it with a sudden snap forward and plastering it down into the hollow of the sea from which it rose. He noticed that one or two of the watch on deck, who were making all snug for a flick before clearing up for the nightly wash-down, were as interested as himself, in this new play of the water.

There could be no doubt that something of unusual violence was moving out there beyond the purple.

"It seems to begin with red," he muttered, "then it comes on with purple, and after the purple comes black and destruction."

A fragment of a ballad, half remembered from a terrified reading years before, came up into his mind.

> *"Then first there came the red blood,*
> *And then there came the blue,*
> *And then there came the black blood,*
> *That brought the Life there-to."*

Something with a very black and evil blood was gathering to smite whatever crossed it out there astern. Someone on the other side of the deck, stopping a coil of gear into the port main rigging, quoted the familiar couplet:

> *"When clouds come gathering, quick and fast,*
> *Look out sharp for sail and mast."*

Surely no sailor had quoted those words? They rang and clanged as though they had been intoned to trumpets.

They might have been screamed by some great, shrieking figure in the scud. He looked aloft for such a figure but only saw the topsails, very awful and almost black as they rolled and whined in their rush across the heaven. Here Mr. MacLerrinnan put an end to his havers by ordering in the main topgallant sail and mizen upper topsail. The watch came skating aft to the gear. Dick thought it wiser to hop below to the half-deck to see about supper before all hands were called.

The half-deck of the *Hurrying Angel* was an iron deck-house just abaft the mainmast. It measured sixteen feet long by fourteen broad by eight high. At one time, it had been "certified to accommodate twelve seamen"; the legend still could be read on one of the beams. Before the War the thrifty owners had saved the ship's expenses in sea-men by carrying ten or twelve boys in this half-deck, ten in bunks and two in hammocks, and contriving that each of the ten or twelve, while working as an ordinary seaman, should pay a premium of four or five pounds a year for the privilege. Outwardly, the half-deck was painted pale green, like the other deck-houses. On the top of it, in the space not filled by the mizen-staysail, were a small central sky-light and chocks upon which the ship's two scows, pram and skiff were secured. In heavy weather, one entered the half-deck by the skylight: at other times, the entrance was in the after wall of the house, facing the poop.

As the house stood in the waist at a point frequently deep in water, the coaming at the door was carried high up, two feet six from the deck, nearly to a man's thigh. The door was little more than a half door, and he who entered had to

clamber over the fence. This was a great nuisance, but the
fitting was well designed; without it, the house would have
been swamped twenty times a day whenever a sea ran. As
there were ingenious scupper holes in the sides of the house,
Dick had often thought that the designers of the house must
have made a voyage or two to sea.

As the ship was running almost dry, sending on board
nothing more than a few spirtles of spray from the freeing
ports from time to time, the door of the half-deck was
hooked back, open. Dick clambered over the coaming, lifting his hand automatically to his head as he did so; he had
no hat, but the other two were at supper and old sea-custom
called for the salute.

The half-deck was painted white internally.

"White," the Old Man had always said, "white is the
colour for the boys' house. Then if the young devils start
getting dirty I can see it at a glance and rouse them out in
the watch below and make them sand-and-canvas it."

At present, though very clean, it was in need of repaint-
ing, which was to come to it later in the voyage. The lower
bunks (those certain to be flooded if a sea came in) had been
stricken down into store. There were now only six bunks,
two on each side, two on the forward bulkhead. Dick's
bunk was aft on the port side. There were now only five
bunks in use, as the sixth boy had cleared out in Melbourne to try his luck at the gold-fields. His bunk, opposite Dick's, now contained the white canvas sea-bags of the
other five. Each of the bunks in use had been fitted with
bright blue linen bunk-curtains which hung by brass rings
from stretched nettles.

On each side of the door, against the after bulkhead, was a small table, one for each watch, measuring just four feet by three; it was hinged to the bulkhead and could be let down when not in use, but it was kept up while at sea. It was a tightish fit for three at meals. On the forward bulkhead in the spaces not now filled with bunks were two small water tanks, one for each watch. On each side bulkhead, in the spaces not filled with bunks, was a locker for food, one for each watch. There was no other furnishing or plenishing: no thought had been given to warming or drying: there was not even any recess with hooks in which dripping oilskins could be hung. The boys had been allowed to cleat their sea-chests to the deck to keep them from skating about in heavy weather: this was the one concession which had been made to them, no very great one, seeing that they did the work of ordinary seamen and received no wages, but at most some returned proportion of what they had paid as premiums. The chests made convenient seats at the two tables and elsewhere. The washing basins of the boys (used only every other day) were kept in the spare bunk with the bags. Part of an old mirror nailed to the port bunk standard sufficed for whatever hair-brushing they had to do: at present none of the five boys needed to shave, but sometimes did so in port. The mirror served also for this. The mirror had originally been wrenched in a foray from some penny wash-and-brush-up place in Belfast. It had been so securely nailed to its standard, with long wire nails bent over and beaten in, that no one had thought of stealing it. Only about a third of its glass remained, and even this was marred with that kind of black fox which seems to affect cheap mirrors everywhere. There was no attempt anywhere at decoration. The place was lit after dark, and when the watches were called, by a small binnacle lamp in a little brass lighthouse screwed to the starboard bunk standard. This, like the mirror, had been stolen by some boys in a foray from a yacht in Falmouth and would no doubt be stolen from the ship. It was an excellent lamp, easy to light and to keep alight. As no provision for lighting the half-deck was made by the ship the boys had had to provide this for themselves, and to supply oil for it, which they did, generally, by robbing the lamp-room when the Mate's back was turned.

When the blue bunk curtains were opened, the visitor could see that the bunk of each boy was a sort of little shrine or home. Each boy had a small wooden shelf fixed to the ship's side and fitted with a rim to keep things from rolling off it. Here were stowed pipes, books, tobacco, matches; the photographs of the best and second best girls, the half-made shackle for the chest, a snapshot of a ship or two, and perhaps a relic or so, a knocker wrenched from a door, a policeman's whistle, a bit of coral, part of a shark's jaw or backbone, or a flying fish's wings.

Dick noticed one thing as he clambered into the house, that the steel bulkheads were sweating freely. Drops of condensed moisture were trickling, stopping, gathering way and finally running down them, leaving little tracks on the moist paint. He was used to this kind of thing, but had learned to take it as a sign of worsening weather.

"Come on, foretopman," Guller said, "before the skilly's cold."

He seated himself on the end of his chest, with his back to his bunk. Guller and Kit shared Guller's chest a little further along. It said much for all three of them that they had been living at close quarters there for the greater part of a year and were still able to meet at meals on friendly terms. Dick got along with most people from good-nature, and from his interest in another man's point of view. He was one very hard to ruffle. He had made no attempt to have the mastery in the half-deck, but had received it by tacit consent. Physically he was no stronger than Guller (or Newbarn in the other watch), but both boys knew that he was a better man than either of them, a much better navigator and a far wiser seaman, even though Guller could make a handsomer shackle, and Newbarn had been told that he would always be able to make a living as a sailmaker. It was something pleasant in Dick's nature that made him get along in the half-deck; it was his presence that made the others get along, too.

"What's for supper?" he asked. "What has the chef sent us?"

He knew very well that all that there was for supper was what he hadn't eaten at dinner and didn't want to keep for breakfast. Guller shoved towards him a tin plate on which lay a small piece (about the size of the usual breakfast sausage) of very fat, cold, salt pork, still in its dirty hide. Similar "whacks" of this dainty had been theirs for dinner, but Kit had eaten all his at one sitting, and now supped on ship's biscuit with a little brown sugar. Guller and Dick had saved some of their whacks till this moment. Dick meant to save some of his for breakfast, which was the meal he liked best: Guller was a supper man. There was an old japanned tin bucket on the table. It had been fitted with a wooden lid and painted with the ship's houseflag of alternate blue and white vertical stripes, with the initials T.H., for Theopompous Harker, the owner. This bucket contained bread, or ship's biscuit, now by no means the kind of dainty it had been a year before. In addition to this, there was a big old battered tin coffee pot containing skilly, or a brown, hot liquid, which the crew called "tea" at night, and "coffee" in the morning. A battered square biscuit tin containing the boys' private stores of brown sugar completed the meal. This was now Thursday evening. At the supper of Saturday evening when the week's whacks had been served out there had been a little (liquid) butter, some marmalade, vinegar and mustard, as well as a few dry beans, but growing lads doing hard work and invariably half starved, had finished their week's whacks by Monday at noon.

"That Old Man of ours has been lifting his elbow again," Guller said. "Coo, you could tell his brand of drinking when you got to leeward from him. Just like my aunt's spirit vaults."

"It was about time he took the topgallant off her," Dick said. "She was jumping about like a cat on the tiles."

"He never takes sail off when he's had a drop," Kit said, "and he won't let Mr. Duckswich take it off."

"He'll take off some soon," Dick said. "He'll get more than he wants to-night. I wish I knew what the barometer is doing."

"It's falling," Kit said. "I heard the MacPorridge tell the Duck that she was down a tenth."

Dick drew a circle with his finger on the table and considered for a moment.

"You can see for yourselves," he said, "what we're running full tilt into."

"It's just a bit of a flick," Guller said. "Aylton said the red is volcanic dust from one of these islands which are always going pop."

"Dust be damned," Dick said. "You may tell Aylton to tell you another. You never saw a sky like to-night's, nor did I, but I know very well what it is, and so shall we before we're much older. We're in a cyclone sea in a cyclone season, and that's a cyclone coming, and the Old Man's heading straight across its path just as though it were the South East Trades."

"It may not be a cyclone," Guller said. "What makes you think it's a cyclone?"

"Well, isn't it obvious?" Dick said. "The swell's all over the place, the glass is falling and the wind is rising."

"Yes, but in a cyclone," Kit said, "you'd have the wind shifting. This wind isn't shifting."

"No, because the cyclone's coming straight at us. The swell of the sea's confused, but the wind is true."

"But it can't be true if it's part of a cyclone."

"Wait till we've finished supper," Dick said, "then I'll get out the Manual and show you. If the cyclone comes straight the wind blows true. If you'll just draw a circle you'll see that the wind in front of it must keep across its path."

"Well, why quarrel with the Old Man?" Guller said. "He's running across the path of this one, in front of it. He'll get across and be out of the way of it before Eight Bells to-night."

"Well, let's hope," Dick said. "But as a matter of fact he won't. We've been doing eight to ten, trying to get across; it is doing nearly double that, coming towards us. We're shortened down, now, and shall soon have to snug her right down, and heave her to. All that the Old Man will have done will have been to put his ship right plunk in the worst possible place at the worst possible time."

"Says Captain Pomfret, Fellow of the Meteorological."

"Says anybody of the smallest knowledge."

"Well, it's my belief," Guller said, "that all this talk of laws of storms is simply theory, when all is said. Some fat cove in a club says 'What-ho,' and all the rest say 'What-ho,' but the chap who has to do the work isn't any the better for it; the sea isn't any drier nor the wind less. I'm going to have a smoke and a turn-in, and when the cyclone rages you can call me, Mother dear."

He wiped his knife and fork on the mess-clout, emptied his pannikin, shoved his tin dish across to Kit who was messman for the week, and turned into his bunk, which was on the port side just forward from Dick's. Here he lit his pipe, puffed for half a minute and then fell asleep.

"God help the poor sailors on the sea," Kit said, as he started to clear the table. "I suppose we'll have an all hands job at Eight Bells."

"Or before," Dick answered.

"Me mother always warned me against a roving life," Kit said.

He sluiced his own plate and Guller's plate in a bucket of salt water and dried them with the mess-clout. He stowed the plates in the port locker, with Dick's plate, which still had a bit of pork on it, on the top. He emptied the tin pot into the bucket and hooked it, with the panni-kins, into the locker. Then he went out on deck, emptied the bucket over the side, returned, shoved the empty bucket into the cleats which held it, saw that the breadbarge and sugar tin were firmly chocked on the table, so that no roll of the ship could fetch them away, scraped up a few biscuit crumbs with the sharp of his hand and pitched them out on deck and so finished "clearing away." Usually at this time he tried his hand at his one tune on the whistle or played a kind of Patience which never could be explained or completed.

"It's called Algebra Patience," he would explain, "and nobody ever got it out the first time except Lord Kelvin."

However, to-night, with Guller turned in, the whistle was not to be thought of, and something in the air, or the menace of the storm, kept him from the Patience. He turned into his bunk, and sat there, bent forward, with his legs dangling from the edge.

"Me sister done well in the world," he said, plaintively. "She married the Sergeant Major in our Salvation Army. 'Don't you go to sea,' she says. 'Sailors is sinful; awful; such language; such revolting habits. You come in the Army, along of my Dick, and you'll be a corporal almost

before you know it.' But I was all for Sin in my young
days, and look at me now."

"Chuck it," Dick said. "You'll wake Bill."

Dick was sure that there would be a call for all hands
before the dog-watch was out. He took out his oilskins
and hooked them near his bunkhead, pulled out his sea-
boots and sea-boot hose and laid them in his bunk ready to
put on when called. As there was little chance of much
sleep that night, he slipped off his shoes and turned under
his blankets "all standing"—i.e., in his clothes.

Usually, like other young sailors, he would be in deep
sleep within a minute after turning in: it was not so this
afternoon. He found himself oppressed by the memory of
the sky, and though he did not like to own it, frightened
by it.

"I'm queer, or dotty, or sickening for something," he
thought. "It seems to me that some of the upper atmosphere has come down, or some kind of air unlike any I've
known. I'm all so prickly and so jumpy. They say you
get this kind of feeling before an earthquake. Whatever
happens, it's going to blow an appalling gale. And there
can be no doubt that he's heading straight into it. Old
Duckswich is no good: he's a broken man: the Old Man
just tramples on him. Why doesn't Dudley Mac speak,
though, and tell the Old Man to heave to in time?"

There was no answer to this question; the matter lay
with Destiny. Dick knew, from the work going forward
on deck, that Dudley Mac was alive to the danger and
making ready as far as he was allowed, stopping up gear
and getting extra lashings on to the spare spars. For half

an hour he felt the ship much eased by the taking off of the sail: she was plainly steering more easily and no doubt going faster (from not burying her bow so much). Presently, as he tossed about in his bunk, he knew that there was an end to the ease; she was again overloaded and complaining, thereby making men like himself, who were one with her, overstrained and anxious also.

He took down his Barometer Manual from the shelf, and refreshed his memory with it. There was no doubt that his judgment was right: a cyclone was coming down upon them; they were in the Dangerous Quadrant of it, and standing across the Centre's track. Lying there in his bunk was almost worse than being wrenched to and fro at the wheel; there he was dealing with the situation, here he was waiting for worse to happen. He was angry with the Battler for being so purblind and pigheaded. Of course, the Battler was in what the Press called a race, and had backed his ship to win "for a new hat and a supper at the Pie-House." Of course, he had snatched at a fair wind, and had drunken to its coming till he was drunk. The time dragged on, as though it were no longer time but eternity. His shoulder prickled and tingled, his skin shrank from the tickling of the hairs in the blanket. There was an oppression in the air although it had fallen much colder. The blocks, banging on the mast just outside the house, with their regular thumping clack once a second, only varied when the chain pendant, not the iron blocks, struck, were enough to drive a man mad. Two Bells came, then, after a long age, Three Bells, with the men on deck perhaps a little busier, and the wind and sea a little more vicious.

Certainly, the ship was feeling the weather more and moving with a greater trouble; more water was spurting through her freeing ports and with a greater savagery. Sometimes, too, a sea of some power seethed up, checked, and seemed to snarl as it held back before flinging a spray on deck. Always these sprays fell with a lead-like thud, as of a coil of rope flung down from the pin.

"That is what we ought to be doing," Dick thought, "flinging the ropes from the pin, letting go and cluing up and making all snug."

He had no doubt in his mind that at Four Bells all hands would have to shorten her down to a storm stay-sail. All the noise of storm was already on them, or had his nerve completely gone? Time stood still for an age, while a strange light, as though the ship were on fire, came upon the half-deck skylight and thence on to the bulkheads. Dick sat up and stared at this, thinking that a sail must have caught from a spark from the galley fire. Then he saw that the glow, whatever it was, had nothing to do with light, any more than Hell has, but proceeded from some intensity, of horror, such as he had never before known.

"I must turn out and have a look at this," he muttered.

Whatever it was, it brought with it an uneasiness which was felt both by Kit Pillows and Bill. At the moment of its appearance both were sleeping; now both roused uneasily, drew back their curtains, peered out with blinking eyes, and asked, "What on earth is up?" As they did so One Bell was made aft and repeated forward. Almost on the stroke Aloysius Rue, the stalwart, stumbled in over the coaming.

"Come on, you damned heretics," he cried. "Out you come here; One Bell. What? All turned-in in the dog-watch? Well. Turn out and come and see what's happening."

"What *is* happening?" Dick asked.

"Judgment Day is happening," Aloysius said. "Nothing less, my son; and now you mouldy old Prots will get it in the neck as you deserve. Out you come, you, Bill, and Kit, no more slumber, but rouse and stir. My boys, we're for it. But for me, who belong to the Old Firm, it's 'muy bonito.' It's you filthy heretics that'll do the howling."

"Chuck it, Alley," Bill growled. "Are we shortening sail?"

"Out you come," Rue repeated. "We're flogging the clock for an all-hands job. You're to be on deck in five minutes. Get your oilskins on, muy pronto; out you mizzle. Leg it."

He hove himself over the coaming, back to the deck, and there paused to hook back the door, letting in the glare which made the three boys look at each other curiously: they had seen nothing like it. All three turned out and proceeded to pull on sea-boot-hose and sea-boots.

"Looks like a fine weather sunset and no mistake," Bill said.

"Not much fine weather here, my son," Dick said.

"That's one of the signs given in all the books," Bill answered.

> "*The evening red, the morning grey,*
> *Are certain signs of a fair day.*"

"Yes," Kit cut in.

> *"When evening's grey and morning's red,*
> *Wise sailors stop ashore in bed."*

"We'll wish we were ashore in bed before we're much older," Dick said. "But one thing's sure, we'll see what a cyclone is before we get to bed again."

He pulled on his oilskin trousers over his sea-boots and belted them very tight. He then plucked rope-yarns from the bunch in his belt and with them tied his trousers just below his knees and round his ankles, outside the boots. Then he slipped on his oilskin jacket, clipped it tight at the throat and wrists, buttoned it, fastened his southwester under his chin and went out on deck. When out there it took him half a minute to get the hang of things.

He found the ship weltering on uneasily under too much canvas; she was groaning and whining and cracking in every inch of her. It must have rained heavily, for the gear was dripping and the scuppers still running with it. A full gale of roaring was in her rigging; yet it struck Dick that the noise was somehow more than the wind warranted.

"What the devil is happening to-night?" Dick asked Staplow, who had already come on deck. "There's a noise all round us, as though we were in the middle of a battle-field."

"It sounds a bit like a battlefield," Staplow answered, "except that it's steadier."

Dick could see that it was like enough to a battlefield to

have made Staplow, the old soldier, uneasy. There was no battlefield, of course, that was all absurd, but far away there must be a battlefield, for surely those were guns. He told himself that it was all fancy, yet, on listening again, there came the repeated crashes of great guns. Half a dozen big guns fired one after the other, then batteries in salvo, then a barrage, then drum-fire, then the solitary guns again.

The wind in the rigging came aigu, never ceasing, and the gear flogged; but over all those noises came the distant cannon.

"It's giving warning," Dick thought. "Or am I wrong about that? Doesn't it sound as though the guns had come almost all round us and were firing to get the range? But it can't be cannon, it must be the storm. The roaring comes from the storm and is echoed back from the air all round us. It is blowing already somewhere like the roaring and soon it will be blowing here; and what kind of wind can it be that roars like that?"

He had read in old books of the wind blowing "great guns." Why, the men who made the phrase had never heard a great gun: their biggest was a forty-two-pounder. They had spoken imagining what great guns might be. Somewhere away to windward those great guns were now in battery, millions upon millions of them, and all that noise was the warning, the cry to look out and stand from under, for when the blast fell it would rip steel from rivet, screw from socket and ghost from bone. All Nature was crying "Look out! Look out! This is beyond all my madness. I am coming to blast and gulf and null."

Dick saw that Dudley Mac had stowed the mizen lower topsail. He had not noticed them doing it, so knew that he had had a brief sleep while in his bunk. It was all to the good that it was in, of course. Dudley Mac had been clever to get it in without splitting, but then he would have had the Idlers, Sails and Chips, to help out the watch. Finding himself near Sails (the Sailmaker), a very fine seaman named Cantlow, he said:

"Did you have any trouble with the topsail, Sails?"

"All the weather leach is split right down," Sails answered. "They ought to have had it in before, and these others. We've got it saved, but we'll have to shift it."

"It's coming on thick."

"It's bad. I'm going to nip below, to lash up."

Most of the watch was forward with Dudley Mac doing something or other about the fo'c's'le head: the men of the Port Watch were already on deck, some of them were bearing a hand forward, the rest were waiting about, anxious and active, staring at the ship and her setting.

She was driving on, sore-pressed, under her two lower topsails and fore-course. It was too much for her. All these sails were strained to the utmost, dark and stretched with rain-squalls, bellied-out stiff, with tugging gear and flogging blocks. The weather rigging screamed; there was a sag in the lee-rigging. It was plainly time to ease her: something would go if they didn't.

All these things Dick absorbed, as a sailor will, at once and as one, the condition of the ship and her sea: they came into him, as it were, through his pores into his soul; the ship was suffering and crying to be helped. But when he turned to look to windward there came upon him an overwhelming knowledge that she was running before the hounds of hell, who would soon have her down.

He looked, and at once said to himself:

"This has got her. She can never hope to escape from this."

A few moments before, while in the half-deck, he had noticed the glare on things, and had wondered what it was. Now he saw that the upper air had been changed to something that was neither air nor cloud. It had become a thickness or murkiness of red, which hurried and was full of omen, and gave the impression of being solid in its upper reaches and about to descend. It did not threaten danger, but extinction.

Looking round, Dick saw redness everywhere, glaring and grim, shutting the ship into a space hardly a mile across. The sea within this space was all livid, evil and unexpected, with shoots, spouts and spittings jerked from it and flung out. Away ahead to leeward there was a lightness in the redness, as though somewhere in that direction there might be light, life and beauty. Astern the red deepened down from blood near the zenith to old blood midway down, and to the blackness of the pit on the horizon. This blackness was extinction coming to swallow the world. Nothing could survive the power coming there.

Dick had a lively love of the beauty of sea and sky: it was a joy to him the more to have beauty in the scene in which his days passed. This to windward was not beauty, but something which annulled her, as it killed light and extinguished life. This was the Enemy; there he was, in all his power, coming out of hell to hunt everything down.

Dick was scared, but could not keep from staring at it, and as he stared was sure that he heard guns; the air rocked and roared with guns. He had heard the guns of the War far inland in England as a distant surf. He had seen their flashes winking on the night like faraway summer lightning. Here for a moment he saw only a few flashes, the redness was too thick for light, but the devil's own batteries were banging. He knew that thousands of naked devils must be strained at giant guns there, flinging in shell after shell, and sending them with a crash to scream and howl, while they, screaming and howling, flung in others.

He moved from the rail, just as Botloe came aft, carrying a maul.

"Did you see the birds?" Botloe said.

"Birds? What birds?"

"On the spare spars there."

He waved a hand towards the spare spars. Dick, looking in that direction, saw that they were peopled with a dazed and ruffled lot of birds, twenty-one in all he counted, nineteen shearwaters, a Cape pigeon and a small grey gull.

"I've got to tomm home the wedges here," Botloe said, beginning to hammer at the wedges of the main hatch. "Them birds began to come in an hour ago, all dazed and done."

"Where from?" Dick asked. "Where do they come from?"

"They've been blown from far enough; hundreds of miles perhaps," Botloe said, "trying to get away from the weather. There's a lot of them on the fo'c's'le, and got in under the windlass. They'll let you pick them up and do anything with them."

It was true. Dick could stroke the little heads of the exhausted, scared birds that had had all the wildness beaten out of them.

"They've been through something," he said, "or they wouldn't be in that state."

"I saw those birds, the redshanks, like it once, on the Bodmin Moor, in the year of the great snowstorm," Botloe said. "They didn't come out of their daze; they died: so will those. A wild thing lives by its wildness; if you break that it dies."

He moved on, to tomm home the wedges on the other side.

"I wish Botloe hadn't said that," Dick thought, "that they'd been blown trying to get away from the weather. This ship's in exactly the same state. She's been running from the weather, and soon she'll be dazed like those, and won't come out of her daze."

The job forward, whatever it was, had not yet been finished; and though most of the Port Watch were now on deck, Four Bells had not been made. The Old Man was aft there, sucking at a cold cigar, waiting, probably, for Dudley Mac to come aft. Old Mr. Duckswich was just outside the alleyway, hitching the beckets of his thigh-boots to his belt with rope-yarn. He had his long oilskin coat laid on the coaming of the doorway. When he had secured his boots, he took up the coat. The spectral face of Mince, the Captain's Steward, appeared in the alleyway. He was an old, haggard, fearful man, once a dare-devil third mate in a clipper-ship, so people said, but now all broken by a fall from aloft, so that he moved and looked like a ghost. Long experience of mates had taught him that the mate is the steward's enemy. The poor creature tried to propitiate even the broken, gentle old Duckswich by all manner of little tender services. He had come now to help Mr. Duckswich to put on his long black oilskin coat. He himself was in the long white linen coat in which he laid and served the meals in the saloon. No doubt he was almost ready to serve the cabin supper.

Loach, the sideways man, was in the main rigging close by, stopping-up coils of gear out of the way. Dick saw that he needed a hand, so hopped up into the shrouds beside him and held up the coils while Loach secured them.

"Coming on pretty hard," he called.

The sideways man looked sideways and said:

"Powdered brick."

"Does it remind you of the War?" Dick asked.

The sideways man looked at Dick sideways, then at the weather sideways, and then said sideways to nobody:

"Like over a village in a barrage . . . all powdered brick. The war to end war. A general's idea of beauty."

Loach had spoken from what he had seen. Dick felt that he had described the case exactly. It was as though

millions of red bricks had been blown to fine powder and
then sprayed so as to cover heaven. Under this murk,
which yet had a glare to it, the sea was rising irregularly
with a snap and a snarl in a jagged unusual way, with the
waves running into peaks, not into combs, and being
slashed or plucked off and then flung down by what
seemed like the act of invisible devils. It was all a savage,
brooding purple colour with bloody smears upon its foam.
In the hollows near the ship were sudden phrixes and
frissons scuttering and scurrying. They came in darken-
ing, flying ripples that spattered and foamed. It was as
though the invisible devils were pelting strips of the sea
with shot or hail. Again and again, quite near the ship,
there came the scuttering swift, shuddering spatter.

"Some shrapnel going," the sideways man said. "But
'our brave fellows laugh at shrapnel.' Not half, they
didn't."

There came a desperate, seething spatter right under
Dick's feet as the ship's roll brought him well down within
three feet of the sea. Then he saw that the twisting ripples were caused by fish, moving in shoal before the storm.
What fish they were he could not tell, but many of them
that leapt out of the water were tiny. Round the fringes
of the shoals were the writhings of paler things which may
have been fish-of-prey devouring.

"See the fish?" he said to Loach.

"If we could get a bag down," Loach answered, excited
suddenly into looking straight, "we'd have a fry of some
of them; but with Old Brass Hat cocking there what
hopes?"

They had finished the job in the weather main-rigging. Dick hopped down, and finding a loose end in the scuppers coiled it on its pin.

From time to time a desolate and exhausted bird sped down the wind. All round the ship, at varying distances, the redness deepened in patches to purple, from which lightning flashed and streams of rain descended in fine black lines. There could be no doubt that all hands would have their hands full for the rest of the watch.

While he coiled his rope, the door of the round-house opened; the Sailmaker came out, lashed-up for heavy weather. He moved across to the fore-brace-bumpkin and stared to windward. He was quite close to Dick. A moment later the Carpenter came from forward and joined them.

Richard Cantlow, the Sailmaker, wore no oilskins, but a marvellous suit, made by himself, of Number One Storm Canvas tarred over. He was a tall, fine, active, elderly man, with a face all mottled with freckles, some of them as big as threepenny-bits. He was a friendly, merry man. In his childhood he had run away from his home in the Blasket Islands because his father had been drowned and his stepfather was too free with his stick. He had been for fifty years at sea, but still talked of the Islands as Lucifer may have talked of Heaven, as a state not perhaps for everybody, but Heaven to those who could stick it.

The Carpenter, Mark Okle, was a grave, elderly, sad-faced, slow man, with a pointed beard. He had been in the ship for many years, out of devotion to her. In early days, when she had carried passengers, his job had been well-paid, and he had had two mates under him for the rigging and striking of cabins in the 'tween-decks and the making of necessary gear for messes and families. Now he was just "Chips," under sentence to go ashore for good when the ship docked.

"What was ye doing forward, Mark?" Cantlow asked.

"Seeing the windlass all clear for running."

"For the love of Mike, what for?"

"It's what they teach in the books."

"Was it Captain Cobb sent ye?"

"No, Mr. Mac. It's his job and he does it. He's a good, forethoughtful young seaman, always looking ahead."

"Are ye going to rig a sea-anchor?"

"He would, but Captain Cobb won't have it."

"He might never want it," Sails said.

"He'll want all the help he can get, before midnight," Mark answered.

The Cook, Tom Coggins, a pug-nosed, little, red-haired man, always thrusting himself forward into dispute or fight, always sure of himself, somewhat of a mock among the crew, but popular because he would dry wet clothes for a fellow and knew and sang a great many comic and sentimental songs, came suddenly out of his galley to join the group. He was in the midst of preparing the cabin supper, but that could wait for a moment.

"Ho, girls," he cried. "Pity the poor matloes. Hey, boys, no sleep to-night. Marriage-night to-night, by gum, all up and doing. Gee, sons, we're going to cop it; we'd best put flannel next our skin."

"I've never seen anything like this before," Mark Okle

said, very gravely. "I never thought there could be anything like this. It is like Noah's flood again."

"Noah's flood was when Balaam's Ass spoke," the Cook
said. "He said, 'Boys, this is great weather for life-belts,
but hell on my umbrella.'"

"I wish our Balaam's Ass would speak," Cantlow said.
"He's split one new sail already by hanging on. Any one
of these gusts might take the rest, if not a spar with it.
He'd best put her head under her wing while he's a wing
left to do it with."

"I must get back to me venison soufflet," the Cook said,
"or it won't get that soupsong Ritz. I shall serve a cold
breakfast to-morrow, me lardships, and so I warn you. If
I have a range left I'll be lucky."

As he went back to his galley, Old Duckswich joined
the Old Man on the poop and spoke to him. Evidently
he said something which the Battler did not like, for the
Battler removed his cigar, looked at him and said something which made him wilt and move away. The Mate
moved aft to the bell and made it Four Bells, then leaning
forward shouted:

"Call all hands on deck."

Hands in the waist, who had been expecting the call,
shouted, "Ay, ay, sir," and ran to the fo'c's'le to repeat it.

In a minute the crowd was mustering at the break of
the poop. Some of the men were still fumbling at but-
tons and straps, growling that the bastards had flogged
the clock on them.

The roll was hurriedly called, then the Mate called to
them to make fast the upper topsails. The Mates went

to the topsail halliards to let them go, the men ran to the downhauls and buntlines; and as the great sails thundered with ominous slattings the sharp, quick, scared cries of the hurrying haulers rang out fore and aft, as they snapped the stops and started snugging them. Two or three fierce lifting heaves shook the sails and their masts, then the gear strangled them as the yards came jolting down. Bulging bags of rain-blackened sail strained out between the buntlines. Those below could see the yards buckle as the strain on the downhauls was countered by the lift of the sails in the gusts.

"Up and make them fast," the Battler shouted.

He had his speaking trumpet now. No doubt he had loaded up with a drink or two before coming on deck for the occasion.

He repeated his shout of "Up and make them fast," with the spur, "before the damned things blow to hell."

The crowd needed no such spur. They knew very well that the ship had been overdriven and that if they were not quick in mastering the sails the sails would go and perhaps the topmasts with them. They rattled up the weather-rigging as fast as men in sea-boots could trot, in a rush to be there first, shoving any laggard aside, and damning any man above whose heel kicked any head as he swung over the top-rim to the topmast-rigging.

With oaths and jokes they went over the top-rim to the fury blowing aloft, and out, somehow, by catch-ratlines, or by a swing from any handy gear, to the topsail yard with its mad balloons playing hell there. They had nine men (counting Mates and Idlers) to each sail, all bent on reaching the weather yard-arms first. Anyhow, it was only a reefed upper topsail in each case, no matter if it had been left too long: it was fun to get hold of it and punch its silly face in.

Dick was on the foretopsail yard. Being light, quick and what his mates called "ambitious," or eager for work, he was out near the yard-arm, leaning well over it to get a good grip of the sail.

It was a wild scene that he looked down upon. Below, was the thin flèche of the ship's deck, and the surging, plunging bow and bowsprit shearing open an array of old blood. Sprays were flying high from under her foot and going in sheets across her fo'c's'le-head. All the air seemed to be growing thicker and redder every instant with thickness and redness coming up from astern. For an instant, he would notice all these things, then with a wallop the sail would fly up, so that his whole world was a flogging, mad sail tangled round his head. Then, he would beat the sail in under his chest and catch a glimpse just below him of the belly of the blackened lower topsail blown out hard as iron, with every hair from every cringle and buntline blown out stiff as wire. It was comical to see his mates, in their dirty old oil-skins, bent across the yard while the wind behind them blew up their coats, flogged their trouser flaps and strove to pluck away their southwesters. Then, after a glimpse came a crash. Then at them, in front of them, over them, and sometimes under and all round them was this devil of the upper topsail which should have been stowed at Eight Bells. Now it gave a roaring flump and broke away from them. Then it would take a downward, mad, sickening, backward leap as the ship descended and smite under the yard at the foot-ropes, and kick at all the feet there ranked, before flying up and hitting their owners across the faces. They cursed it, they beat it with fists and punched it down on to the yard. Then, some standing or sitting on the lower topsail yard, others leaning far over, they passed the coils of gaskets, while the devil that possessed it beat away the tethers and won loose again.

Beating it at last, for when all was said it was only a reefed upper topsail, they laid in, and then out to the other yard-arm to snug that. It did not take long, though it seemed long, for all there felt that this might not be a storm but the very end of the world. Dick was next to Aylton and passed the gasket for him. Dick knew that Aylton was one of the bravest and steadiest men on board; he had served in Q ships during the War and had been through some tough times. Aylton was as strong as an ox. He had a quiet, resolute and even beautiful face, such as a painter might have taken as a model for that of any-one who has endured. Yet Dick could see that Aylton, like everybody there, had a look of horror in his eyes.

"It looks like dirt," Dick shouted.

"It looks like hell," Aylton shouted back, "and I shouldn't wonder if it won't be hell."

Up there in the blow they had a taste of the strain on the gear. At each gust they could see the play on the fore yard-arms as the topsail-sheets lifted them. They knew that everything there was strained pretty far: a very little more and . . .

However, the sail was stowed, they laid in, and down on deck, all a bit stiff in the straddle. Looking up, they saw that they had made not at all a bad stow of it; but the chaps on the main were at it still. The younger hands hurriedly coiled up the gear clear for running, while the Old Man bellowed through his trumpet to them to "Up and help them schoolgirls on the main."

They left the gear as it was and ran to the weather main-rigging. They saw that the Starboard Watch had furled their weather yard-arm and were struggling with the lee. They had it, so Dick thought, well in, under their chests, all conquered and ready to bind, yet even as he looked there came one of those gusts that somehow always brought terror on this night of storm, and away the sail went from their hands, all the lee side of it loose and triumphing. Snap went the gaskets on the weather side, up went the weather side, too. It flogged up, royally, once, twice and thrice, at the third time snapping its reef points, till the whole sail was loose and away, shaking the mast, and looking magnificent against that sky.

Dick saw it flog, then saw sky through it in a spreading streak: the next instant it was all tattering pennants flying from the jackstay, being cut adrift by the watch.

"There she goes, sons, a new main upper topsail," Bill Guller called, "worth fifty quid and more."

"Mister," the Captain shouted to Duckswich, "what are you staring there for? Stow the lower topsail. Main lower topsail: stow it."

"Stow the main lower topsail, ay, ay, sir," several voices repeated.

A squall of rain came drenching down upon them, making them duck. The old Mate went to the weather sheet, the men tallied-on to the buntlines and cluelines and lifted her as the sheet slacked.

"Up and make her fast," the old Mate called, and gallantly led the way, old and lame as he was, only to be shoved aside at the futtocks by younger and stronger men.

He went down on deck to the lee gear. Dick found himself next to Sock Staplow near the weather yard-arm, where the clue was thumping and romping in a game of its own.

"Who says the bunt's the place of honour?" he shouted.

Staplow hadn't been long enough to sea to know why the bunt had been the place of honour. He damned the flying clue for one of the Lord's mistakes.

"Get the leech in and jam it under your belly," Dick shouted.

"Come on here, under my belly," Staplow called, wrestling with the leaping leech rope. It did not come for the call, but leaped aloft among oaths, cheers and anger. Suddenly the sail lifted all along the yard, for the Starboard Watch had now come down to help and the Mate with the few on deck had slacked the lee sheet and manned the gear.

A rainsquall coming up behind them suddenly smote their backs like coils of ropes and filled their eyes, mouths and ruffled clothes with water.

"Pick her up, now," someone shouted.

The arms grabbed, gripped and hove. The sail in a bundle came up on to the yard in man's control. Dick got the yard-arm gasket from Staplow, caught the stirrup, lowered himself down, and swung the made-up gasket under the yard and up for Nick Cradley, the man on his left, to catch and secure. It is a position of danger, to hang on by one hand to a stirrup while sitting on a jerking foot-rope in a gale of wind some seventy feet in air. Dick did not love the job, but it had to be done on all bulky yards, for the gaskets could be passed in no other way. Nick missed the flying bunch the first time. Dick had to gather it again, then again to jerk it forward for Nick to catch. It was while he was doing this that the trouble happened.

The men were fumbling under the rain for the gaskets; three other men, sitting on the foot-rope, were doing as Dick was doing, trying to send the bunched-up gaskets to them. The rain was coming down as the devil went through Athlone, "in standing leps." Then, suddenly, for no apparent reason, the ship checked, bowed her weather side under a mountain of sea, took a packet of it on board along her rail, while at the same instant the wind, which was following the rain, blasted out upon her in a gust more violent than any which had come. The sail was lifted from the men's hands. The wind plucked it from them and sent it up till the yard bent like whalebone. It threshed and thumped, and then, coming aback, flew under the yard and knocked Dick off the rope.

He had hold of the stirrup still, got his other hand to it, and was back on the rope again in three seconds, but he had had a scare such as comes to few: he had been within an ace of death. The Battler had seen him, for there came the hail of:

"Pomfret, there . . . Pomfret . . . What in hell are you playing at?"

Dick, knowing that he couldn't be heard, shouted back: "Leap-frog, ducky," and again swung out the gasket.

As he did so, he saw a flash of fire below him, a running stream of fire, tearing along the lower yard and down the side of the mast. The chain sheet had broken and unroven with a rush of sparks. As Dick watched, it reached the foot of the mast with a crash. There was nobody there for it to kill. It had gone because the clue had gone. In two seconds more the sail had split from clue to yard, in half a dozen seams at once. Dick saw some of it flying away like a dirty old sheet of a newspaper. It skimmed, stooped and lifted, going half a mile before the sea got it. That was the end of their main lower topsail.

They salved what they could of it, cutting adrift some of the madder tatters and frapping the rest to the yard. Then they began to lay in, glad to have done. The wind was fast increasing. It was coming at them with leaps of violence, which became the tempo of the gale until the next leap raised it. The redness of the sky above seemed to grow nearer to them and to deepen in the colour of its horror. As they laid in and scrambled down, they noticed that it had gone suddenly much colder: it was now bitterly cold. Dick kept saying to himself:

"What has happened, of course, is a down-draught from the upper atmosphere. Well, if it's like this, I don't wonder that life can't exist there. Golly: it's a beastly night."

He was glad that the other men were all round him; he had not quite recovered from his shock.

"Ah, Pomfret," Cradley said, as they reached the deck nearly together, "you had a close call up there. This Pomfret had a bet, you fellows, to see which was the harder, his head or the deck. I tell him not to try."

"I knew a fellow, one time, come down from sitting on the foot-rope," the melancholy Pencome said. "His bones went three inches into the deck. His girl asked for the bit of deck after, to remember him by. 'My Woozlie's death-bed,' she called it, but the owners sold it over her head to a wax-works."

"Lay aft, you," the Old Man shouted. "Up here, half a dozen of you, and secure these mizen topsails."

Indeed, the two mizen topsails were showing signs of breaking loose from their gaskets, as sails sometimes will. Ominous puffings and rufflings were jobbling up in bulges along the stow of the sail. There was not much time to lose if the sails were to be saved. When once the wind gets into a stow it usually takes charge very quickly and sends the sail to glory. About a dozen men, Dick among them, ran aft at the order. Cantlow, who was ever fore-thoughtful, dived into the sail locker for some lengths of gasket-stuff, before going aloft.

As they ran up the mizen-rigging, the brick-coloured air began to sparkle with sudden fires. No man there had seen anything quite like it. Pencome, who had been at Newport News in the summer and had been impressed by the fireflies there, said:

"Fireflies, boys; we're going to get it hot."

It was on a much bigger scale than the sparkle and extinction of fireflies. It was as though lightning were continually trying to get through the reddish murk and always being baffled. Perhaps in that dull, glowing glare, nothing of light, not even destructive fire, could exist. A glimmer of brightness would light up and leap and then be smothered. Another and then another lit and sped, was choked, then flashed, and then died in the murk. All the vast purple, orange, scarlet murk was stabbed and shot by the muffled sparklings, which now appeared and sparkled and disappeared along the yards and chain-sheets close to them. The men did not wait to discuss what the sparks were due to. They got out on to the yards to smother those bulging sails, beat them into their skins and lash them fast. As they worked and cursed, the thought passed among them that the sparks were like fire on a fuse, which sputters and struggles, yet surely burns on to the charge. The charge was somewhere behind them where the guns were banging. They could not doubt that presently those fires would reach the charge and blast sea and heaven into one.

It was not a long job to secure those two doubtful topsails. They lashed them down "for a full due," and then laid down on deck.

Dick, being up among the first, was among the last to leave the yard. While he waited for the men in front of him to step away and leave room for him he cast a glance aft and astern.

The overdriven ship was crashing on in front of an

appalling sea. Just astern of her was something that looked like the line of the Downs from Liddington to Lollingdon, not coming as the comber comes in the Western Ocean, but with sidelong lurches as well as the forward march; for there was not one evil in this sea, but many. The comb toppled and thrust sideways, and from time to time overtook. One awful hill came within a few feet of Dick as he looked, but the ship rose to it, and it went roaring away.

"Poor Torrent at the wheel," Dick thought. "There he is, not relieved yet. Golly, they might give him a lad at the lee spokes: it's no picnic steering in this."

As he thought this, he had to laugh at the sight of Paddy Suckley going over the top-rim just below him; his southwester had blown off his head so that it only held by the chinstrap, which Paddy had caught in his teeth just in time to save it. The southwester was flapping in his face so that Paddy could not see. The gale at the same instant had got inside his oilskin coat, and blown it out over the belt like a balloon. There he stood at the top-rim, like a fish out of water, half in and half over, blown out and helpless, with the southwester tearing at his teeth to be free. The trouser-end of Paddy's outstretched leg was beating on his boot like a flag blowing to tatters on its halliards.

"Do look at old Paddy," he cried to Staplow.

"Gotsake, old Paddy," Staplow said. "To it, Paddy. Sick him, boy. Hold tight. I never saw the beat of it."

Paddy waited for the roll, got his southwester back in place, and disappeared over the top-rim; the others followed. The Old Man was no longer on the poop, when they got there.

"Gone down to crook his elbow again," Staplow said. "I wish I'd some of his complaint: he must have necked a bottle since breakfast."

As the rest of the hands were streaming forward, they followed. Though they had heard no order they judged that Mr. Duckswich was going to stow the foresail. It was time, too, and more than time. The question, now, was what chance had they of getting it in unsplit? Another question was what would happen when the Old Man tried to heave her to? There was no doubt now that the full fury was coming on fast.

Barty Berrow clapped a hand on Dick's shoulder and pointed out a strange effect, as of floating fire, on a sea that had run on ahead.

"See that," he called. "That's a Corpse Light. Well-named, too, for our old Bucko Corpse Light is going to run this hooker under and corpse the lot of us."

"I'm beginning to wonder whether he won't," Dick said.

While he was wondering, the ship's stern lifted to a big sea, which had plainly overtaken her. Her stern lifted clear, but the sea running on came on board on both sides at the waist, rolled all that it caught clean off their feet and put Dick down under water in the port scuppers. He picked himself up as the sea went roaring onward. The decks streamed, gurgled and bubbled and at last cleared themselves. Dick saw the hands gathering themselves from where the sea had put them, some from the scuppers, others hopping down from pinrail or bitts. It was the first

big water which had come on board. It was plain that
more would come in a very few minutes.

Old Duckswich called to them to get the foresail off her.

This was now no light task for all hands. It was a new
sail, all the stiffer for being drenched; the gale was now
blowing full, and the chance of splitting the sail and
springing the yard had now become a probability. Still, if
they did not take it off her, she might either sail them all
under or whip the foremast out: the chance must be taken.

"Get on to the lifts here," Old Duckswich called. "Get
what you can here."

He took the weather lift-fall off the pin; Dudley Mac
did the same on his side; the men tallied-on to them and
got all they could on both lifts.

"Get your watch on to the lee gear, Mister," Old Duckswich called.

They went quickly enough to the buntlines and clew-
garnets: the sooner the job was done the better for all
hands. They saw Mr. Dudley Mac go to the sheet, ready
to ease it away "judgmatically," so as to take some strain
off the sail before the tack was started. Everybody knew
that it is a ticklish job to take in a new course in an over-
run ship in a gale. Some there disagreed with the Mate's
method, which was, plainly, to ease the sheet, then haul up
the weather clew and gear, before snugging up the lee side.
Some would always quote the lines:

> "He who strives the tempest to disarm,
> Must ever first embrail the lee yard-arm."

Others would reply that the right reading is:

"Must never first embrail," etc.

Both schools got hot about it, both methods had something in their favour. The yard-arms are gone from British use, but the problem still remains and has its partisans. The weather clew-garnet was taken off the pin and stretched along. Mr. Duckswich and Aylton were at the tack, peering across the side ready to signal to the Second Mate. In another ten seconds the orders would have been given and the sheet started. In the ten seconds the Old Man appeared from aft, with a flaming face and angry eyes, to quarrel with the Mate.

"What is all this, Mister? What are you thinking you're doing?"

"Taking the foresail off her, Captain Cobb," old Duckswich answered.

"Time, too," the man Loach said, without moving his lips.

"Who in hell said 'Time, too'?" Cobb asked.

"No man of my watch, Captain Cobb," Duckswich answered.

"Which of you said it, there?" the Captain roared. "Mr. MacLerrinnan, which of your damned packet-rats said 'Time, too,' then?"

Dudley Mac, who had been on the other side of the fore-bitts during all this, had seen and heard nothing of it. He happened to notice the Captain's presence for the first time and saw that the Captain was speaking to him. He knew at once that the Captain would not be forward without very grave cause; he loped up to windward and said:

"What is it, Captain Cobb, sir?"

"Which of your push of toughs gave me lip, then?"

"I didn't hear any man, sir." He cast an eye over the men present. All there hung their heads and looked like the mildest of sheep; but each man there was enjoying the scene and hoping that it would go on. "I was over on the port side, Captain Cobb," the Second Mate continued. "I could not hear any word that was spoken."

He turned directly to the men of his watch, all clustered under the fore-rigging by the fife-rail.

"Did any of you speak, then?" he asked.

"Yes, Mister," the Captain said. "One of them did. You think, you men, because you've won the War you can sling what lip you like. I'll teach you different. One of you spoke. You know which one. I'll ride the lot of you down like the damned fore tack till you make that one sick he ever breathed it. And what are you taking the foresail off her for, Mr. Duckswich, without my leave?"

"Because I'm the Mate of this ship, Captain Cobb, and it's my watch on deck."

"And I'm the Captain of this ship . . ."

"Certainly, Captain Cobb . . ."

"And I'll decide what sail comes in."

"Very good, Captain Cobb, since you come forward I'll go aft. There can't be two Mates to a watch."

The old Mate caught a turn or two with his gear and started to limp aft.

"Come here, Mr. Duckswich."

"No, no, Captain Cobb," he answered, without turning, "one Mate's enough in any hooker."

"Come here, when I call you, Mr. Duckswich."

Mr. Duckswich paid no attention, but proceeded aft, walking with the limping waddle which the sea and his broken bone, ill mended, made necessary. Just abaft the main hatch he took his pipe from his pocket, tapped it out on the fife-rail, and began to fill it as he walked on. He had meant this to madden the Captain. It succeeded. The Captain had been watching his every step and gesture.

"My good God," he gasped.

He leaped aft, after the Mate. A tremor of joy ran through all the crew, as they craned to see what would happen.

"Get you on to the gear there," Dudley Mac called to them. "It's none of yeir business. Tally on to these wee bits of string."

"Are we to haul the sail up, Mr. MacLerrinnan?" old Purple, the Boatswain, asked.

Mr. MacLerrinnan had been considering the matter. The Captain had plainly decided against the foresail's coming in, and the Mate, whose watch it was, had gone aft. Plainly, it was for the Mate or the Captain to make the decision and give the order.

"Hold on, all," he said.

They waited, casting curious glances aft to the break of the poop, where Captain and Mate were having a set-to, the Captain furious and full of gesture, the Mate at last stubborn and defiant. Dick was on the side of the Mate. The Captain had been brutal to him for months on end, and now found that his weapons no longer bit. Dick liked old Duckswich and was sorry for him. He was as good a seaman as the Old Man any day, only, being a broken man, he could not keep his end up against the Captain's savagery. The crowd were divided in their opinion: though they liked the Captain to be insulted, they still felt that old Duckswich was too much of an old fool.

"Get the brooms out," MacLerrinnan said, suddenly. "Broom down the deck there, where it's wet."

Half a dozen of Dick's watch got brooms from the Boatswain's locker and broomed away the film of water slipping and sliding on the wet deck. They hoped to be able to sweep aft, so as to hear the row still going on under the break of the poop, but MacLerrinnan kept them well forward of the main hatch so that they should not. Dick, sweeping in the waist, had a fine view of the seas, which came racing along and threatening her and boiling up and away.

The wheel had not been relieved yet. There was poor Torrent still at the helm, after two-and-a-half hours of it.

"Why on earth couldn't they relieve the wheel, or at least send a second hand to it?"

The thought was in the minds of all the Starboard Watch. Dudley Mac had been considering it for some time. He wanted to relieve Torrent, but did not want to weaken his watch by sending away a man until the foresail was in. However, the steering in that sea was no joke and all depended on it. Plainly, it would be a job for Newbarn.

"Newbarn, there," he called.

"Sir."

"Get to the lee wheel."

"The lee wheel, sir; ay, ay, sir."

Newbarn slipped over to leeward and trotted aft, probably glad at heart, for, on the whole, half an hour, or three-
quarters of an hour, of the lee wheel would be a shade less
unpleasant than stowing a new foresail, thoroughly wet, in
such a gale as this. The others watched his going, thinking that probably they would get some crumbs of the row
from him later; for perhaps he would hear something of
what was being said. The older men of the Starboard
Watch were growling together that these two damned
tom-cats were keeping all hands on deck while they were
holding their damned concert; and why couldn't they save
it for some other time? All hands were being held on
deck for an all-hands job; why couldn't they get on with
the job? If they wished to scratch their eyes out let them
do it in their spare time.

Dick, who had finished brooming, stowed his broom and
went back to the gear under the weather forerigging. He
glanced aft at the poop, where the row was still proceeding. Newbarn was moving to the wheel when the Captain called him over.

"Now he's got the poor kid on the mat," Staplow said.

They saw Newbarn cross to the Captain, halt, look
sheepish, and take off his southwester, while the Captain
swore at him.

"What the hell's he ticking him off for?" the men asked.
"He's a good lad. He'll be a fine seaman when he's got

his strength; a better seaman than that old tank, who keeps all hands on deck while he wags his silly chin."

Newbarn was popular with the men; he was one of themselves.

"What's the poor kid done, to be told off for?" they asked.

There was no doubt about the telling off; Newbarn was getting it hot, and taking its injustice none too well. What it was all about, they did not know, but after it was over they saw Newbarn go, not to the lee wheel, as Dudley Mac had ordered, but up the side of the charthouse to the spanker boom. They saw him bestride the boom, and jockey himself along it, facing aft, till he was just over the cabin skylight. It was a horrible position, he was nearly blown away, he was facing into the gale and staring at the following sea.

"He's put him to ride the wooden mare," Barty Berrow said; "a kid like that."

Old Duckswich came forward to them, taking his time. As he was now smoking, all hands concluded that he had "turned in his job," and no longer counted himself as on duty.

"That's the New Seamanship," he said bitterly, waving his pipe aft. "Puts a poor boy astride the spanker boom for not taking his hat off quicker: and this after running his ship to hell, endangering masts and crew. Mr. MacLerrinnan, and you, men, if you don't take that foresail in, muy pronto, the Lord God'll do it for you in a way you won't like."

He watched the effect of his words. He had not been

much liked as Mate; he was not better liked as Mutineer. "Well, you can tell Him I told you," he added, and moved aft again.

MacLerrinnan had not answered. All hands, gathered at the weather fore fife-rail, watched him going aft, and then watched the sails above them and that lifting of the fore yard-arms in the gusts, which told them that the spars were in danger. Then they looked to MacLerrinnan for an order, while he looked aft to see what the Captain would order.

The Captain was now at the poop-rail, sucking his cigar; he had probably had a drink or two since putting poor Newbarn astride the boom. As Duckswich reached the break of the poop, he stopped, took off his southwester to the Captain, and no doubt made some insolent remark, perhaps asking, "Did that hat come off quick enough?"

The Captain seemed to make no reply: after some other remark the Mate moved on to the alleyway door and went below, slamming the door behind him. Even those forward heard it slam and jangle.

Mr. MacLerrinnan was much too good a sailor to watch a ship endangered without protest, and much too good an officer to let his men be kept on deck without need. Besides, his order to Newbarn had been interfered with. He now told all hands to stay there ready for a call, while he went aft to speak to Captain Cobb. He was a favourite with the Old Man and from careful study of his moods had learned how to deal with him. It was now plainly time for quiet sense to interfere. As his great body swung swiftly aft with the grace of movement which Dick had so often noticed, the growling of the crew broke out again.

"What in hell is he keeping us on deck for?"

"Why don't you get the foresail in, Bosun? Then if he wants it set let him set it himself."

"Old rum-tank. He's been lapping it, all afternoon."

"Get to it, Bose; let's furl it and get below. She'll be dismasted if you don't, sure as hell."

"Stay where you're put," old Purple answered. "When you're ordered to do a thing, you'll do it."

"Obey orders if you break owners."

"There Dudley Mac goes up to him. I'd give a plug of tobacco to hear what he says."

"He's a gent, Dudley Mac, and knows how to put it."

Dick saw Dudley Mac explaining the situation to one who was resolved not to heed. Dudley Mac pointed to the gathering midnight to windward. The Old Man, it was plain, did not see the storm as the young man saw it. He appeared to be unmoved. To the surprise of all hands they turned to walk together, up and down the weather-poop, with a glance now and then at poor Newbarn, still riding the saddle-less mare.

"What in hell are they talking of?" a man growled. "Society noos and that?"

"Ah, trust Mr. Mac. A madman and a drunkard and a beauty, you must humour all three."

"The hell with humouring. This mast'll go, next thing. It'll take more than humouring to clear a wrecked fore-mast."

"I was in the Navy in my young days," old Purple be-

gan, "in a corvette, as we called them, barque-rigged . . .
what was her name now? We'd a Scotch lad in her used
to crook his elbow. He used to save his rum; I don't know
how he did it; but he'd be canned when no one else would
have a smell of it. One summer evening, when we were
in Queenstown, a boat came under our bows with a party
of Paddies singing 'The Wearing of the Green.' They
shouted all kinds of things at us; and this Scotty, who'd
had his full whack and beyond, he heard what they said.
'Ah wull na take yon lip from any Paddy,' he says; so he
nips a pin from the rail and overboard he went, clothes and
all, to go for them. He could not swim. He'd a very close
call for being drowned. When our cutter got to him, to
pick him up, being canned, he thought we were the Paddies he was to go for. He gave our bowman a nasty clip."

"There it is, Bose," Bill Aylton said. "A sailor ought not
to mix business with pleasure, like our young Scot and his
Nibs, there."

"There's a hell of a following sea there," Barty Berrow
said. "Whose wheel is it?"

"Tom Torrent."

"He ought to have someone with him."

"He ought. What in hell is happening now?"

"It's the Steward."

They saw the frail figure of the Steward creep up to the
midship line of the poop and stand there in the attitude
of a suppliant, waiting to be noticed, while the Captain
and Dudley Mac paced past him. They passed him twice
without paying heed. At the turn for the third time Dudley Mac seemed to call the Captain's attention to the Stew-

ard's presence, for the Captain halted, heard what the Steward had to say, and then continued his walk.

"Your supper is ready, Captain Cobb, sir," Kit Pillows said in a mimicry of the Steward's manner.

"To hell with supper. It's our watch below," a man growled.

"Now he'll go to supper," Barty Berrow said, "and forget there's a ship in the business."

The Captain paced the deck with Dudley Mac, passing the Steward, who still stood cringing there, fumbling with his cap in his hands, plainly longing to be gone below, for he was not in oilskins, and at any moment might be soused. At the third or fourth passing the Captain seemed to notice him; he paused and spoke, both to the Steward and Dudley Mac.

"That's got it," one of the men said. "He's giving an order."

Dudley took the Captain's speaking trumpet, stepped with it to the poop-rail, and shouted:

"Morritz, there."

"Morrissey," Purple called, "it's you, me lad; answer, will you?"

"Yes, sir."

"Come aft to the lee wheel here."

"Can't he get someone whose watch it is?" Morritz growled, as he ducked down his head and started to shuffle aft.

"Ah, hell, think of these swine aft," Loach said, "keeping all hands on deck . . . why it's Two Bells now, or gone, and poor Torrent there has been at the wheel three hours

... and now they send Morrissey to the lee wheel, as though it were still his watch on deck."

No one there liked Morrissey, but an old custom of the sea was being broken: every man there was against the after guard who broke it.

"It's time someone went to the lee wheel," Bill Guller said.

All hands stood waiting under the weather forerigging for the orders which did not come. What had been daylight was now fast fading into something which promised the extinction of light and air for ever. All to windward was now an advancing Death, which would have been black but for the glare upon it. Dick had the fancy that Light had been murdered and that this was the blood of the murder. Out of that Death there came a long, sweeping, whistling, hissing noise, as though a myriad snakes were suddenly rushing at them. A whitish, greyish, wall or curtain rushed towards them from to windward, caught them up and swept over them in a cold fury of rain, so intense that they could see nothing, and so cold that it took away their breaths.

It ran over them and drenched them, and at the same time stung them, for there was plenty of wind behind it. What impressed Dick was the overwhelming horror of the hissing, as it struck ship or sea. He felt that half an hour of that awful hiss, as of steam escaping, would be an unbearable suspense, one would so long for the relief of the explosion. Either the world had gone mad, he thought, in which case perhaps the sea-serpents might be loose and coming at them, or perhaps the sea's bottom had given way, let in the sea to the central fires and prepared a crash like the end of the world.

"As soon as steam has been generated," he thought, "the whole top of the earth's crust will come off like a blown cylinder head, and that will be the end of some very good seamen."

Perhaps fifteen minutes passed before the hissing ceased. When the rain squall had rained itself out, or gone on, drenching the seatops, the deck was running a foot deep and spouting from the scuppers. As the rain curtain thinned, the murder colour in the sky deepened over them. Now, certainly, from to windward, the gods of the underworld began to howl at them.

"A kennel full of dogs there," Aylton said to Dick, nodding aft.

"God, it does sound damned like dogs," Purple said.

"It *is* dogs; nothing else could make that noise," Aylton said.

Where the dogs could be was another matter. Near at hand they had an infinity of noises; it was all roar and clack and thunder, with the washing of the seas as undertone. But over all these noises, from somewhere, not exactly there yet, but drawing nearer, from somewhere to windward, where it was darkest, where it was most hellish, someone great (or many who were very evil), barked, barked and barked, or varied the barking with howling. What curse or madness was it that made such power speak like dogs? What was it that was there? What was it that was coming?

Wind, plainly, wind and sea together; for here they came

together, the great heaped sea striding, the wind in quick, gathering, growing gusts, which bowed the ship over, sent sheets of spray, all glimmering like lightning, high over the fo'c's'le head, and seemed to tear at her masts. She tore forward, spouting where she struck the water, and bending her yards.

"Hell, Bose," Barry Berrow called. "Let go the sheet. She'll take the masts clean out of her."

"The hell she will," old Purple said. "Go take a quid of tobacco."

But even old Purple didn't like the look of things. He looked aft anxiously for a word of command, and finding that none came, walked aft a few steps, peering (for he was short-sighted) towards the poop. All hands stared with him. It was time that the folly aft ceased.

"Ease up the tack, Barty," someone called. "Slack the sheet, Bose."

Perhaps if they had done so it might have helped matters and saved a good deal of future trouble. The sail would have flogged to tatters. The letting go would have passed as an accident. But the suggestion came too late. When it came, Barry's mind was not on the tack, but on a sudden dancing of corpse lights on masts and gear. Down all the lightning conductors, along all chains, down the lifts to the yard-arms, and away along shrouds and stays, lingering always especially about the hanks of the staysails, and then away by the guys and jib hanks to the jib-boom end were multitudinous dancing flickers of bluish light. It was almost as though it were being scattered from above. Some of it seemed to hop from the bumpkins on to the fife-rail and along it from iron pin to iron pin. Dick put his hand on to one, and felt nothing and caught nothing, for it was gone. Looking aft, he saw a running flicker of similar fire on a sea rolling up from astern. It was a big sea, such as made him hold his breath. It came on very quickly, overtaking the ship fast, but she rose to it and it ran by them, dark with death, on both sides of her and glimmering with the flashings. Almost as soon as it had gone roaring on ahead, another was there advancing; it came rolling up astern, showing all its teeth, toppling over near the ship's stern and sending a wash of spray over her poop. It, too, just failed to strike the ship, and roared on, dropping some tons of greenness into the waist as it passed.

"Waves come in sets," Dick quoted. "Three or four big ones together."

The wash from this one surged forward on the 'scend to the men at the fore-rigging. They swung themselves off the deck to let it pass. It had been glimmering with the corpse light in all its approach. At the instant of its dropping over the rail it seemed to take fire; the strange light spread, winked and disappeared as the water washed into the crannies, over the hatches and away into the scuppers. The men dropped their feet to the deck: another big sea, then another, roared up, and passed on, each flinging something to the deck.

Usually a man can tell beforehand when a sea is going to be something out of the common, bringing danger with it. Such seas are very rare, and usually give one a little warning. Sometimes they come when the ship is not ready to receive it, through some momentary disadvantage of position, when she is down, when she already has her decks full. Sometimes they send out avant-couriers, and proceed by climax.

Dick suddenly knew that something appalling was coming. He saw what seemed the side of a downland heaving itself up and up and up, directly astern, dark against the black of the storm, yet danced on by fire and topped by teeth. At the same time, he knew that some of it had already numbed the ship, that she was not ready for it, that her way had been checked by it and her stern in some way plucked down by it. All hands knew, even before they saw the thing, that this was the wave of the set that would put them under. Dick saw Dudley Mac leap aft towards the wheel. The sea rose up, up, up.

"Popped, by God," Aloysius Rue said. "That's done us."

"I think it has," Dick answered.

He was not scared, he was not in the least scared, only interested: all hands were interested: it was intensely interesting: only it was so slow, it took such a hellish time.

Suddenly, the foresail just behind them flogged backward at them with a thundering slat. Dick saw the leech of the topsail quake as the sea took the wind out of it. He knew that the sails would go; but that was nothing now. Something flashed in the sky above; something shook the ship, as though she were a rat, worried by a dog; something cracked and collapsed far aft, but this last he could not be sure of, it may have been the top of the wave blotting out all that part of the ship. He felt the ship become a stone under his feet and begin to sink like a stone. There was to be no ship now, only an enormous, raging, grey-black, red-black, glimmering, corpse-lit, awful water, bigger than the downland, that hissed and cackled and slid in little horrid laughs, and spat itself forward at the top and moved like a mountain crumpled forward by an earthquake. All hands were in the fore-rigging or fore-bitts, crouched against it, ducked to it, gripping with all their might, catching turns round themselves. Some said, "God," some said, "Hell, boys." Dick caught four of the biggest breaths he could. Then, very suddenly, and with appalling weight and speed the mountain of water was over them all, shutting out all knowledge and all sense.

Dick felt that the weight would break in his chest, and that things would be a great deal pleasanter if he let it. He opened his eyes; he was in deep blackness of water. No ship could live under such a weight. He felt that the ship was sinking with him; down, down, down, never to see the light again. No ship could rise from such a blow. No deck, no hatch could stand that weight of water. This was no doubt Death, a great pressure on the chest and a smarting on the eyes, weight, pain, blackness. Then that changed to something quite pleasant and pretty, of a corn-field bright in the sun and ripe to the harvest, with a clear swathe already cut in the corn, so that he could walk uphill, always uphill, in the light, to something well worth going to. Then this suddenly changed to something purple across the eyes, then red in the eyes, then golden, while the roaring in his ears whirled and whirled into something that was not roaring. Suddenly his head was

out of the water; he gulped a couple of breaths and then
was splashed by a cold spray in the face.

The deck was full of water; he was in water up to the
chin; a wallow of water went over him again. He felt the
ship to be without hope, settling like a stone beneath him.
He had never felt that hopelessness in her movements before: it was unlike anything that he had ever felt. She had
so plainly given up the ghost; she was beaten to death.
The water passed from his face; he got a good gulp of
breath, two or three together, though the ship was full to
the rails with enormous seas toppling about her.

"She must go down, now," he thought. "She can't get
up from this."

But then there came a kind of stirring beneath his feet,
a kind of labouring effort in the fabric which gave him
the lie.

Once, a year or two before, on a Saturday night when
in port in London, he had gone to see a boxing contest in
Whitechapel. He had seen the boxer of his choice put
down, rise, sorely hurt, having been punched over the heart,
and then again go down from a second punch in the same
place. He remembered the count going against his man—
five . . . six . . . seven . . . while he lay on the floor, and
then, at eight, he had slowly risen, contrived to get into a
clinch and hung on, and covered up and got out of the
way, perhaps not knowing in the least what he was doing,
and so fought out the bout, avoiding the knock-out. Even
so, now, in the stricken ship, a life stirred. Very, very
slowly she lifted with the monstrous weight upon her. She
rose spouting and streaming.

"God, she'll do it . . . the good old slut," the man Suckley said.

"I do believe she will," Dick answered.

"The mizen topgallant's gone," Suckley said. "Where the hell's the man at the wheel?"

They did not see any man at the wheel: there was none. The mizen topgallant mast had gone at the cap, taking both yards with it. Dick could not see them: they were gone.

A darkness of water and wind came down together upon the ship, so that she seemed to lie down and beg to be spared. Dick had seen beaten horses and cattle act in just that way. The poor thing seemed to be pleading with something that might perhaps be moved. While he crouched there, hanging on, still over the waist in water, he saw the mainsail, that lay stowed in storm gaskets along the mainyard, fling itself out of the gaskets into tatters. It was exactly as if the poor thing had put out hands in supplication, waving, piteous, ineffectual baby hands, stretched for mercy. There was not going to be much mercy.

The gust that had put them down suddenly deepened so as to pin them down, while a new cataract, full of gleams and fury, swept them off their feet and soused them. They rose from it as it passed, all out of breath, expecting another. It had seemed nothing of a sea to the big one, but it finished what that had begun.

As Dick got his chest and then his waist out of it he saw that foresail and foretopsail had gone from above him without his knowing it. All that was left of them were these pitiful, flopping and flogging hands, still flying from the yards, and two cloths, in rags, spinning round and round the foretopmast stay, with a piece of the chain tack that had tied itself .in knots.

"God," Suckley suddenly said, "it's got the mainmast."

What one of all the countless strains had been the last unbearable strain they could not tell. Suckley could not tell afterwards what it was that had made him speak. Some sudden movement, no doubt, that told of a backstay gone. As Dick looked, at Suckley's sudden cry, he saw that the mainmast was nodding its assent to its own death.

"Look out," he cried. "Stand from under, all hands."

All who had been watching had already scattered "from under" to the shelter of the fo'c's'le-head; Dick leaped after them, and there turned, to see what was to happen next.

The mast staggered a little: it waggled. With a snapping, stripping, splitting noise, unlike anything that any of them had ever heard, yet plain above all the roaring, it seemed to drop and shorten itself. Then it seemed to hesitate or waver (it only seemed) as the roll changed and began to gather. Then with a rising rush of noise, with its two steel lower yards, each weighing over three tons, its doublings, its topmast, its upper topsail yard, its topgallantmast with the two topgallant yards, and all their weight and tracery of wire shroud, backstay and batten, gear, lifts, braces, halliards and tackle, its countless blocks, fairleads and cringles and flying tatters of sail, fell as a tree in a wood falls with a splittering, thunderous crash, which carried all before it, snapping the lee foretopsail yards and carrying the ruins with it to a shower of sparks, splinters and collapsing mess from the port main-bitts to the fore-rigging.

Probably not one man of the crew saw more than the first blow or shock as the foretopgallant yards were flung flying and the foretopsail yards snapped at the slings. When the final collapsing crash came they were all back behind the windlass, crying "O God Almighty," while the flying fragments of wire, chain, iron and wood whizzed, clanged and settled.

That was only for a moment. A minute later they were out "from under" to see what remained of the ship. The mainmast was gone. It had snapped off its topgallant mast at the cap and flung it overboard, where it now dragged.

"Mainmast's gone all right," Alfrick said. "The foremast will go, too."

"We can save it," Dick said.

Alfrick pointed. "You can't," he said. "Half the port shrouds are gone."

"No, no," Dick cried. "Come on down the forepeak and get up a hawser."

"Hawser? What for?" some asked.

"Preventer stays," Dick cried. "Get a hawser round the masthead and set it taut by the capstan. Come on, now."

Then men looked at him with a kind of admiring pity.

"Come on," Dick cried, moving towards the forepeak hatch in the darkness there, "we may just save the mast."

In his mind already there was a plan for sending down a topsail buntline for a gantline, getting a hawser middled to the cap and set up taut to the heel of the bowsprit or the fo'c's'le bollards. He knew that it was a desperate plan, and that there was not an instant to lose. He had talked of it with Dudley Mac once, as the thing to do, if it could be done at once. Dudley Mac himself would be leaping forward to it, even now.

There came the slow, lingering, growing, roaring wallop of an enormous sea rolling in along the rail. The ship was in the trough, no longer under command. She ducked her head down so that a cataract shot over her bows and cascaded from the fo'c's'le head. Dick had to hold on to keep on his feet. Alfrick had him by the arm and spun him round.

"This will get her," he said.

He spoke from a fullness of knowledge and certainty of instinct. As she lifted her bows from the plunge she put the greatest possible strain on the stays and the shattered port shrouds. Dick saw the shroud cases strip and give. There came violent reports over his head, and then a clanging crash, as though the bows had been stove-in. He knew later that it must have been the stays stripping and the steel bowsprit springing, as the weight of the foremast came upon them. Then the entire foremast tottered, shuddered and cracked, with a burst of flying sparks at the mastcoats.

The fling of the ship to starboard hurried what might have been a graceful fall. The steel tube gave a kind of screaming whistle from the wind howling in it. Then down, falling aft with a crashing, collapsing, clumping, crumpling wallop, came mast, topmast, topgallant-masts, with the five yards and the whirling whips of stays. It fell so as to crash down the forward starboard corner of the fo'c's'le, and to cover the starboard main-deck, far aft. It struck with a blow that shook the ship in every plate and

rivet, and with a crumpling lift and rebound of bending
tube and splintering spar. Flying splinters, hanks, cringles,
fairleads, blocks and wads of chafing scattered in all directions. At once, as though the hurt thing were crying and
pleading, the few untattered sails burst from their bonds,
leaped into trailers and beat and beat and beat in the wind,
like flags of distress, like hands imploring, till the tempest
ripped them away and flung them far.

The crash had been so near and so awful that for an
instant no one spoke, though all those shaken men craned
from their shelter to see.

"God, boys, that's a general average," Aloysius Rue said.

A few minutes before the ship had been running heavily,
keeping a course, shearing the sea, with great sails set and
checked and three pinnacles of masts each a triumph of
skill and strength. Now they looked aft at a confused,
helpless, loitering, weltering wreck, broached-to, in the
trough of the sea, washing hither and thither, deluged by
floods on each side at each roll, her decks jammed, heaped
and tumbled with thirty tons of split, cracked, dinted iron
tubes, and other tons of broken, splintered, sprung wooden
spars, jammed together, pointing up, down and all ways,
messed, bound and tangled with wire and hempen rope,
iron shackles, chains, blocks and twisted iron spreaders,
and the whole decked out and flagged with flopping, mad,
careering, tattering strips of sail, some of them twenty
feet long, free of all bonds and flying loose ready to flick
anybody's face off. Out of this appalling mess a jagged,
cracked, hollow, sharp tooth of yellow iron, some thirty
feet high, rose up: it was the stump of the mainmast.

Beyond and above this rose the mizenmast, with topmast and yards still standing, all streaming sail in tatters, but with the topgallant-mast gone at the cap. It did not seem likely that this mizen would remain long aloft with the ship rolling as she was.

Alfrick made the first remark.

"That new band for the braces has saved the mizen yards for us."

"You bet your life it has," Barty Berrow said.

"They'll go in two more ticks," Pencome said.

"Every boat gone," Suckley commented. "Not a toucher left of any one of them; a clean sweep."

Dick had had enough to look at, he had not noticed this; he noticed it now: all four boats, the two on the skids aft and the two on the fo'c's'le had been wiped away. He had had a stunning blow, and only now began to realize what had happened. This was the case with each man there; and to each, as clear thought became possible, some part of the disaster became important.

"That knock she took when the mast fell," Barty Berrow said, "that will have split the deck; sure to. She'll fill, you see; she's half full already."

This was offered to the ship's company who were apathetic about it, though one or two muttered, "The hell she will."

About a minute passed in a stunned way: it seemed a long, long time. Dick wanted to scream with laughter at the naked look of the ship without her masts and rigging. If he had laughed he would have wept, too, for it was a shaky kind of fun.

He edged over to port, for a recurrent, dull, shaking thump on that side seemed like Death knocking to come in. It was now fast falling to night, though the twilight had still the glare upon it. Dick could make out that some great trailer from the mainmast was adrift on that side, possibly the topgallant-mast with its yards, which could not tear free, and, therefore, smote as the seas brought it home. Thump it came, and then again thump, somewhere near the fore-brace-bumpkin.

By this time, Dick had recovered himself; discipline and instinct together made him a sailor again; he moved out on the starboard side as far as the bitts to stare aft. What was happening or had happened aft? Why was not an officer tearing forward to lift this flock of sheep into life, to try to save the ship? Why was not the Old Man forward? Surely Duckswich would have forgotten his quarrels, now that the masts were gone? Dudley Mac, where was Dudley Mac? In the past Dudley Mac had only moved fast when there was trouble; then he had leaped into the thick of it, "like his weight in wild cats."

He had heard no single order, seen no trace of life aft since the big sea came aboard. There was no impulse forward to do anything; his moving out into the open was the first stirring of life in the stunned ship's company. It was as good a ship's crowd as would be found in a sailing ship anywhere, but it waited always for the order.

"Clump. Thump," came the wreck on the port side again. No plates could stand that for long, yet no one aft shouted an order. The men were looking aft and looking from face to face for an order.

"It's for me to call them," Dick thought suddenly. "I'm the man. I may be the only one left."

"Come on," he shouted. "Chips, and you, Berrow, and you, Suckley, get axes and try to cut that wreck there clear. I believe they're all dead aft. Sails, Boatswain, there, Kempley, and you, there, lay aft. We must set the mizen staysail and get her out of the trough. Roll your tails, sons; slippy does it."

He did not wait to see who obeyed or disobeyed. He saw Okle, the Carpenter, Cantlow, the Sailmaker, and half a dozen others leap to the word, with loud echoings of his bidding: "Cut the wreck clear," . . . "Set the mizen stay-sail," etc., etc. He meant to be first, to give the lead and set the pace, in the two vital things—to get the ship out of the trough and to cut away the wreck before it holed her. He set out at a run, feeling sure that long before he got to the mainmast stump the officers would be in charge again, making men stamp and go.

"They've been stunned," he muttered. "They've been knocked out."

The only free running space in the ship's deck was between the fo'c's'le-head and the fore-rigging. When he reached the fore-rigging, or what had been the fore-rigging, the nakedness of the ship struck home. She was all bare to the elements with no cover from the glare, no screen from the fury. The wind could get at her now; the sea could really sweep her now; both were doing it. The wind thrust her down, the lee-scuppers were under water. The sea rose up and hissed down upon her; there was no order in the sea: it struck from both sides often at once, so that the seas fought upon her hatchway.

Only a few moments before the deck on which he moved had been a clear ship's working deck, in sea order. Now, all that space was filled with a ruin and mess almost indescribable. Among the broken frame of the bitts the butt-end of the foremast lay. It had snapped off clean at the deck, almost as though sawn through there. The mast had fallen so as to jonch the whole starboard deck with ruin. As he started to clamber over the first of it, he took a shrewd note of it, knowing that the light was soon to go. Indeed, the night was on them.

The great weight had come down, God alone knew how. He had seen trees come down, he had seen this come down, yet what had been the procedure? It had smashed the bitts, of course; it had bent, crumpled and dinted, in a strange and awful manner, the strong forward wall of the starboard fo'c's'le; it must have rolled on that, bending it almost in, till it rolled off the edge and thundered prone.

The main upper spars in falling had snapped the fore topgallant and upper topsail yards at the slings. The fore lower topsail yard and fore yard, being steel tubes, had not snapped, but a terrible (though broken) blow had come upon them and had bent their trusses awry and tossed their starboard yard-arms skyward as cockbilled as an ancient mizen.

When the foremast fell these yard-arms were the first to hit the deck, into which they drove, so that some of their bands were started. Their great steel pikes now pointed slantingly up, streaming with sail and gear. The topmast was still securely fidded at its foot, but the shock of the fall had burst the cap asunder and allowed the doubling sufficient play to crumple the futtocks, the top, the spreaders and topmast rigging screws into a kind of iron mat. The upper topsail yard had snapped at the slings and lay one half on each side of the steel topmast, but was still held together by a bent jackstay and some gear.

Over all this hideous, heavy jumble and smash the net of the shrouds lay, crossed by its battens, to trip everyone who tried to pass. On each side they lay like a grid of rigid bars (however much bent), still secured to their screws; odd strands, and odd wires in other strands stuck out in jags so that in every yard of the deck there was something to catch and tear a man's clothes or flesh.

Dick crawled over and through this mess, noting it for future use, and eyeing it with anxiety, lest at any of the heavy rolls this ruin should fetch away and crush him against the ship's side. It was moving. Twice or thrice a minute he heard the wreck on the port side thumping the ship. From the waist opposite the thumping he saw a great spar rise from the sea, smite, and fall back. He had to hold on; at each roll water wallowed over and cascaded in. As he clung there, under the wash of a heavier sea than usual, the wreck alongside smote twice; he felt the deck tremble beneath him, and saw the ruin of the foremast roll.

He crawled out of its way to more wreck. In front of him the starboard main-rigging of stripped and twisted box-screws had been flung aloft "like iron railings by an earthquake," as he put it. Just beyond this railing lay the foretopgallant-mast with its yards, all broken, sprung, splintered and jagged, the truck on the deck, the heel on the boat-skid (now bent into a capital V), the yards leaning partly on the rail, partly on the roof of the half-deck.

Having reached this point, he had to hang on to let a set of waves pass over him. They broke on board from both sides. They rose up, high above his head, and tipped the ship this way and that, filling her to the rail. He was up to the chin half the time, but did not relax his purpose, to get the mizen staysail set, and the ship out of the trough. He counted seven waves, thinking that at the seventh there would be a smooth. At the ninth he heard as it were a screaming of thousands of hounds with a ripping of fire out of heaven. Multitudinous flashes ran out of the sky, like arrows on fire, streaming horizontally, so that he saw all the after part of the ship clearly lit, with water washing into spray against the poop bulkhead. As the flashes died, a darkness rushed down upon them all mixed with waves of the sea and this screaming of hounds. This noise could not be wind. This was some new, untested, unknown force coming into the world for the first time.

"Golly," he said. "Now we've got it. I never knew anything like this before."

He had started to wade towards the half-deck, for the mizen staysail was on the top of it. This new force took him by the shoulders, while the waters took him by the knee and shoved him with a gathering speed till he fetched into the half-deck with a bang. He caught hold of the rail that ran round it, somewhat dizzied by the darkness and the rage. The ship went on rolling and rocking, tipping this way and that, scooping herself full. Dick heard the foretopgallant-mast, just overhead, slithering and crashing near him. A cold wave of terror ran through him that at any instant it might roll in on him and crush him dead.

"Let's get out of this," he muttered, "anywhere clear of that rolling spar."

Where the others were he could not tell; they were swallowed up in the darkness. They might have been within a yard of him, or down under the sea.

Crawling away from where he was he thought, "Why, the officers may be in the half-deck. They may have been swept down here. . . . They may have brought Newbarn here. . . . Of course: why haven't I thought of that before? That is where they will be, washed clean off the poop, down into the deck, with a bone or so broken, and that's where they'll be now, waiting for someone to help—Captain Cobb, old Duck, and good old Dudley Mac, that glorious Scot, and Newbarn, saddle-sore from the boom." Dick was still a boy. Though the sea had given him manhood before his years, he still hoped as a boy. "Oh God," he prayed, "please let them be all there."

He hung on to the rail and hauled himself round to the doorway, which was screaming shrill from the tempest. Here was more ruin; the house had been gutted. The door had gone from its hinges, the skylight had been lifted off. He could see from the glimmer that two feet of water was washing about inside.

"Is anybody here?" he called, hanging on to the lintel. "Is anybody inside here?"

No answer came to him, except the wash of the water

moving with the roll to flood the lockers, and that shrill
shriek at the skylight. There was a horrible lesser noise
of click and clink, like bones rattling: the draughts were
plucking the curtains of the bunks and jangling their rings.
Suddenly the blast seized all the curtains together and
flogged them out at him as though someone were rushing
to shoo him away from the door. Something like a corpse
rose up in the water at him. He started back, but then
recovered; it was only a chest, or one of the tables or something. Everything in the house was awash or adrift or
broken.

"Is that you, Captain Cobb?" he called. "Are you there,
Mr. MacLerrinnan?"

He knew very well that no one was there; but it cheered
him to shout. Heaven broke in pieces above him and
spurted fire over him, so that he saw that near him, to
port, was a pile or jam of wreck, made up of God knows
what relics. On the top of it was a shifting sea-chest, black,
with big white letters, ED NEWBARN, stamped on it.
It had been floated and flung there with a mess of other
matters: bodies perhaps, who could tell?

The light died. A sea suddenly plucked him from where
he was and swept him into the lee-scuppers, where somebody already was. Somebody else said, "Keep your feet,
son," and had him round the waist with a powerful arm,
which drew him up to his feet. It was Barty Berrow, grinning as usual when there was nothing to grin at.

"Keep your feet, son," he shouted. "This isn't swimming
lesson."

They had vivid glimpses of things in the flashes. They

hung on together there. Bill Guller, hanging on a little further forward, let go his hold to come to them; the sea rolled him over and washed him past them to the starboard poop ladder (which still stood). Here he righted himself. Both laughed at his comical look. There were other men nearby, hanging on, waiting for the sea to wash away. Dick shouted in Barty's ear:

"Seen Old Man? . . . or Dudley Mac?"

Barty bellowed back, "Over side, son. Bad business. Good seamen."

Dick's heart sank, but he resolved to try to set the storm staysail.

"We'll cast loose the staysail," he shouted. "Mizen staysail. You and Guller man the halliards, soon as sheet's aft."

"Mind your tip, son," Barty shouted in reply.

Something big was coming: it was mounting there like a hill to windward, and the ship was rolling over to meet it, with an uncertain lurch which showed that it had caught her unprepared. Dick knew from her way that it would be a bad one and had hardly taken hold before it was on them up to their necks, with the news that what had been before was only flute-playing and prelude, but that now there would be a storm.

As he held on the darkness seemed to come out of the air on all sides at once, with a cry in it like hounds, "like bloodhounds and owls together," he muttered. The cry shrilled to that of screech-owls, with an increase of wind to something unbelievable. A flash of lightning, coming with the gust, brought a brightness that seemed to stream, and no doubt did stream, down the tooth of the mainmast for twenty seconds. Its glare showed Dick half a dozen men hanging along the rail, waiting for the seas to run off, and the mizen staysail, that new, Number Nought, storm staysail, which they had come so far to set, blown from its gaskets into tatters. Light sparkled on its empty hands, and on the hands of the topmast staysail above it. There went the sail which might have brought the ship out of the trough.

The worst of the water on the deck settled itself away somewhere. There were Cantlow, Barty Berrow, Kempley and the men of the half-deck near him.

"Got a weathercloth, handy, Sails?" Dick shouted.

"Yes. Two," Cantlow shouted back. He seemed to point to the sail-locker.

"Set weathercloth in mizen-rigging," Dick shouted to two or three. "Get her out of trough."

The *Hurrying Angel* had been built to carry passengers, both aft, under her long, roomy poop, and along her spacious 'tween-decks. She had carried no passengers for many years. Part of her cabin space had been converted into paint-and-lamp rooms and a big sail-locker. The sail-locker door was close beside them under the break of the poop. There was a hand-rail along the bulkhead to it. It was a big steel door, with a heavy teak latch fitting close into a steel catch. They crept along by the hand-rail to the door. Dick could not budge the big teak latch, but Berrow and Cantlow together beat it out of the slot, swung back the door and hooked it open. A fugg of hot air, sour with the smell of new sail, came out at them. They clambered into the locker.

"Where's the weathercloth?" Dick asked.

"Down here," Cantlow answered.

The room was pitch-dark, save for running glimmers of lightning, which showed the bulges of giant sails in confusion to all but Cantlow, who knew each one as a shepherd knows his sheep. He was on his knees in a corner to starboard lugging at something.

"Give us a hold of the bastard," Berrow said.

He and Dick got at it with Cantlow and roused it out. It was a small square of new Number Nought canvas, fitted with ear-rings and robands, and stopped up ready for instant bending to weather shrouds in emergencies.

"Catch a hold of this," Dick called. "Get it up the starboard ladder: the other's gone: then across to weather mizen-rigging."

He caught a glimpse of faces as the glimmer of lightning ran round. He saw beside the two stalwarts, Bill Guller, Rue, Kempley, Aylton and Staplow.

"Where are Chips and Suckley?" he asked.

"They got axes to clear the wreck that's hitting her," Kempley answered. "To clear the wreck overside."

"Right. Catch hold," Dick called. "Aylton, you and Guller go to the wheel, and ease her down as we bend this. It may be that she'll answer."

"Ease her down, it is," Aylton answered.

"Ease her down," Bill said. "She needs some easing."

They did not question Dick's order. In emergency obedience takes any order. Sails, Berrow, Dick, Aloysius

Rue, Kempley and Staplow tallied-on to the roll of weathercloth. Watching their chance they stumbled out over the rolls of sail, paused half in, half out, of the door, while flashing water lipped over the coaming; then, staggering, tripping and swearing, they stumbled out with it and contrived to shut the locker door. Then they set out, knee-deep in sea, blinded and buffeted by the gale, gripping the roll, clutching the hand-rail, falling and getting up, blown suddenly one way, then rolled the other, and so to the poop ladder and up it into the unchecked blast.

They reached the poop with it and re-formed, bent double there, with their heads down before lunging across to windward.

"God's sake," Sails shouted. "Charthouse gone."

The lightning lingered long when it came. They had all seen before Sails called that the small teak charthouse just abaft the mizen-mast had been wiped away, save for a jag or two.

"Come on, across," Dick shouted.

"Away hay," they shouted, as they dived up to windward. They were six of them against the wind, but it was all that they could do. The storm caught their clothes, beat back their southwesters and made the roll of sail in their arms like a young dragon or python. Now and then, as they struggled, the gale was like a charge of young bulls beating them back, sometimes even hurling them back, with a bang into the lee bulwarks of the poop.

As they clawed the sail there and struggled to their feet, the ship took in a bigger sea than usual, so that she was stunned and stilled as though about to sink bodily. The ease of the instant was like death after mortal pain. As she floundered under it, she made a steady platform, poor thing. While this stayed they beat across to the weather shrouds with their sail and crouched down, under the bulwarks there, to lash the flying ear-rings and robands to the box screws of the shrouds.

Cantlow shouted to Dick to haul taut aft, low down, below the sheer-pole. As all three knew, their task was to lash the head of the weathercloth low down against the shrouds, cut the rope-yarn stops which kept it rolled, and let the fury of the wind unroll the sail upwards against the shrouds. Then, before the wind could flog it to ribbons, they would have to leap up the shrouds and lash it as well as they could. Dick had the word from Berrow, who was next him, that the head was secure. They cut the stops. Instantly the sail flew up with a bang, flinging out its trailers of robands and ear-rings, which the men gripped and lashed as they could. As they clambered up to do this, the wind pinned them flat against the cloth, so that they could feel how terribly the shrouds were strained. They lashed the flying ropes' ends, then painfully crept down, foot by foot, praying that the cloth might budge her from the trough where she lay.

They crouched under the cloth. They had set this cloth aft, so that the gale, driving against it, might force the ship's head towards the wind, where she might perhaps lie to. They waited for perhaps half a minute, praying that the wind, drawing ahead, would show them that the ship was shifted. They felt no such drive on their left cheeks. Berrow shouted to Dick:

"The cow won't shift. She'll not do it."

"No," Dick thought, "she's stuck in the mud and needs more power than we've given her."

Then, he thought, "Those two fools may not have got the helm down, or the rudder pintles may be jammed or bent, or gone, for that matter."

It had been impossible for them to shout to the wheel, and for the helmsmen to shout back, with any chance of being heard, and in this blindness of darkness, only lit by flashes, no one could see, or depend on seeing. He crawled aft below the poop bulkhead till he could barge across into Aylton at the wheel.

"What a matter?" he shouted. "Is the helm down?"

"Getting it down, by tackles," Aylton shouted. "The wheel's broken across. Feel."

He put out a hand, felt nothing, then, groping, found the wheel. It had not gone at the spindle; that was there; but nearly half of it had been knocked away, possibly by Torrent's body being knocked across it. The gratings had gone from the wheel-box, but most of the box was left. The flashes showed that the binnacle was there, but the big cabin skylight, with the brasswork which he had so often polished, had been taken right out of its fittings, leaving a hole.

"Don't you go down the hole," Guller cried. "I nearly did."

They groped together at the tackles; groping, heaving and slacking, to get the helm down. It was joy to have Aylton's strength in that moment and place, when physical strength was so much needed. He was a wonder, Will

Aylton, strong as an ox, nimble as a weasel, resourceful, crafty, able to get at anything that jammed and to coax it clear, or heave it clear. But for Will Aylton they would never have done it. Probably, he was the only man in the ship who could have done it. All the time that they were there he was the one who both knew and did. All the time that he was working he was cursing and laughing. Little chuckles and bits of blasphemy reached Dick from time to time.

They got the helm down. Aylton shouted:

"You don't want her hard down. No. Not hard down. She'll fall off too much. A bit down. Not more than three points down."

Dick waited with a sick heart, hoping to feel her draw out of the trough, for no ship could stand the bucketing that they were getting. There was no change: she stayed down in the hollow, being rolled to glory with her decks full.

Little decisions are often hard to make: the big ones may come on such feelings that they make themselves. Inspirations come seldom, and happy thoughts not often. When they come, they may be only memories.

Dick groped his way to the bulkhead, and along it to the weathercloth. The storm swallowed up Aylton and Guller from him, shutting him from sight and sound of them. He was not thinking of them, but of a dodge that would be good to try. Into his mind, as he crawled, there came one or two dodges recommended by the books, the sort of answers which examiners would expect: unfortunately, they weren't to be applied here. How could he "brace all the yards up and shorten sail"? How could he "reef the mizen staysail and set it"? His yards were mostly down on the deck and his mizen staysail was in little rags five miles away. He had hoped that the mizen and its yards would have shoved her head up, but they had not. Then, suddenly, there came to him some memory, or half-memory, of something read long before (he remembered clearly where), of English seamen, desperately pressed off Cape Horn, trying something which beyond their hopes succeeded.

It came into his mind with a curious, sudden happiness, like water of life bubbling up in a desert. It was life. Life had been put into his mind. As he came under the weathercloth he caught Cantlow's arm and shouted into his ear, then into the ears of the others:

"Come up . . . above weathercloth. She'll do it."

They understood him at once. Their six bodies were to be an extra sail in the rigging above the weathercloth. It might be that the extra force would drive her head up; it might be that the extra strain would send the mizen-mast down like the others. It was a chance: there was no other chance: the ship could not stand such batterings much longer.

They swung themselves over the shrouds and up above the weathercloth. They were blown up, as it were, the side of a penthouse. They were pinned flat and beaten breathless. Their toes dug into the sail, which was like a wall: their hands steadied on the shrouds, which were like iron bars. Then presently, they were above the weathercloth, treading on battens, holding to the wire while the fury on their backs was like a cataract.

They were shut off from anything and everything. They were nothing there: inhuman, impotent, lifeless, valueless. They were specks in nothing but fury. There was no ship, no sky, no sea, that they could see. There was nothing but roaring and wetness, fury and streaming. All that they were was that they were neither of these.

It seemed to Dick that if he stayed there long his soul would be blown out of his body, and then blown small, and then blown tiny and then blown to nothing.

A splitting, cracking crash just over his head came with a blinding, great glare of light which lasted vividly, yet glimmeringly, for half a minute. The noise of the crash had been enough to terrify the strongest, and the awful light was like the ship on fire. Yet there was Barty Berrow's face alongside his not a foot away. Dick thought at first that he was being sick, but not so, he was roaring with laughter.

"What's—joke?" Dick shouted.

"Sails," Barty bellowed back. "Lost his bloody southwester."

Again the joke shook him. Dick could see by the glare Cantlow's bare head on the next shroud; the famous tarred canvas hat, Cantlow's own make, the envy of all hands and, therefore, the butt of all jokes, was gone with the mizen staysail "to be broken by the seas in the depths of the waters." Had Barty plucked it and flung it?

"His Sunday cadi gone off his old crumpet," Barty yelled. "Sails's Sunday cadi."

The light suddenly ceased; they were swallowed up again in blackness and fury.

How long were they there? Not long, probably. Under Dick's feet there was a movement of life suddenly, as the log beneath them that had lain in the trough trembled into being as a ship. He felt her emerge, as it were, and rise up, very slowly but very surely. Then the wind, and the wet which flew upon it, which had been smiting their backs, now caught them edgewise, as though striving to hurl them aft.

"It's done it," he shouted.

Barty Berrow, who was already clambering down, shook his leg from beneath him as a sign that they need stay no longer.

"Good old sea-cow," he shouted. "Good old bastard of an Angel."

They crouched together again under the weathercloth. He waited, wondering for a few minutes. She had climbed out of the trough; she was a ship again. He knew that for a moment the helm and weathercloth would keep her alternately coming up and falling off in reasonable safety. But in this wind it could hardly be for long: much more must be done, but what? The weathercloth would not keep them half an hour, perhaps: either the cloth would split or the mast come down. How either stood it he could not think; he had never dreamed that wind could have this force. What could be done if the sail went or the mast fell?

"Sails," he shouted, "could you rig a drogue?"

"Eh? What say?"

"Could you rig a drogue?"

"In this?"

"Yes, now."

"What of?"

"Spanker boom; staysail; killick."

Sails paused. "How get it over?" he asked at last.

That was a problem. How would they unship the spanker boom, lash or nail a staysail to it, weight the staysail with a boat's chain and anchor, secure all to a hawser with bridles, and launch the lot overboard to windward in the teeth of this that was beating on them? How could they lead the hawser aft, outboard, on the weather side, clear of all obstructions? It would be an all-hands job, even in daylight, in this gale, with all that slipping wreck and breaking water in the waist. Could they rig the drogue and launch it forward? Was there a space anywhere forward, not jammed and messed with wreck, where the drogue could be rigged? Was there any unbroken spar forward big enough for the ship to ride to, yet not too big to be man-handled over the side? If they had a drogue out, and the ship would lie to it, why then they might go to sleep.

He remembered an old sailor's remark to him. "The trouble with a mess at sea is that everything else has to be done first." This was a mess at sea and everything else *had* to be done first. Probably they would have to clear a space forward first, if they could, so that they might make their drogue: and how make it in blind pitch darkness, raging wind and flying water?

Well, first, perhaps, they could get oil-bags over, or

dripping from the lavatories. Oil would be the thing, good, thick oil from the donkey engine. In any case, he must get oil over: oil was the thing, oil now.

He caught the Sailmaker's arm and shouted:

"We'll get oil-bags over. Then rig drogue."

At this instant, he felt the ship tremble to another *Thump* from the wreck alongside. He and his gang had been so busy, so intent, toiling so hard aft there, that they had lost all thought of the wreck alongside. It had banged so little since the ship had come from the trough that he had not bothered about it. Now, *Thump*, there it was again, in that same space in the waist. Why had they not cut it clear? Where was everybody? What were people doing? The oil-bags must wait till that wreck was cut clear. He caught at men's arms and shouted in ears:

"Get over to the ladder. Down to waist—port side. Cut wreck clear."

He thought that they understood. They sheered off. He remembered that a very good fireman's axe had hung in an oilskin case inside the Captain's teak charthouse. Every voyage it had been taken down, its helve sanded bright, its head polished, then smeared thick with grease and returned to its cover and its clips. It had been in the ship ever since she first went to sea, and had never once been used; there had been no need for it in all that time. Now the same sea that had made it necessary had probably taken it to Davy Jones. If not, it would be a godsend now. He beat his way up to the site of the charthouse. The house, coamings, mattings, bulkheads, banisters for the little hatchway, locker for the code-flags, Captain's table, bunk, lockers, chart drawers, protractors, sextant, telescope, speaking trumpet, tell-tale compass, sofa, everything, had been taken right out of it, off it and away. There was nothing there now but the hole of the hatch, leading down to the saloon, with wind whistling up it bringing the noise of water slopping. *Thump . . . Bang . . .* came the blow of the wreck again. There was no axe, nor any of the wall from which it hung; yet axe or no that wreck must be hacked clear. He remembered that down in the sail locker Kempley had said that Chips and Suckley had axes. With this third axe gone, they would be short of weapons.

"Never mind," he thought, "we can take turn about, as men get tired."

It was likely to be dangerous down there in the waist, where the seas were breaking; but a great deal less dangerous than that wreck would be, if left to batter the side much longer. *Thump . . . Double Thump . . . Wallop . . .* came the thunder of its blow.

"Stick it, old bird," he cried to the ship. "We'll save you yet, if men can do it. My golly, old bird, you are some ship to stand it." He felt an exultation from the gale. All that fury of energy had in it an elemental life and joy, which tuned him to it, while it made him defiant of it. "Blow winds and crack your cheeks," he cried. "I'll beat the lot of you, please God."

Often before, he had felt an exhilaration from a gale; now, at this new one, so much more terrible than any he had known, he felt, for the moment, uproarious. He let the gale fling him (against the roll) across the poop to the ladder, and then prepared for battle. Why, down there, in the darkness and danger, where the wreck was thumping, he would find the missing men. Dudley Mac, the Battler, yes and the Duck, would all be where the danger was worst. Barty Berrow could not know that they were overboard. They would be there where the dragging spars were thumping the midship plates asunder.

Often before, he had seen men lifted beyond themselves, to deeds of frenzy and bravado, by the fury of a gale. He had seen them go down the leeches of sails, and out on the pennants of braces, hanging on by eyelids, with the end of a rope in their teeth, to reeve new gear. They had swung on the brink of death, grinning, spitting and cursing, and had come back damning because they'd dropped (perhaps) a tobacco plug or wetted a box of matches. Now he was going out into something as dangerous as a leech and as far from safety as a brace block.

"Golly, I'll show you," he cried. "Come on, the lot of you."

He was down on the main-deck now, up to his knees again, fighting across to the stump of the mainmast. He won to the bitts there (what was left of them) and hung on there. Seeing his time, he struggled cautiously over to windward from the stump, till he was staring into pitch blackness near where the wreck had been smiting. He was staring into fury that was mixed with water. All Nature, except himself, seemed going the one way. In the blackness were oily gleams of running fire in waves breaking on board. Over and through the blackness the lightnings ran livid, so that he saw all sorts of things for dreadful instants: scud (or was it black smoke?) galloping across mad heaven: a sea split, blasted, broken, going in all ways, only the smashed-off tops going the wind's way; the weather-rail, all flying ropes' ends, lipping down to collapsing cataracts, and men at the weather rail, three, no, four men, lashed there—they must be lashed there—half drowned or wholly drowned, up to their necks as he watched. The lightning ran round; he saw their eyes gleam in the lightning; no; not their eyes; they had something bright with them; very bright.

Darkness came down again, so that he saw nothing more save the moving, warmthless, greenish fire smeared within the water that curled about him. He remembered reading in a book how some fishermen had told somebody that this effect was always a sign of wind coming.

"Not much more than this can come," he thought; but in this he was unfair to Nature.

He waited in the darkness; there was still too much water in the waist to risk that dash to the rail. The seas ran off a little; then the lightning streamed again, showing him Cantlow, bare-headed, quite close to him, hanging on to a ringbolt against the roll. Once, twice, thrice she rolled, with her decks green with liquid fire in the darkness. Then she relented. The lightning blazed out again and showed him Cantlow making his dash. Dick took the instant too; now was the time to snatch a chance, clamber over ruin, hang on, hold tight, make a dash, slither, slip, and arrive with a bang. He and Cantlow did the trip together thus. There they were at the post of honour, uncomfortable even as posts of honour go, gripping for ends or bights of brace (they were near the fore-brace-bumpkin), to secure themselves against the next cataract, which soon came. They were with the men who had come there to clear the wreck. As the water poured away and the lightning shone, he saw Okle, the Carpenter, Alfrick, Suckley; the fourth might be Staplow. The light lapsed; the noise of the sea so near, and so devilish, was almost more than man could stand in the dark.

Somebody shouted, "Ahi, you bastard"; and a thrill shot through Dick's heart as the sea leaped at them all bodily, with a blaze of light upon it. Out of the sea the main upper topsail yard rose, as though Somebody were in the sea going to whack them with it as with a club. Up it went, at them it rushed, crash it struck, just beside them. It was fast by chain sheets, wire pennants, best manila halliards, and who knows what gear. Crash it came, and then again crash, while Okle and Alfrick struck at the gear of it. Dick at instants saw above the gleaming water two tools flashing, an axe and a chopper. He saw men wielding them, other men tugging at jammed gear, all striving, no doubt, all swearing; then the sudden light would lapse, with an odd effect of black heads above a black surging sheer of ship, which eclipsed suddenly into night. The men with the tools felt for the wire pennants that held the yard to the ship. These slipped and surged to and fro on the wet, rounded moulding of the bulwark top, as the yard tugged them. Often, as the men had the lifts in position for a chop, the ship lurched and flung them askew, or deluged them with sea. Dick and Suckley had hold of a wire lift which was like a mad eel. They tried to steady it to an iron pin in the rail. Sometimes it was loose to their hands, all slack and gone: the next instant it was away again, surging and sheering. The axe and the chopper made hacks at it and sometimes struck it, sometimes struck the teak fife-rail, and often just missed their heads. All there were often off their feet, under water. From time to time the yard swung in and smote. It was a time of mad confusion, effort and struggle; they were unable to see; they could only grope, whack and struggle.

"What we want," Alfrick shouted, "is searchlight, steady."

Dick came to think that Suckley could see in the dark, just like a cat. He himself had good eyes, but they were nothing now, whereas Suckley seemed to know what was happening.

After some twenty minutes of this it dawned on Dick that the wielders of the axe were weary, and that even if they hit the gear they did it little harm. Somebody thrust into Dick and shouted:

"What is it's holding her?"

By a flash he recognized Aylton, who, by the same flash, recognized what was wrong.

"Never do it this way," he shouted. "Get all the gear into one place. Avast axeing."

He had a chain from somewhere. Barty Berrow appeared from nowhere. Cantlow, Dick and those two got the chain passed round much of the slipping gear. It tugged them this way and that and struggled to be gone. They cursed it, and almost let go, they cursed each other, and shouted, "Hang on to her. Don't let her go." They did not, quite.

There came a lasting glare of light on a windward roll, when all things helped them.

"Heave now," Barty shouted. "Heave." Then, as they hove, he cried, "Hang on to her," and got his bundle nipped together and the chain round an iron pin. "That's got her," Barty shouted. "Will, you're a wonder."

After this, they had to hang on, while the sea went over them and the great yard smote. It was the most terrifying thing, not to know, within ten yards, or half a minute, where and when that ram of death was going to batter. Slowly the smooth came. Barty was waiting for it. He was at Chips's side, yelling:

"Give me axe . . . I'll get this son of a gun."

They could not see what he did, nor could he. He was, by much, the strongest man in the ship, and one of the stupidest, but here was the kind of job he loved, to whack at something with all his might.

"Stand from under," he shouted, shoving men aside.

He had Chips's axe. He wormed his way up to a good smiting-place, and jammed himself in, one foot at a ring-bolt, one inside a deck staunchion. Then he squared-off in the dark, taking both hands, knowing the exact site of that griding bundle of gear upon the rail.

"I'll teach you, you son of a gun," he cried. "You think you're somebody. You think acos you cut loose you're the Emperor's tart. You're not, I'll show you. I'm Barty; see? I'm Berrow; get that? I'm B. Berrow, gent. I'll teach you. That'll learn you. None of your lip with me, you cast-iron son of a gun." Swinging his axe, he smote, and smote again, then smote again, again and again.

"Twanky bloody dillo," he shouted, warming to the work, in spite of the shocks that ran up his arms, and the quite frequent misses. "Down you go. Out you come. Away, hay, hay, hay."

The lightning glared out on a long burn, so that they saw him smiting, and he could see to smite. All there saw the topsail yard in the sea rising high above them, as the ship plucked it to herself. Then, suddenly, there were sparks and a stream of fire. Dick felt something vicious whizz past his ear, just missing him. Suckley, who was standing just beside him, fell heavily against him and knocked him down. As Dick picked himself up, Alfrick called:

"Barty got her. She's gone."

Okle shouted, "All gone. I saw the yard go clear. She leapt out . . . like a fishing-rod."

Cantlow called, "Some of that gear unrove and flew back."

"Here's a dead man," Alfrick shouted. It was Suckley collapsed in his brace-bight from a whack on the head. "That chain, unreeving, got him," Alfrick shouted.

"Get him out of this; he'll drown," Dick shouted back. "Get him . . . fo'c's'le."

They unlashed his fastenings. Whether he was dead or not they could not tell; he was a dead weight to drag and pull along the deck, over the mess of mainmast, and through the washing waters. Over the unseen jam and tangle of gear they had to stumble and trip, dragging and shoving the unconscious body. Any little light would have shown them the way: they had no light. Sometimes they all fell prone, barking shins and elbows, scratching and tearing on jags and splinters.

"Nothing like a corpse, to weigh heavy," Staplow shouted. "They weigh half as much again as a live chap. Fact." They were now up to the fore-rigging, near the fo'c's'le door, only waiting for a smooth. "I been in the War," Staplow shouted.

The ship steadied for an instant after a run of heavy rolls. Dick felt that now was the time.

"Up with him," he called.

They hove up the body, dragged, pushed, shoved and lifted him over the mainmast doublings, only to find the fo'c's'le door jammed by a bent steel yard flung across it sideways.

"I know," Staplow cried. "Get him up top, and down skylight."

He was up the iron stair to the top of the fo'c's'le in a few brief seconds; Aylton followed him. There had been boats there that afternoon; boats and their chocks were gone. Lying down flat, the two men stretched arms for Suckley. Dick cut a rope for a sling, got it round Suckley's waist, and handed it up to them, then, they hauling, with Dick, Alfrick and Okle lifting, Suckley went up on to the fo'c's'le.

Crawling up there after him, Dick had much ado to keep from blowing overboard. Groping, he found the skylight gone, clean razed away by the sea that had lifted the boats. The wind made a whistling note on the edge of the hole. Down below the fo'c's'le seemed clear of water. Some old sailors down there had doubtless drained it, cunningly watching the rolls, and brooming to the scupper holes when she leaned to them. Aylton and Staplow dropped down into the fo'c's'le. After an age of pain and lying prone and hanging on they got Suckley down and swung themselves down after him into the pitch dark sodden room, where one could at least speak, in spite of the noise on deck.

"Anybody got a light?" Dick asked.

No, nobody had a light. Every match there was sodden; the one lamp had gone with the sea.

"Find an empty bunk," Dick said.

"Here's one," Staplow said.

"Hold on," Aylton said, "till I get a light. But there's a blast here enough to blow your head off."

Under his oilskins somewhere he had a briquette, with flints and tow; he pulled this out and contrived to light with it the stump of a tallow dip stuck in a jam tin. The sides of the tin kept the flame from blowing out, but also kept the light from spreading. However, it served to make the darkness visible. Dick could see the rows of bunks, wet clothes swinging to the roll, and odds and ends of gear skating about the deck.

"Get Suckley into the bunk there," he said.

Lifting him, they sidled him into the bunk and propped him in it. It had a high edge; there was no chance of his rolling out.

"Let's have a look where he's hit," Dick said. "It must have been his head; it just missed mine."

They took off the southwester and felt the skull. The bone was not broken, but there was a big, swollen, bloody bang on the side of the skull above the left ear. Suckley was coming to himself now and saying that he couldn't find the clip-hook; if he could find the hook, he could cut the mousing and cast loose . . .

"All right, son," Staplow said. "You're all right. You lie still and get your strength. We've cast loose the clip-hook. You'll be all right after a lie down. Funny thing about a clip on the head," he said to the others, "the tosh it makes you say. I was in the C.C.S. at Arlicourt when they bring in the Brigadier who'd stopped one with his brass hat. The Brig. kept saying he was a little dicky-bird; he didn't half make chaps laugh; they thought he'd been having one over the seven. It's the same thing really, pressure on the brain and that. And it don't half make them sick, sometimes."

"You keep quiet here, Suckley," Dick said. "You'll only lay yourself out if you try to work after that bat."

"I'm not going to lie up," Suckley said, starting up violently.

He sat up so suddenly, and with so little sense of where he was that he struck his brow on the bunk above him and fell back upon his bruise.

"You just stay quiet, son," Alfrick said. "We'll call you at One Bell."

Suckley seemed to understand this and lay still.

Barty Berrow's big body came trundling down the skylight to join them; he was followed by Kempley. Barty had the axe stuck in his belt at his back, so that he looked like a big-tailed ape.

"Here's your axe, Chips," he said.

"Some of it," Chips said, looking at the edge and feeling it with his thumb.

"That was a good chop of yours, Berrow," Dick said.

"I got the bastard," Berrow said, grinning.

"We got the main topgallant-mast and the yards away," Okle said. "We could see to chop, then; and they were all so smashed, they were held by very little. But that top-sail yard . . ."

He sat down upon a chest, rubbing his thumb along the edge of his axe, yet with one elbow hooked into a bunk, to keep himself from being rolled away. He was tired, and thinking how he would like to get that axe-head on to a grind-stone, to put a new edge on to it before turning-in for the night.

"Have you seen anything of the Captain or the officers?" Dick asked.

"No, nothing," Chips said. "We've been cutting this gear all the time. Haven't you?"

"They're not on the deck aft," Dick said. He looked about the dark room, thinking that somebody there might perhaps have seen something of one of them. "Has anybody here seen anything of Captain Cobb, or the Mates?" he asked.

There was a sort of murmur from those present, which grew louder as certainty came to them. "No, they hadn't seen anything of any of the three."

"Nor the two at the wheel, poor Torrent and the man Lefty?"

"No," the men agreed, none of those present had seen anything of them.

"They might be below, aft there," Kempley said. "They might be hurt, with broken bones; or they might be forward somewhere. They'd be in the starboard fo'c's'le, both of those two."

"That's true," Dick said. "You're a Starboard Watch man, Kempley, would you go into your fo'c's'le to see if they're there, and if they're hurt, and bring me word?"

"Yes, I'll do that, poor souls," Kempley said.

He leaped for the skylight coaming, got his foot on to a bunk, and swung himself up into the storm.

"I don't believe, Pomfret," Alfrick said, "I don't believe that we shall see any of those again; Captain Cobb, and our Mates and the two at the wheel. Ah, no. That big sea must have got them, up there on the poop. That will make five gone."

"And Newbarn?" Dick asked. "What of him? Has anybody seen Newbarn?"

No; nobody had seen Newbarn.

"That will make six gone," Alfrick counted.

"Where is everybody? Who has seen anybody?" Dick said. "Where's the Boatswain? Has anybody seen the Boatswain?"

No; nobody there had seen the Boatswain since they had been forward with him when the masts came down. It was the Boatswain's job to be on deck and to see that all hands were on deck. He was an old man, but tough and strong enough, and certainly no slacker at his job. Since nobody had seen him the chances were that he had gone, or at the best been hurt.

"That will make seven gone," Dick thought. "And Suckley laid out here makes eight."

"Is anybody turned-in here?" he asked. He did not wait for an answer, but went along the house feeling in the bunks. He pawed in two empty bunks: the third had a sleeper.

"Here's someone," he cried. "Whose bunk's this?"

"Evesbatch's."

"Rouse out here, Evesbatch," Dick said, shaking him. "Come out. On deck. Rouse and bitt."

Evesbatch was a dangerous customer, but Dick had always got on well with him. They had been in the same watch since the ship left England. Dick had had many talks and done many jobs with him; he knew him for a real plug-ugly, who would burgle and bash and perhaps kill, yet with a kind of faith, deep down, that made him almost grand. Evesbatch as a citizen was a misfit, as an enemy a danger, but as a friend in a tight place he was a rock of salvation.

"Oh, it's you, young fellow-me-lad," he said, rousing. "What are you doing in the fo'c's'le? I thought you weren't allowed here."

"I'm not," Dick said, "but I want to get some oil-bags over. Come on out and get some oil over."

"Who the hell has pinched my plug of tobacco?" Evesbatch said, as he turned out.

Dick went from bunk to bunk: he found two other men of his watch turned-in, Nick Cradley, the cheery one, and old Nab Wallers; they both turned out at his bidding, that is, they sat in their bunks, tying their trouser legs with rope-yarns over their sea-boots. He could see the gleams of light on the oilskin trousers and knew that was what they were doing. He waited on for a few minutes, for Kempley to come back with a report about the helmsmen from the starboard fo'c's'le. Kempley did not come back.

"Kempley's a long time bringing the news," he said.

"Bert Kempley always does what he's told," Cradley said, "but he does seven other things first."

Dick remembered, too late, that this was the wandering Kempley's way; he wished that he had sent Alfrick. He reflected that in this storm a man disappeared the instant you lost sight of him, and that having disappeared he became involved in a fight for life which put even an urgent order into second place.

"Hold on, all," he said, "till we get this clear. Who have we got here? Alfrick. Aylton. You, Chips. Sails . . . did Sails come?"

"Not here," the Carpenter said.

"Who else, then?" Dick asked. "Staplow, Berrow, Evesbatch, Cradley, Wallers; eight; myself, nine.

"What we've got to do is to get oil over, to ease the ship. She's getting such a welting she may start something. The oil's forward, as you know, in the Boatswain's locker. I want a colza drum in each lavatory-pan, fore and aft; that'll give her a chance perhaps. Evesbatch, will you come with me to get a drum aft? Aylton and you, Alfrick, take a second drum aft. Staplow and Cradley, one drum forward, port side. Berrow and Wallers, one drum forward, starboard side. You know how to get a drum going, job the bottom with a marler, so that the oil will seep out.

You'll find marlers in the rack above the oil-drums. Is that all clear?"

"Yes," the men repeated, it was clear and would be a very good thing; there was nothing like oil for drawing the sting out of a sea.

"If you won't mind my suggesting it," Alfrick said, "it's always a good thing to have an oil-bag out aft, on a long span, well out to windward, as she drifts. The oil will make a smooth, oh, twenty yards from the ship if you pay it well out, and be twice as good value as an oil-bag forward."

"I see it would," Dick said. "Thanks for the tip. I'll try that. The sooner the quicker, then."

He swung up to the skylight as Kempley had done. There he was in the fury once more, gone from the shelter, the light and companionship of men, into the blast, the pelting and the roaring. He was crawling to the iron steps to the deck when Evesbatch joined him.

"Good night for a job of work," Evesbatch shouted, meaning a burglary; "all the cops under cover and so much noise nobody could hear the safe pop."

"How many safes have you popped?" Dick asked.

"I was never one of them ducks," Evesbatch shouted. "Too many expenses. Too much outfit. Motors. Acetylene. Mug's game, popping safes."

Dick slid over the edge of the fo'c's'le, and so down to the deck. A little water came over his feet. He remembered suddenly with a pang that there, close alongside of him, was the hole where the foremast had stood. He hung on to the iron ladder and groped towards the hole with his left hand. It was there, still open, and water was running into it at each roll. How much had gone into it already? Of course, they were out of the waist, where the dangerous water came aboard; still, a running brook fills the pond, and this brook had run for a long time now.

"Waltzing into her," Dick muttered. "There's another thing that ought to be done first. I'll do the oil first."

There was not far to go. He hove himself uphill along the side of the donkey-house, ever forward to the fo'c's'le-head, where the sprays gleamed as they cataracted over all. The sheet of their falling soused him as he beat through it into shelter. He had arrived. There in the pitch darkness by the windlass it was out of the blast, out of the beating water, a man could breathe. He stumbled over a body who had chocked himself on deck against the windlass, and was sleeping there.

"Turn-to," Dick shouted at him. "Turn-to. Get oil-bags over."

The man, whoever it was, rolled over and stood.

The ship was taking giddy plunges and then lifting high. All that tottering iron cage of the bows was whining, cracking and whickering. At times, the bow-sprit, broken but not yet free, whanged and banged as though it would rive the bows apart; then the ship would shove herself sickeningly down, down, down, till with a whumpf a sea would burst under her figurehead and collapse with a crash above their heads and come streaming down. If oil-bags didn't ease that, one of those dives would end her.

Yet what could men do against such force? This wasn't a storm: this was the end of the world: ships weren't built for this kind of thing.

There wasn't any light: all had to be groped for. Under the fo'c's'le-head to each side were the men's lavatories, one for each watch; forward from these were the Boatswain's lockers. On the port side, the Boatswain's locker was used as a coal-cellar for the galley and donkey-engine. On the starboard side it stored the wash-deck pump, tubs and brooms, the blocks, small stuff and marlers for use about the deck, and a wide variety of gear, including paint-tins and brushes, drums of colza oil, blocks of holystone, a tub or two of sand, and many bundles of old sail for the scrubbing of paintwork.

Dick had gone to this starboard locker daily for something or other, ever since he had joined the ship. He knew where each thing was, but was not prepared for what he found. As he entered, he trod on one body, stumbled on it and fell on two more: three men had been tightly chocked there, fast asleep, jammed between lockers and bulkheads.

"Come on, turn-to there," Dick called. "Out you come, now. Get oil-bags over."

The men rose up, growling and muttering. He did not know who they were and could not see. He thrust past them and roused out the oil-drums from the rack. He was afraid that his oil-bag company would melt away from him in the darkness.

"Are you there, Evesbatch?" he called.

"Just by you," Evesbatch answered.

"Right. Catch-a-hold here. We'll take all we can manage. Aylton, there."

"Present," Aylton answered.

"Here's one for you. Who's that that I trod on?"

"I'm Tom Coggins, the chef," a voice answered.

"Catch a hold of this tin of soup, then: job a hole in it and set it to simmer in the pan."

Tom Coggins growled that he didn't belong to the deck department, by rights, and that it was his time to Kipp. "Glory-ho," he said. "I have my all night in, like any other Idler. It isn't a night for the Doctor to be out in. I'm only forward here, because of the draught in the round-house. I can't sleep in a draught, all the world knows that. Till the skylight's repaired, I'll have to sleep any place where there's no draught; for a draught brings on my catarrh. However, now you *have* woke me, as it's you, Pomfret, what gave me that pair of socks, perhaps I don't mind for once, but it's not my practice, mind."

He took the drum and marler like a good fellow and soon returned in great glee.

"I took that oil along, next door," he said. "There was that Mat Penk, sitting there, all lashed against falling and just dead-oh, snoring.

" 'Out you come,' I sez. 'We need that place for the oil.'

"He got up and sez, 'Is the ship sinking?' he sez.

" 'Yes,' I sez, 'sure to.'

" 'Oh,' he sez. 'Doctor,' he sez, 'I shan't see her again.'

" 'Who?' I sez.

" 'Why,' he sez, 'my darling Millie, that married the oil and colour shop.'

" 'No,' I sez, 'you won't.'

" 'My ghost will, though,' he sez. 'It'll be near my Millie whatever happens.'

" 'That'll be a picnic for her,' I sez, 'to have your ghost baa-ing round her. But come on out of it,' I sez. 'This oil's got to go there. And the sooner you give up mooing about a married woman, my lad, the better.' "

"Is Berrow there?" Dick called. "Barty, there." There was no answer. "Lord, he's gone again," Dick said. "Well, catch hold of this other drum, Doctor, and set her flowing across the way. Is Guller there? Pass the words along; is Guller there?"

Guller was there; had been there all the time, he said.

"Stand by, Bill," Dick said, "I want you to come aft with us. Catch-a-hold of a drum."

"Here," Evesbatch said, "don't think you'll carry these drums aft in your hands; you'll not. You'll need both hands to hang on by. Sling them by a double line on your shoulders, pass one line over each shoulder, then back under your arm-pits, round the drum and knot across your chest. Then, whatever happens, you can't drop them."

This seemed sound sense. They helped each other in the dark to sling their oil-drums.

"Bill," Dick said to Guller, "when we've got this oil over I want to search for the officers."

"Haven't you seen them?"

"No."

"Right-ho, then. But they're dead, Dick, or they'd be searching for us."

"They may be hurt," Dick said.

"This doesn't *hurt*.. It kills."

"We'll prove that. Come on. Keep close, Evesbatch."

"Shove ahead, son."

They shoved ahead, out of the shelter, into the pelting. The roar of the wind was, if anything, louder, but was there not some ease already from the oil? Dick knew how swiftly and blessedly oil will work in heavy seas: usual things were gone from the world to-night, but surely the waves were smiting with the palm now, instead of with the clenched fist?

A big figure stopped them as they came from under the shelter. It was Alfrick.

"Don't you try it, the lee side," he shouted. "The wreck's got a play on it."

"How d'ye know?" Dick called.

"Tried," Alfrick answered. "Nearly got scrunched. It's all right weather side. All jammed there."

"Heave ahead, then," Dick shouted back.

They set out, gingerly, to the donkey-house, their first port of call; they made it without trouble, and got from it to the fo'c's'le.

"Over the top of fo'c's'le," Dick shouted. "Dodge the main yards that way."

As he bent to climb up to the top of the house, the water dribbled over his foot. He remembered suddenly that the water was still going into the hole where the mast had stood.

"Waltzing into her," he repeated. "My God, if she gets a head sea she may fill ker-wallop."

He jumped down from the rung and fell over somebody

at work in the narrow space between the fo'c's'le and the
donkey-house. There were two or three there.

"In the name of God," Cantlow's voice called, "is it taking to raining seamen?"

"Are you plugging the hole?" Dick asked.

"Damn to hell," the Carpenter shouted. "Stand off this
hatch-cover. Can't you see we're plugging the hole?"

He was tired and hot, as well as exasperated by the diffi-
culties of the job in that narrow space. In that blackness
no one could have seen that men were there. The running
lightning showed them for an instant.

"Good-oh," Dick shouted. "Come along, Evesbatch."

The oil-bag party went up the steps to the top of the
fo'c's'le, and then crawled on hands and knees along the
roof, hanging on to whatever they could catch of the wreck
of the boat-chocks, and the mesh of main topmast back-
stays. Something that Alfrick had said made Dick edge
across to the starboard side of the house. Craning there, he
heard, at the lee-rolls, a grinding, griding scraunch, above
the roaring of the wind. It was quite true, the wreck of
the foremast had "a play on it"; it was moving. In a
lightning-flash, he saw it move: not much, of course; it
was partly jammed, partly, no doubt, stuck in the deck,
but the scraunch that it made showed the power of the
play. He knew, very well, how sometimes a great weight
will break loose on deck, and take an impetus, in a series
of rolls, such as no power of man can check. This weight
was checked or chocked for the instant, but for how long?
Suppose she fell off again, as she was sure to, and began to
roll her silly guts out? All those twenty-odd tons of iron

would go racing across decks, playing hell's delight. Who
could lash, or chock, or wedge them, when once they took
charge? They would roll one way and stave the main
hatch in; they would roll the other way and burst her side
out.

"Well, if they start," he muttered, "we can't stop them;
we've just got to stick it and take it. In the meantime, I
must get this oil aft."

Crawling aft, he reached the end of the deck-house,
where he butted into Bill Guller, who was waiting to go
down the ladder.

"Evesbatch is rigging a life-line," Bill shouted, "from
here to the half-deck."

That was a great idea, to have a life-line across the waist,
to hang on to as one crossed. He knew that Dudley Mac
had rigged life-lines, in that past life when they had had
light, but the falling masts had taken them. He blessed
Evesbatch for the thought and the deed. The waist was
the open space between the mainmast and the deck-house
where they crouched. In the midst of it was the main
hatchway. It is at the waist that the main seas come
aboard. "Wet work in the waist," is a proverb. It was
wet work in the waist at this moment, as Dick could see
by the gleam in the waves below him.

It occurred to Dick that Bill was funking. Why was he
not down with Evesbatch helping to rig the life-line? He
clapped him by the arm.

"Come along, then, Bill, old horse," he shouted. "Come
on, the fore-top."

"Come on," Bill shouted back, and followed him down the ladder.

Sure enough, Evesbatch had rigged a life-line of old three-inch rope from the iron ladder towards the darkness aft. It was not very taut, but it made a world of difference to them. Dick shouted to Bill, "Good King Wenceslas," but Bill either did not hear or did not understand. Dick sang as he hauled himself along:

> *"Mark my footsteps well, my page,*
> *Tread thou in them boldly."*

He was up to his thighs in malevolent, gleaming water full of horrid fire. This was wet work in the waist, all right. He had heard Old Purple, the Boatswain, call the waist "the Slaughter House" from some old naval seaman's name for it, in days when ships fought side to side and converged their fires upon it. Dick feared the fires that were on it now, for who could tell? Might not sharks be in this depth of water on deck? Each one of those twisting gleams might be a shark. He had heard lots of tales of sharks at Melbourne; how they will come right in, to shallow water on the beaches, and pluck people away. He thought how they would break the news to his sister: "He was unfortunately eaten on deck by a shark while carrying aft an oil-drum. His end was peace and regretted by all, especially the shark."

They reached the main-bitts, or what was left of them, in safety. There they caught the hand-rails of the half-deck, steadied themselves an instant, and clawed by them, hand-over-hand, round the house, till they faced the break of the poop.

"Good old Evesbatch," Dick thought. "My God, he is a good man; he's run us out a life-line over to the poop ladder."

He clawed out and felt that Bill was beside him. It was not the moment to plunge yet, for the ship was working up to another big series of rolls. They waited there, hanging on, while the ship rolled, as though she were going to roll over. Big water came over and round them, savage swirls of it rushed along each side of the half-deck, swerved at the angles, met where they stood, clashed, debated, and then roared away together to whichever side had the vote.

Dick thought, "As there isn't a mess of wreck just where we are, perhaps the mizen-mast still holds."

He was not sure of it. No man could see. He could not even be sure that the howl above him meant that the stays were still there. The mast might have fallen in any direction at any time during the last hour, yet no man forward could have seen or heard of the fall. Probably, the mast still stood, because the ship was still pointing up; therefore, the weathercloth was set still; and if the weathercloth were there the lower mast at least must be standing.

Whether the wind were shifting or not, he did not know; the ship was coming up to it anyway, which was the main thing. What was the wind? Who knew what direction it was coming from? Who cared? It was Force Twelve, Beaufort Notation, or "such as no canvas could withstand"; but by all accounts the worst came later: this thing was only the prelude: this wasn't the storm yet.

"Well, now," he thought, "now I know why they write with such respect of cyclones."

They had seemed very beautiful, orderly little things in the diagrams in the books. This outrageous fury was only the beginning of one; what in God's name would the thing's manhood be?

The rolls were heavier than usual. There was so much noise that he could not tell whether the wreck on deck had begun to roll or not. The roaring of wind and sea were such as he had never heard: even if the masts had started to dance he could not have heard them. The rolls were so heavy that he kept saying:

"This will take the mizen-mast out of her. No? Well. This one will. No? Ah, but now it must go; no gear, no mast, nothing made by man can stand this."

Had it stood it? He thought so, but how could he tell? The mast might fall within a foot of him without his hearing it or seeing it. Suppose it went, as it must? What could they do when the mizen-mast went? Rig a drogue. How could they rig a drogue in this? How would they launch it if they could? Why had they not a drogue all ready made and bent, as a part of the ship's standing equipment? Because it would be in the way in the whole passage in nineteen voyages out of twenty. He remembered a wise American's remark about nations being armed. "It's like a man's carrying a gun . . . you may never need it, and you ought never to need it, but if you do need it, you'll need it so badly that you'll be glad to have it." He would have been thankful for a drogue now: a good, strong, solid one, with chain-bridles, away out there on a good span with an oil-bag on it. Well, he hadn't one and couldn't rig one. If you haven't eggs and flour and a fire you can't make pudding.

There came a comparative smooth; the boys snatched their chance and followed the life-line to the ladder. On the poop, the saving line led to the mizen-mast and thence to the shelter of the weathercloth, where the lightning showed them Evesbatch lashing his oil-drum to a life-buoy. They launched it presently on a long span of the main braces, and had the blessing of it within two minutes: the teeth of the sea seemed drawn.

"Got her," Evesbatch shouted. "We'll lash the spare drums here." They did so.

"I'm for a doss," Evesbatch called.

He had a length of boat-cover: he rolled himself in this and lashed himself to the mizen shroud-screws. He was asleep in twenty seconds. He was a hard case, Kruger Evesbatch.

"Come below, Bill," Dick called. "Look for officers."

The boys crept across to the companionway, once roofed by the chart-house, now a hole in the deck up which a blast of air came piping. Dick slowly stepped down the stairs, with Bill behind him. When they were below the level of the deck, he paused, for the intense relief of being out of the deafening, blinding thrust of the wind. Here the roar was diminished; a shout could be heard; one had not to yell. Plenty of lesser tumult was going on below, however. Somewhere down there in the cabin quarters doors were slanging and banging, wreck of some sort, with metal or glass in it, was washing to and fro, not only in the cabins but in the alleyway. A blast of air was whistling up, water struggled, gurgled and slopped, or sometimes swept with a great, laughing wash and rush across the foot of the stairway. Bang . . . Clang . . . the swinging doors went; scutter, gurgle and wallop went the water. The wind piped, whined and shrilled. All the bulkheads of the cabins went whack on the cracking stretch at each roll. All the grunt and crash of the rudder-head and of the seas under the counter rang out here, with the many whines of complaint of the ship's structure. Down here, too, unexpectedly they heard what they had not heard on deck, even a few feet from it, the death-bell clang of the poop-bell striking in the heavier rolls; and something much more ominous, the grinding of a grim weight on the starboard deck.

Dick had gone slowly down the stairs, not knowing what stairs had been swept away. It was pitch dark down below there. Bill caught him by the shoulder to keep him from pushing further. Bill was scared of what they might find there: Dick was not too happy. He kept thinking:

"Very likely I shall step on somebody's body."

"Dick, old man," Bill called, "how the hell does the mizen-mast stand?"

"I don't know. Thank God it does."

"It must be damned good gear."

"It's all that," Dick answered. "Come on down, now. I'd give something for a light. The Steward used to have an electric torch and refills. Do you know where he stowed them?"

"He had them on a shelf near the pantry door till he found I borrowed them from there," Bill answered. "He kept them on himself, after."

"They might be in his bunk," Dick suggested. "We'll look there."

"Give a call first, old man," Bill asked, for the horror of that deserted cabin had taken hold of him. He was thoroughly scared.

At the foot of the companion Dick stopped again and shouted:

"Is anybody down here?"

They heard no answer to their call among the many noises of the place. The water sloshing and loitering in the alleyway suddenly made a rush towards them, and then, meeting a rush from the cabin, splashed and washed back. It was as black as a pocket down there. As Dick trod from the last stair into the wash of water a lasting glimmer of lightning lit up the alley at that point, so that he saw, and noticed with particularity, a fretted beading or moulding running along the bulkhead opposite. It was of some wood painted to resemble walnut, perhaps it may have been walnut, for the ship had once been, according to her owner's prospectus, "the last word in luxury and comfort, in the Australian Passenger Trade." At any rate, the commonplace, repeated dark fretting, each fret exactly the same, and resembling nothing, except perhaps the works of a piano, impressed themselves on Dick's brain, so that he saw them often, after that, like hieroglyphs suddenly lighted, like Hebrew or Cuneiform writing, something of great importance set there for him to read, yet with no key given to the script.

The Steward's pantry and cabin, which had once been two first-class cabins (described as "state-rooms" in the prospectus), were just opposite the foot of the stairs on which the boys stood. Both the doors were gone from the door-posts, wrenched clean off, so much the lightning showed before it lapsed.

"Doors gone," Dick said.

"How could the sea get at them down here?"

"It struck a big blow, that sea. Are you in there, Steward?"

He knew as he spoke that the Steward wasn't there. He moved into the cabin. Part of the door was broken on the floor of it, shifting to the roll. The wreck on the floor of the pantry, which opened into the cabin, was jingling with broken china, and a loose tin kettle. The sea had made a fair sweep there.

"He kept the torch sometimes on a little shelf to the left of the door," Bill Guller said. Bill knew a good deal about the cabin, for he was a skilled food-thief.

"No shelf there, now," Dick said, after groping. "There's just a chance it'll be in his bunk."

"I think he had it on him always," Bill said. "I used to be scared of his flashing it on me when I came scrounging."

"I wish he'd flash it now," Dick answered.

He groped to the bunk in the pitch-black little cabin. Bits of the door and some of the Steward's clothes were floating about on the floor. Dick probed with a leg this

way and that to test if the Steward were there, too. He
did not seem to be. He felt in the bunk; it was wet of
course, it had been drowned like all the rest of the cabin:
there was nothing under the pillow. As he patted the pillow, to make sure, a vicious sea smote the little bull's-eye
port, with a noise between Sumph and Spatch. Perhaps it
was the sudden shock of this noise which made him think
that the Steward would not have had the torch upon him
during daylight; and it had been daylight, of a sort, when
the sea came. No, he would have hidden it somewhere,
in his pantry-drawer, in his chest perhaps, or in his sea-
bag, or why not in the bunk under the clothes? It was not
under the clothes, even at the foot, but something made
Dick turn the poor, thin, sodden straw mattress, and there,
under the foot, were the cartons of refills, and (after pat-
ting here and there) the small square tin case of the pocket
electric torch, which had cost perhaps three shillings and
sixpence, yet now seemed, to Dick, worth its weight in gold:
the buying of it surely the one thing in all the Steward's
life which had mattered to the ship, though he had been
in her for twenty years. Bill was already groping in the
pantry. Dick pressed the switch of the torch, and instantly
in the flash saw what he thought was the Steward's body
hanging from a hook. It was one of the long white over-
alls or coats, such as umpires used to wear at cricket-
matches, which the Steward always wore when waiting at
table, such being the Captain's pleasure.

Dick turned the flash upon the cabin floor: a shoe, two
socks, and a couple of sabots were floating there.

He knew the sabots well; he had often seen them in the

Steward's room. Once, when helping the Steward with some cases of stores, he had asked him about them. They had been given to him (no doubt as a sweetener or commission) by some ship's chandler eager to do business, at the port of St. Nazaire, when the ship had been there years before. Mince had kept them ever since. "When I go home to my daughter's," he said, "in Shell Street, Wapping, East (that isn't the common part of Wapping, Pomfret), I wear the sabots for me little grandchildren. When they hear the clack, clack on the pavement, then they know it's their grand-dad coming."

Dick thought of this now: it brought the tears to his eyes. The better part of Wapping would clack no more, let the grandchildren listen never so.

He moved into the pantry, which communicated with the cabin. There was Bill, already munching raisins.

"I've got the light," Dick said. "I suppose the Steward's not here?"

"No. Have some raisins; they're a bit salt on top, but all right inside."

"I'll have some presently," Dick answered. "The cabin crockery seems to have caught it."

Indeed, there most of it was, in bits, swept from its hooks to smash, chinking in the wash underfoot.

"Come on out, now," Dick said. "There's lots to do."

He turned the light on to the alleyway towards the forward end. The door at the end had been wrenched off one of its hinges, and now clanged and flung about more like a port lid than a door. As it moved to the roll Dick saw through its gape a glimpse of lightning on white foam rushing across the outer deck. He lowered the beam on to the water in the alleyway. At once he caught sight of a body.

"Here's somebody," he said.

Near that alleyway door, trailing in the water and lifting, falling and washing about in it, was a body, face downwards, plainly dead. The two boys struggled through the water to it. Dick turned it over with one hand, while he held the light with the other.

"Mr. Duckswich," he said. "He's dead, poor old man. Let's get him into his bunk."

His bunk was in his cabin, which was just at their side, on the starboard side. They had but to drag him out of the alley and then give a lift.

"He can't be dead," Bill said. "A bit stunned, Dick, or partly drowned."

Dick had moved the poor head, to identify it; he knew better. He had felt the broken bone and knew.

"He's dead, poor old man," he repeated. "The big sea flung him and broke his neck. Poor old Duck; he was often damned kind to us."

The Mate's cabin was in a worse state than the Steward's. The door was gone; the drawers had been pitched or washed out of the lockers, and now floated with their contents all broken and foul. The tin basin had fetched away from its rack and pealed a merry note as it went to and fro.

"We can't leave him quite like this," Dick said, after they had straightened the limbs. "One of these seas might roll him out of his bunk. I'd hate that to happen." By the torch-light he saw some amberline on a hook at the bulkhead. Dick passed a couple of turns with this, to keep him from rolling out. "Poor old Duck," he said, "we didn't think this would happen when we came on deck at midday to-day: that is, if it still is to-day."

"He would never have come this voyage," Bill said, "if he hadn't lost all that money."

"Rather different, I expect," Dick said, "this last night of his and his first. Then, I suppose, he had his mother and the midwife; they had night-lights, I suppose, and a fire going: the doctor looked in and Mrs. Jones from over the way. Since then he has been fifty years at sea. Knocking round the world, and now here. But come on, we must look for the others."

"Do you think they're all drowned?"

Dick knew from the question that Bill had lost his nerve. Bill caught his arm.

"We're going to be drowned, Dick, aren't we? Tell me the truth, now," he pleaded.

"We shan't cheat the gallows as easily as all that," Dick answered. "Come on along now, to Dudley Mac's. We must finish down here and get on deck."

It was but a fish-captain's walk to Dudley Mac's cabin. He was not in it, but it took them some time to make sure of this. The cabin had once been described as "a palatial stateroom, replete with every modern convenience." It was now as palatial as it had ever been, and it was replete, for what the great sea had gathered aft it had flung here all smashed and crushed, three doors, part of the skylight, a bit of the wheel, some of the pigeon-holes of the code flags, three broken revolving chairs from the cabin table, a tin trunk, the Captain's topee-case, and a spare bunk-full of wooden blocks, all unstropped and now sent sailing hither and thither, with a tin basin and jug and all Dudley Mac's kit of clothes. Sea had washed down here from the sky-light and hatch; it had also washed in from the deck: the place had been afloat, but Dudley Mac was not in it.

"He was on deck when the sea got us," Dick said. "We'll find him on deck, now, under some of the gear perhaps. We shall soon see, now that we have a light."

"Let's look in the saloon," Bill said. "He might have been pitched down the skylight. Good Lord, there's the cat, in the upper bunk."

It was true; the cabin cat, Polly-Wolly, was in the upper bunk, crying loudly for sympathy. She was all draggled with the sea; no doubt, she had had to swim for it. She was terrified at the noise. Her three little kittens, aged about one month, were all gone. Like an hysterical woman, she tried to fling herself into Dick's arms.

"Get back, pussy-cat," he said. "You stay where you are, old girl. Keep in this upper bunk. It's no weather for little cats. All your little kitties drowned? Well, you'll soon have some more."

He stroked her wet and staring fur, and rubbed her throat. She whined with terror at the roaring and bang-ing. Her mouth hung open, like the picture of a shell-shock case: the big sea had broken her nerve. She was very different now from the bold Roxana that put such a flutter in the Toms down East London Dock way, that moused in the wool bales of South Australia, and had been the standing toast of the cats of the Orient mail ships these last three years. Only the day before she had lain on her mat in the saloon, in a patch of sunlight, with her three kittens, drowsily purring, but now, poor thing, she was terrified.

"You stay there, pussy," Dick said. "It's the best you can do. Come on aft, Bill; we'll look there."

Anyone who had been on the poop when the big sea came aboard might have been swept down into the saloon when the skylight went. The boys waded aft to the saloon, and stood in the doorway, gazing at the smash within. The sea had dealt it death.

Long custom had given them an awe of the saloon. It was a place that one only entered bareheaded, with the greatest respect, at rare times, when dining with the Captain or on some special service, taking the sights, or asking for slops or medicines. They felt that awe still, and hesitated to enter: they stood in the entrance while Dick turned the light hither and thither, looking for bodies. There were no bodies there, only smash and mess.

A withering gale was blowing down the hole where the skylight had been. Plainly the blow that had taken that great structure had followed it with an appalling weight and force, smashing all that it could not carry. Formerly, the saloon had been the big dining-room for many passengers: it had been decorated for them and still had some of its first fittings. Its forward bulkhead had been hung with big mirrors in gilt frames; its sides had been panelled with a wood painted white and stencilled with green and pink. Its after bulkhead had held a big painting of the *Hurrying Angel*, done by a Chinaman in Hong Kong; below this had been two big mahogany chests, bound with broad bands of brass, which the Steward had kept like shining gold. One of these chests was the medicine chest, the other the ship's library (of sermons, 1840–1850). Both chests had once been parts of the equipment of an East Indiaman and had been at sea for nearly a hundred years. On each side of the painting there had been racks containing carafes of water, thick sea tumblers, and the bright green fire extinguishers (like hand grenades), which had been there since the ship first sailed. The bulkheads aft and to the sides had doors in them, leading to other cabins. In between the doors had been stands of arms, mostly old service rifles (of 1880), bought cheap when the Army was re-arming, for possible use against pirates in the China Sea. In the centre of the room, under the skylight, had been a big dining-table, with revolving chairs for ten. The table had always had upon it a white waxed cloth. The chairs were of bright yellow wood with green leather seats, a little worn with service and the sun. It had been, on the whole, the finest saloon in the British sailing fleet; and seamen who had seen all its wonders had talked of it with awe as something not easily matched. Sometimes it was the stencilling which won them, sometimes the fire extinguishers, sometimes the Chinaman's painting or the green leather seats. But now all these glories were like the ruined Tyre described by Ezekiel.

The table had been smashed in three and wrenched from its supports: only one chair still stood: parts of some of the others were trundling about as the ship flung them. Half the doors were gone from their supports and were washing on the deck. The mirrors had been torn away and flung down and smashed. The racks were broken, and their contents spilled and smashed. The weapons had been swept from their stands. Dick saw one old rifle with the barrel bent into a V shape, and another with the barrel flattened into a kind of sword-blade. An oil lamp, which had hung from gimbals in the after bulkhead, was now upside down, swinging from one screw. It had dropped its oil on to the water on the deck, which now shone with colour from it in the light of the torch.

"A mess for someone to clear," Dick said.

The door to the Captain's private cabin, on the starboard side, was swinging about with the roll, banging and crashing, sometimes shutting-to upon its hook. Dick waded across and hooked it open, so that it should not bang itself to bits. He flashed the torch into the cabin: no one was there. The place had been flooded and had still a foot of water in it, but the locker containing the ship's chronometers had not been swept away. There were other cabins, the doors of which were still shut. Dick left these unexamined. He was eager to get forward again, to see if the foremast coat were plugged. If he could get forward by the port side, he might find out on the way if there were other bodies washed under the wreck. In his heart he gave up the missing men for lost. If the great sea had killed Mr. Duckswich, who was down below, sheltered from it, what chance had those who were on the poop, exposed to its full fury? He remembered the aspect of the sea as it came on board, vast as a down, higher than the mizen topsail. Why, those poor chaps may have had forty feet of water over them, enough to drown them and bury them twenty times. As he turned from the cabin to go on deck, he felt that he would give one hand to see one of the officers coming up the alleyway.

As he turned, thinking thus, with a word to Bill to come on out of it, for it was dreary down there in all that smash, he saw one of the officers (as he thought) enter the alleyway from the deck.

"Golly," he said to Bill, "here's the Old Man."

It was like the Old Man, just his height and build. Dick's heart rose at the sight; he knew now how much he longed for someone to be in command. He turned the light on to the alleyway, then on to the figure. It wasn't Captain Cobb, but Alfrick, who hailed them.

"I'm glad you've found a light," he said. "You'll need it. I've found Captain Cobb."

"Alive?"

"Oh yes, but badly hurt."

"Did you find any others?"

"No," Alfrick said. "We shan't find any others."

"We found poor Mr. Duckswich. He's dead."

"Ah? Dead? He ought not to have had to come to sea at his age. You got your oil over by the feel of her. She's a lot easier than she was."

"Is the wind letting-up at all?"

"Not a let. It's worse, if anything, and will be a lot worse before it's better. We've got the mast-coat plugged, forward there. Now, if she ships one over the bows it won't sink her."

"I'm glad that hole's been plugged," Dick said. "I've

been worrying about it. You'd a job to do it, in that narrow place, with the sprays flying over you."

"There wasn't much room," Alfrick said. "The stuff on deck isn't shifting too badly."

"What do you think?" Dick asked. "There are some spare chain topsail sheets in the forepeak. Could we catch a turn with them round the foremast, at the doublings, say, and snug the whole mast home by the capstan, to the main hatch?"

Alfrick considered the point and shook his head.

"Not in this, we couldn't. We'd better let well alone. It is just shifting a little, each way, as it is, and then something brings her up. Leave it at that till we see. If we start heaving we may carry away what it is that is holding her, and set her really going. If she does get going she'll split the deck or stave the hatch. Bring out your light. We must bring Captain Cobb in."

"Where is he?"

"Just outside here, under where the port poop ladder was, in a mess of all sorts of stuff. I only found him by accident. One of those last big seas took me right into him."

"Is anyone with you?" Dick asked.

"Yes, Chips is outside there, and Kruger Evesbatch. It'll take us all to get the Captain clear. He's jammed in there like a bale with dunnage."

"Come on, then," Dick said. "I'll lead the way. I've got a light."

In a minute he was out in the fury once more, holding on to the hand-rail under the break of the poop, with salt water racing at his legs and other water, mainly fresh by the taste, pelting his face. It was blowing harder than ever, so it seemed. He cast a light above his head. The mizen stay still stood. That was the only joy in the situation, that the mizen stood. While one mast stood, she was a sort of a ship, not a log in the sea. It was like a flag that kept flying over a battered fort, this mizen. He stumbled into a man clinging there. It was Kruger Evesbatch, with the lowering, tough face: Chips was just beyond him. Kruger said something inaudible and pointed. Alfrick urged them on to the port side, which Dick lit with his flash.

A good deal of water had come on board and was now wallowing about, running from side to side, gulping itself out at the freeing-ports and leaping at all obstructions. In the angle formed by the break of the poop with the ship's port side was a little hill of wreck that had jammed itself against further movement. The water was rushing round it and flying over it. The wreck consisted of a wide variety of matters. Some of it was the port poop ladder, with three yards of teak poop-rail. Over this were some lengths of the mizen topgallant yards, broken, splintered and so stuck that they held the mass together. Some rags of sail and some rope-ends were flying like pennons from these. On the top, jammed in pretty tightly, yet shifting a little at every roll, were pieces of the poop skylight, some of the charthouse, Ed Newbarn's chest, a grating from a boat, and some of the bucket-rack with two wooden buckets in it. In behind these, pinned by the legs in a sitting posture, was Captain Cobb. How he had got there without being killed and held there without being drowned was something that they asked later, but at the moment took to be the Fortune of the Sea. The Captain was bareheaded. His face was all smeared with blood from small scratches. The rain washed the blood about as it oozed, but Dick felt that there was not enough blood showing for any one of the cuts to be serious. By the torch, Dick made out that the Captain was pinned in the main by a great piece of the cabin skylight, which lay across his legs. His head was propped against a part of the broken lower topgallant yard; a length of chain topgallant sheet was pressed on his chest; and near him, waggling about, sometimes beating him on the chest, was a most curiously bent, kinked triple fold of wire, shroud, stay or backstay, bent, serving and all, into a kind of flattened letter Z.

"We'll soon get you out of this, sir," Dick shouted.

The Captain was ever full of fight. "Why in hell," he shouted. What followed was lost in the gale's roaring. No man could have attended to it anyway at that time, in that place.

Alfrick shouted to Dick, "Keep light on the skylight. We'll shift it."

But, indeed, for three men and a boy to shift that weight, in that confusion, among all that mess, from all the countless knobs of iron, wire and wood in which it had caught was a bit of a problem. A big fourth figure surged up from nowhere. It was Aylton, the cheery man who had cleared the rudder tackles. He came opportunely, just as the others were beginning to despair. As often happens, at sea and ashore, the new man brought a new method, which in this case was the wise one, to use the ship's roll and gravity or the motive force. Helped by these, they contrived to heave

the broken skylight from the Captain's thighs, so that Alfrick could pull him clear. The movement of the ship
flung them all down at this instant; the piece of skylight
skated away from where they floundered to break with a
crash on the lee bulwarks. On its way back to them, as
Dick saw, it met with a new flood surging round the half-
deck, which sent it into the after-hatch.

He saw Alfrick bent over the Captain's body, trying to
lift it. It seemed to him that the body was drooped like a
corpse, but hoped that it was only a faint. He crept up
and took the Captain's legs and knew at once from the feel
that one of them was broken. They tottered with the bur-
den to the door and there, with some supporting, some
heaving, they got out of the blast into the alleyway.

"Shall we put him in Mr. MacLerrinnan's cabin?" Aylton
asked.

"No," Dick cried, "it may be flooded at any moment.
Get him aft to his own cabin. He'll be free from flooding
there, perhaps."

He led the way, holding the torch in his right hand; his
left arm gripped the Captain about the knees. Aylton and
Evesbatch edged along sideways, helping to lift the body.
Alfrick followed with his arms under the Captain's arm-
pits. Bill and Chips followed Alfrick.

When they were in the saloon, Dick called to Bill to take
the light to light them, as he had to shift hands. A change
for the worse had come even since they had left the deck.
Rain was beating in sheets down the hole of the skylight,
making a noise as though hail were falling in water. They
splashed and staggered across the saloon, to the private

cabin's entrance. Dick stayed himself there against the roll, while he shouted directions to Bill and Chips.

"There's no mattress on the bunk. Get the mattress and pillow off the sofa there."

The "sofa" was a hard narrow couch stretched under the cabin port for use as a second bunk in case of need. It was upholstered in very tough, black horsehair, hard almost as wood. Its pillow was a roll of the same black horsehair, equally hard, and kept from rolling out by the board designed to keep the sleeper in bed. Bill and Chips unshipped these things with some difficulty. They had not been moved for many years. They laid them in the standing cot.

"Come on," Dick shouted to the others, "we'll lay him on this for the moment."

"Out of step does it," Aylton said. "Keep out of step and you'll hurt him less. That's what we did with the wounded in the War, only we'd rum then, which mended matters."

They edged the Captain on to the cot, face upwards. Bill brought the light so that they might see.

"I'm not sure he's not dead," Aylton said.

"He's got all his bones pulped up inside him, if you ask me," the Carpenter said. "As long as he stayed quiet he may not have felt it much, but now . . ." He shook his head as he looked.

"I've seen that, in the War," Aylton said.

But at this point the Captain opened his eyes and feebly asked, "What the hell hit us? An earthquake or what?"

"A big sea, sir," Dick said.

"Who's that speaking?"

"Pomfret, sir."

"I thought it was you, you young devil. Squirt that light out of my eyes."

"Certainly, sir. I'm sorry, sir."

There was a pause after this. They waited out of respect for the Captain to speak next: the Captain seemed to be trying to gather strength for speech. At last he said:

"Where's that blasted old woman, my Mate?"

"He's dead, sir," Dick said. "The big sea flung him down and killed him."

There was another pause.

"Send Mr. MacLerrinnan to me," the Captain said.

"We don't know where he is, sir," Dick said.

"Find him."

"Please, sir," Dick said, "I'm afraid the big sea took him overboard."

After a time the Captain said, "It seemed to come on very suddenly. Get the foresail off her."

"Sir," Dick said, "the foresail's off her. She's lying-to under a weathercloth."

"Give me a drop of whisky," the Captain said. "I've had a knock or something. What the hell's this stone thing under my head?"

"It's the sofa pillow, sir," Dick said. He had thought from the first that that mattress and pillow would be nearly as comfortable to a hurt man as the stone slabs in a morgue. "We'll get you something softer, sir."

"No need for that," the Captain said. "Fetch me a spot of whisky. Why've you brought me here? Take me to the charthouse."

"If you please, Captain Cobb," Dick said, "the big sea took the charthouse overboard."

"Hell," the Captain said, struggling up, with a squeal of pain, "take me up on deck straight away. This comes of having a eunuch for a Mate."

The effort was too much for him: he lay back white, faint and sick.

"If you please, sir," Dick said, "you've had a sore knock and banging. You've got a broken leg and arm. Let us get those tied up and then we'll take you on deck."

"The young fellow's right, sir," the Carpenter put in. "We only want to give your bones a chance first. If we can get your bones set and yourself into dry things, we'll take you on deck, never fear."

"We will, like hell," Dick muttered to himself; and then aloud to the Captain, "Where can we find you some whisky, sir?"

"Tell my damned Steward."

"I'm sorry, Captain Cobb," Dick said, "we're afraid the big sea took the Steward overboard, too."

"Mince gone, too," the Captain said. "He said something about supper being ready . . ."

"Yes, sir."

"Well, bring me the whisky. It's in the after-cabin, port side; the aftermost locker."

"The slop chest is there," Bill Guller put in, "you could find some dry blankets for him, perhaps, and a bed and pillow."

"Is not the whisky locked up, sir?" Dick asked. "Will you give me the key?"

"Mince has the key round his neck," the Captain answered. "I can't answer these damned questions without a drink. Get it."

Dick had noticed that Chips had his axe stuck in his belt at his back.

"Come along, Chips," he said. "We may have to force the slop-chest door." He left the cabin; the Carpenter followed.

The slop-chest is a collection of necessaries carried by the Captains of ships on long voyages and sold to needy members of the crew against their wages. Its usual stores are blankets, bedding, oilskins, sea-boots, woollen clothing, straw hats, dungarees, tobacco and matches.

In his earlier journeys aft, Dick had noticed that the door of the slop-chest room had not been burst by the sea and had thought, "That means that the lock is extra strong." Now he thought, "This extra strong lock may take us twenty minutes to smash."

When he turned his light upon the door he was amazed to see that a key was in it.

"Look, Chips," he said, "the key's in the door. What if the Steward's in here, looking after MacLerrinnan?"

He was young and hope leaped in him: Chips, who was sour from fatigue, shook his head.

"The Steward was in there, getting pickles for the cabin supper," he said, "before the big sea took him."

Dick opened the door. The cabin was lit and occupied, but not by the old afterguard. A lantern containing a burning candle hung from the beams. Propping each other on the locker top, so that they kept each other from rolling or pitching off, were two figures. They were Obbie Loach and Bill Purple, the Boatswain. They must have been there for some time, for they had broken open all the lockers and had pulled out for removal several things which had pleased them. The thing which pleased them most was whisky; each held a bottle, from which a good deal had gone. They were shocked for the first instant, thinking that Dick and Chips were the Captain and Mate; but Obbie saw who they were and whispered to the Boatswain, who was a ready old rogue at all times. Instantly, he was on his feet.

"I thought it wouldn't be long before I found you down here, Pomfret," he began. "What are you doing off the deck, me lad? Just you get along where you belong."

"None of that with me," Dick said. "Skin out of this on deck. Drop that whisky. Give it here." He grabbed the whisky bottle from the Boatswain's hand. "Drop it; slippy," Dick said. "Captain Cobb'll be here in a minute, and then God help you."

Purple had been in the Navy; Obbie Loach, for a time, had been in the Army; both knew that when caught in wrongdoing, any explanation, however plausible, may make matters worse. They did not speak, hopped to their feet, pulled off their southwesters, and shambled to the door.

"Put down that whisky bottle, Loach," Dick said.

Loach did as he was bid, but reached for the lantern.

"To light us out," he explained.

"Leave the lantern," Dick said. "I'll light you through the cabin. Get forward where you belong."

He uttered no protest, but followed the Boatswain across

the saloon and down the alleyway. Half-way down the alleyway, he turned on Dick.

"I've forgotten my key," he said.

"Oh, it's your key, is it?" Dick said.

"Yes."

"What's it doing in the Captain's door?"

"It's my key. I want it."

"Right about turn, then. Ask the Captain for it. He's in there. Tell him how you came to leave it."

Dick had his light on the two men, for he half expected a blow at this point. Obbie would gladly have dealt it, but the Boatswain nudged him to come away. After all, they had both had a good drink, and had more stowed under their oilskins. They turned, and went lurching out of the alleyway to the deck. Dick went back to the slop-chest.

Obbie Loach had put down his whisky bottle like a real sailor, so that it was jammed tight in its locker, between blankets, in such a way that none could spill.

"There'll be the Old Man's drink," Dick said. "Those two ducks have had some nerve. Perhaps we'll find some dry bedding in the locker here."

Dick noticed then that the two bull's-eye ports in the cabin had been burst in, probably by the big sea which had pooped her. However, both had been plugged by the Boatswain and Loach, very cleverly, by plugs of blankets held by battens and spunyarn. The cabin and all within it had been flooded, but most of the water had now drained away. An open blanket bale to one side of the cabin felt as though its inner blankets would be nearly dry.

"Here are his blankets," he said, beginning to pull some out.

The ship put down her nose suddenly, then put it further down, then went over on her side and took on board a thundering and awful packet. There came a running hissing, whumpf of water, and in through the door came the wide Missouri, which washed round them, and washed out and then came wandering back with a kettle on top of it. She started to roll, as soon as she could move at all. Over she went and back again; the water washed, the gear smashed, the doors banged. Then with a crash that made their hearts leap something came down on deck just over their heads and brought with it minor crashes into the saloon.

"There goes the mizen," Dick said.

"No, no," Chips said. "The mizen would have made more noise."

"It was noise enough."

"It'll be the gaff and the vangs," Chips said.

"It was too big," Dick said. "It'll be the boom. But anyhow it means that the mizen's beginning to go."

"It's a miracle she's stood so long."

"I don't know how she'll keep to the wind with no weathercloth set," Dick said.

"Give her seventy fathoms of chain out. She might lie to that."

"That's an idea," Dick said. "But we'd never get all clear, for running, in this."

"She's all clear for running," Okle said. "Mr. Mac-Lerrinnan got her clear for running in his last watch on deck. He was a fine seaman, who looked ahead, and took thought for his ship."

He was silent, thinking of another, who had not done so. "They say that a broken leg feels the cold," Dick said.

He added some flannel shirts and woollen underclothes to the blankets; then, both laden, they returned to the Captain's room.

They were surprised to find a light there. A little safety oil-lamp not wrecked by the sea had been found upon its gimbals. The Captain had told Alfrick of it; he had groped for it, found it, and contrived to light it by the Captain's briquette. It had a safety screen to it, so that it had remained unharmed. While Alfrick had lighted this, Cantlow and Bill had found the cabin's scupper-plug, had removed it, and were now brooming the water off the deck, at each roll, using a little rubber door-mat as their squilgee. The place looked sad and wild, swinging and tossing, the men swaying or clutching hold, at the rolls, the lamp leaning to it, the water splashing, and "Neptune's raging fury" in all that remained of the universe.

Dick left his spoils, and then returned to the slop-room for a whisky bottle. He locked the door and pocketed the key. He now wanted water to mix with the whisky, and thought that there would not be any in any after bottle or jug not mixed with sea. Then he remembered that in the pantry, high up on a hook, the Steward usually kept a canvas water-bag, from which he drew icy-cold water for the officers. He had learned the dodge in an Australian port; Dick had tried it in the tropics for the sake of the coldness.

"The bag may still be there," he thought.

Going to the pantry, he found that it was there, still nearly full; there was also an unbroken mug on one of the hooks.

He brought these back to the Captain's cabin.

"I've brought you your drink, sir," he said.

"You've been long enough about it. What have you been playing at?" the Captain said.

"I had to forage for some water, sir."

"I didn't send you for water. I've been in water half the night and more. Water . . . Gottseck, boy . . . we've enough water slooshing. Give me the rum there. Who the hell's been at that bottle? You've been necking that whisky, boy. Come here, till I smell your breath."

"I'm teetotal between pilots, Captain Cobb," Dick said. "As to the bottle, it's the first that I came across: it was open when I found it. Will you please tell me when, sir?"

"My God, you young devil!" the Captain said. "You think you've got me in a cleft stick, but if I don't skin you alive when I get on deck again my name's not Robin Battler Cobb. Battler I was named and Battler I am, and I'll be a bloody battle for you, my lad."

"Yes, sir," Dick answered. "Shall I add some water, sir?"

"Take your water and pour it down the drains it's fit for," the Captain said. He sucked down the neat whisky, smacking his lips over it. "Ha, Chips," he said, "that's the stuff. Don't you wish you was me, drinking whisky?"

"No, Captain Cobb," Okle said quietly, "not me. I've no use for the stuff at any time."

The Captain took this for a reproof. He glared at the Carpenter and then exploded:

"I always said you were a damned old woman, Carpenter. Don't you answer me, let me advise you, what you've a use for and haven't a use for. Gottseck, I've a fine crew, I don't think; but I'll give you a use now. Carry me up on deck where I belong."

Dick saw that he must interfere.

"Captain Cobb," he said, "you're the Captain of this ship, responsible for all of us . . ."

"Hell, you tell me that?" the Captain cried.

"Yes, sir, I do. And you, the Captain, have two broken bones, if not three. We've got to look to those first, for all our sakes, not only yours, sir. First let us set your bones. Now's the time, sir, before they get all astray and lose you the use of them. It won't take long, sir."

"Lay hold of me and take me on deck, all of you, or I'll log the lot of you."

"No, no, Captain Cobb," Dick said. "We hope you won't log us; it's only our plain duty to look after our Captain. Come, sir, please let us strip you, set your bones, and get you into dry things. We can talk of coming on deck, later, when your limbs are saved."

"What do you know about setting bones? What bones?"

"I've had some lessons in first-aid, sir. I can put on simple splints and bandages. Your right leg is broken below the knee and your left arm below the elbow. I should judge, too, that one of your ribs is broken. We ought to make sure of that at once."

"Yes, sir," the Carpenter said. "A broken rib neglected works into the lung: then you cough red foam and die."

"There's another thing, Captain Cobb," Alfrick said,

"and that is moving a man too soon, after he's had a great shock. They moved my old uncle too soon, after a shock."

"Gottseck," the Captain yelled, "I'll shock some of you, just now."

"Come, please, sir, please, sir," Dick said. "We're not going to carry you on deck till we've bandaged you. Take that as final. We only ask leave to help you while you're helpless. Afterwards you can skin us or log us. Think what fun that will be."

"You young whelp. I do think."

"The sooner we begin, sir, the sooner we'll have you on deck. So, please, may we begin?"

With a very ill grace the Captain told them to turn-to and be done with it, to heave round and be damned to them: the work began.

Alfrick and Dick began the job, while the Captain, still fresh and full of fight, loudly thanked God that he wasn't going to have a lot of women pawing over him, "as they do in these hospitals." Alfrick was not very deft. When they had come to the Captain's shirt, Kruger Evesbatch, who had been watching and bearing a hand, took over from him. He was very deft. He had been a second at many rings and an orderly in more than one hospital during the War. The Captain swore a good deal, but became faint from the pain inflicted before he was stripped; he was quiet enough, but for some ejaculations when they hurt him.

They mopped him dry with one of the blankets. He was a fine figure of a man, they thought, with a fine, big, hairy chest, great pectoral muscles, forearms all corded with lines of muscles, and the fat not yet beginning to take charge.

"We'll see about the ribs first," Dick said.

"A broken rib loose is worse than a Dum-dum bullet," Evesbatch said. "The two ends are like two saws working inside you. Now they saw through the stomach, then they saw into the heart."

"Stopper your jaw with your two saws," the Captain said.

Dick's fingers roved about the Captain's chest.

"We'd a man in the *Loughareema,*" Aylton said, "got washed by a sea over the spare spars and hurt his side, so that he couldn't lift. He had to go into hospital. He'd had a rib broken, they found; and it had worked a great bag of water round it, out of the blood."

"I'll bag of water you, just now," the Captain said.

"There's nothing a broken rib won't do," the Carpenter said. "It's when it's mending, it's the worst, for sometimes it starts to corrode, and eats you all out, hollow."

"I guess you've got one in your brain, then," the Captain said.

But here Dick finished his search. One of the left ribs was plainly broken: there could be no doubt of it. Alfrick and Aylton held the Captain up while Dick and Evesbatch swathed him with strips of blanket. This proceeding touched up the broken arm.

"We'll take the arm next," Dick said. "We want battens or something. What can we use as splints?"

"There were the boat-stretchers for the gig," Alfrick suggested. "Four of those. . . . They were with the yoke and lines in the spare bunk in Mr. MacLerrinnan's cabin."

"They'll be washing about in the seven seas by this time," Dick said. "Chips, you take this torch and get what wood you can; cabin table, or rack, or fiddle, or door, or anything. Trim it up with your axe. We want splints."

It did not take long for Chips to find floating wood. He trimmed it for them roughly to the right lengths, wiped them and padded them with blanket strips, and helped the setting of arm and leg, in spite of the oaths and occasional blows of the victim. When they had finished, the Captain was completely exhausted. His surgeons had not been very skilful. They had worked in a theatre lifting, swaying and shifting with such mad, soaring and giddy swooping that often the injured limbs had been dropped, so that the opera-tors might hold on to save themselves.

They drew a rough woollen shirt over the Captain, worked the straw mattress, covered with a blanket, under him, tucked him up with blankets, put rolled blankets beneath his head, and then were scared at the sickness of his look.

"He'll take the full count," Kruger Evesbatch said.

"He looks as though he might die on us," Aylton muttered.

Dick poured out a tot of spirit, with which he restored the Captain.

"That's better," the Captain said, "give me another. I'll be all right in a minute. A noggin of Scotch. I needed a drop of that. I come over all faint a moment. That's better. Now then, take me on deck, you, and lash me to the weather shrouds."

"No, sir," Dick said, as he passed some turns of amberline over the bunk and the patient, to make it impossible for him to be rolled or flung from it, "no, sir; you'll stay here, sir."

"The hell I'll stay here. Take me up, I say."

"No, sir," Dick said. "You've three broken bones and God knows what internal bruises beside. You're not fit to be on deck. Even if you were, sir, it's risking the bones of other men to try to carry you there. And if you were there, you couldn't see, sir, nor give any order; nor if you did could anybody do it. You lie still, sir, and get your strength. We'll tell you when it begins to moderate."

He motioned to the others to get out of the cabin, which they did, though the Captain cursed them, saying that he would log them and get them six weeks hard in any jail in England as sure as he was a Battler. Dick shut the door upon his cursing. He had taken the lantern, leaving only the safety-lamp with the Captain. As they began to shuffle and grope across the rushing litter in the saloon the lantern blew out. On his way through the alleyway he left it hooked to a beam in the Steward's pantry. He showed Kruger Evesbatch and Aylton the body of Mr. Duckswich prone on his back in his bunk.

"He was a good seaman," Aylton said, "but old for a job like this."

Both Evesbatch and Aylton had removed their south-westers on coming into the after part of the ship. Eves-batch stood for a while silent by the bunk, biting his south-wester rim. Dick held the light of the torch on Mr. Duck-swich's face. The big, strange, bent nose seemed more prominent now that the cheeks had fallen, but the sourness of the face was gone: Dick could not doubt that all was very well with Mr. Duckswich. Long afterwards, he remembered that dead face, tranquil in the tumult, lit in the darkness, with all things dripping and splashing, and the tough face of Evesbatch peering, his stumps of teeth biting on the yellow stuff.

"He won't come-to at the gong," Evesbatch said at last. "It slips us all one, sooner or later, just the same. It's odd how things come about. Old Nab Wallers used to see him when he was a young Second Mate. You wouldn't think it, but when he was young Mr. Duckswich fancied himself with the gloves. Nab Wallers' father kept *The Three Cups* off Shadwell Dock Road, with a ring at the back. Often, Nab said, he'd see Mr. Duckswich come in there for a go with the gloves. It was an old pug, called Filmy, bent his nose on him."

Dick noticed that drops from the drowned upper bunk were falling on the dead man's face. He found a wet blue handkerchief (there was nothing dry handy), and tucked it over and round the head to keep the drops from the flesh.

"I'm going on deck," he said, hurriedly.

He was shocked by the sight of the body and the knowledge that Dudley Mac, Ed Newbarn, poor Torrent, Morrissey and Mince were all mute and helpless like this, away out in the sea, far from anyone. Perhaps poor Dudley Mac would be alive still, swimming and swimming; for he was a strong man, stronger even than Aylton or Berrow; a glorious man; and even in Australia, where all swim well, he had been counted a good swimmer.

Dick was only a boy; he had had friendly dealings with all these men; he wanted to get on deck and weep unobserved.

He left them there and slipped hurriedly up the companion into the blast.

When he had come below, long, long before, with the Captain's body, he had thought that it was blowing to the limit of a wind's power, yet he would be sworn that it was now blowing harder. Away, at the first roar of it, went all thought of the dead and useless mourning. His first thought on reaching the deck was for the ship. He turned his light forward; the mizen-mast stood: the weathercloth held. Chips was right; it was the gaff that had fallen. It was no longer in sight: no doubt he would fall over it presently.

"Golly," he thought. "How can the mizen stand it?"

Somebody had said that no gear made by man could stand the utmost that the wind and sea could do. This was standing, therefore the worst was not yet; the worst was to come when the centre came. He knew the symptoms of a storm-centre. The wind would drop suddenly; he would see a clear patch of sky, quite a small patch, overhead, with stars in it, very bright, with, as it were, smoke gyrating round their little heaven. Then, after a minute or perhaps two, there would be a clear sky overhead and no wind at all, not so much as a breath, for ten, twenty or thirty minutes. Then fury would rage again from the opposite point, catching the ship aback and rousing up such a cross sea as no ship could live through. That would be the worst, the worst wind and the worst sea. And they were in the track of the centre, dead across its path. How soon would it be likely to reach them? How fast could the storm be travelling? It had seemed slow in its approach:

"Long foretold, long last,"

but this had been on them now for hours; they must be near the centre. What time was it? Who could tell? Time had ceased in the *Hurrying Angel* when the big sea came on board. The clocks were out and time was forgotten. But it had lasted now for such an eternity that it must be drawing to the climax. He tried to remember the speeds and sizes of cyclones. All sorts of maps from text-books came into his mind, but this buffeting blast of wind seemed to fling them out again. Some of the maps seemed to fill the whole Indian Ocean, all the China Sea, all the Atlantic. He seemed to remember that the little storms were the worst, little compact storms. Yet, how big is a little storm? He could not remember. Was it a hundred miles across, two hundred, three hundred? Say that it was a hundred miles across, how fast would it come? Would it be fifteen miles, or twenty, or thirty in an hour? Or would it vary? Would it sometimes loiter, would it sometimes hurry, would it ever stand still, revolving about its vortex? If it did, this might last for days, weeks even. The lives of some storms were long. Why should not some become permanent? All these things were battered into what remained of his mind, and then battered out of it. He hung onto the bitts of the mizen, and turned the beam of his torch onto the stay which held so bravely.

It was pitch dark everywhere, no glimmer of light any-where, save sometimes a streak of something bluish on a wave breaking over the rail, or some sudden glare that made the air reddish for an instant in one part of the sky. The murk was so deep that it made him feel that the air had curdled and gone thick, so that presently it would choke them as they breathed it. Now as he turned the beam of the torch onto the stay above him he saw what was like a great smoke flying across the stay not a yard from it. It was not smoke but storm cloud, hurtling at any speed, eighty or ninety miles an hour perhaps, screaming as it went and snatching to itself, as it crossed the beam, the likeness of mad white faces, blind with their will to be on. Dick turned off the flash; he was terrified by those faces.

"They are coming down closer," he thought. "They are all the millions of the damned, let loose. Soon they will be the only thing between the firmament and the sea: it will be all rage and destruction everywhere.

"Presently," he thought, "they will get this mizen-mast and then what will save us? Dudley Mac's forethought and the seventy fathoms of chain, perhaps; nothing else." And how could they let go the chain and when, and who would be with him to do it? Where was everybody? Who could tell where anybody was in this blind madness?

If a man moved from his fellow he lost him; the darkness swallowed him away. Where had they gone to, those wise men of the crew? He had been with them, then he had rashly left them, and now where were they? Had they started to go forward? Were they forward? If they had started to go forward, would they ever get there? Any movement on that flooded deck with its shifting ruin brought danger to life and limb.

Young as he was, he felt beaten. He was very cold and wet; he had had no food for eight hours, supposing that it were now about midnight; he had had no rest of any kind since coming on deck, and much of his time had been passed in taxing bodily exertion, struggling with something so much stronger than himself. Then, as he had often found in other lesser storms, a tumult is exhausting. Even living, the effort to draw breath and remain alive, in the presence of so much destruction, and to stand up in the madness of so much violence, is difficult and strains the strength. He longed to be in a bunk, or better still, in a hammock, that remains steady while the ship plays the fool, asleep till this fury blew itself out or blew what the ship could stand no longer.

He flashed his torch about the poop. No man was there. It was all a howling desolation, with the gear streaming and spelters and splatters of water, quarts of wave-top, foam, rain, who could tell, flying not unlike birds over the poop bulwarks and flattening themselves into quivering bubbles on anything they hit. All the madness was shrieking, barking and ringing bells, but above the tumult from time to time came the ominous over booming thunder of a bigger sea than usual in the waist.

How well he knew the symptoms: a roll, a bigger roll, a much bigger roll, with a scraunching Crash of the lee wreck shifting, then a roll that seemed likely to tear her side out, a sudden quick arrest and quiver, then Double,

Double, Double Wallop, a monstrous shipment over the rail that kept her still, horribly still, while he thought, "That stove-in the main hatch; now we are for it."

Listening to these waves coming on board convinced him that he must prepare for the centre passing by paying out that chain, to try to keep her head up. Which chain he ought to pay out he could not be sure: no doubt Chips would know. He would find Chips.

He had left Chips below in the alleyway only a few minutes before; perhaps he and the others had not yet gone forward; he might catch him there. He slipped down the companion and turned his flash along the alley: no one was there. He crept aft and listened at the Captain's door: all was quiet there.

"They've gone forward, then," he thought. "With Evesbatch's life-line it may not be so bad; I'll go after them; though the sea's worse than it was."

Something made him think (for the first time) about the ship's cargo of grain. Grain is a dangerous cargo, apt to shift, but it had not shifted yet, apparently, in spite of the dusting they were getting. The Battler had his faults, but he had stowed the grain like a master stevedore, with groynes and athwartships bulkheads, which were standing the strain. Yet could anything stand much more strain? When the centre passed would not all these things give, and the ship be hurled upon her side, with the grain fetching away in a mass to keep her there? Taking the life-line, he crawled to the lee ladder, and went down it, to a deck full of water. Groping for the life-line to lead him from this point he found that it had gone. Some floating wreck had smashed away the rail to which it had been hitched. He hung on there, waiting. It was blowing like nothing that he had ever imagined. He could hardly look near it; it seemed to slue his head round. The ship was weltering wearily in the sea. Either she had a lot of water in her now, or the weight of water on deck was more than she could carry. More was coming on board at every instant, more than could ever win away. Great volumes of it were cascading over the hatches, over the bitts, and swirling round the half-deck to fetch up like breakers against the ladder where he stood. He stood for ten minutes, unable to step forth; then in a smooth, or half-smooth, he thought to try it, and stepped out towards the half-deck, his torch jammed into his belt, his hands free to catch at anything. When he was near the half-deck-rail, reaching out for it, she put her nose down suddenly, for some reason good enough to her tormented iron, but blind to him. Possibly she shook off some of what was coming to her, but all the rest came on board like a rolling hill, and filled her green to the rail.

Her stoop had brought him down on one knee. Under the swirling water her decks were slimy and very slippery; the plunge took his foot from under him; down he came. He hurt his knee on the deck. Before he could rise he was afloat in a rolling ocean going he did not quite know where. His mouth was full of salt water: some of it went down and made him choke. He felt cold wet run over any part of him that had been warm, if not dry, a moment before. It ran in between skin and under-clothes like pawing hands made of icicles. He hit something round and hard, probably a staunchion, then something flat and hard, probably a bulkhead, then a much greater volume of water took him and drove him feet first into something hard which gave way at the shock. At the same instant an appalling weight of water took him by the shoulders and shoved against them, meaning to complete the job. He knew what was happening. He had been washed half through a freeing-port. His feet and his knees were through it and water was driving the rest of him after them. All a Niagara of water was cataracting over him, trying to get out and to take him with it. He was under water, but grabbed a deck-staunchion. Slowly the pressure of the weight on his shoulders relaxed; he got a gulp of breath; then suddenly all the pressure was the other way; he was sucked back with the roll and carried in the swirl past and over all sorts of things, now in shallows, rolling on slimy deck, now in deeps, swimming, now seeing streaks of brightness, now far under water. He felt the heave of the water slacken and steady. He was in a smooth for a few seconds, the water was loitering before starting its rush back. He groped for something and found a deck staunchion. Painfully, against the suck of the water pouring back, he dragged himself up. He was on the weather side, somewhere near the ruined port poop ladder, as he judged. He was somewhat the worse for wear, banged, bruised and out of breath. His torch was still jammed in his belt, but then it was a real belt. His knee was painful. He was very cold; the water was very cold. Someone had said somewhere that cyclone seas are very cold, being about a third rain from high upper atmospheres. Who had said that? Some seaman. He remem-

bered, now, a man called Ewarts Something, who kept a
pub near Sailortown and had a "mermaid" in a glass case.
Well, there was no doubt about the cold; something as cold
as death had come into air and sea. However, here he was
on the rail. That was the place that the jockeys tried for in
the Derby, to get onto the rails and then come away, if not
interfered with. Well, there he was on the rails, and he
could come away, to the winning-post by the windlass, if
not interfered with. It was a big "if" in that pitch blackness. Who could tell how many feet of rail had been swept
away by this time? Rolling wreck, such as their poor ship
was cluttered with, would take deck-staunchions and bulwarks away together. If he came to a gap of that sort when
she rolled to windward, he might be fifty yards from the
ship before he knew that he was overboard. Well, better
overboard through a gap perhaps than be caught by rolling
wreck and squeezed flat against a deck-house. It was less
likely to be death on the weather side. He set out, clawing
along the bulwarks and feeling forward with his feet, before moving, to be sure that the ship's side stood. There
was a lot of stuff on deck washing around, buckets, tubs,
brooms, gratings, oars, bits of boat, stretchers, paint-pots; he
knew roughly what the things were when they knocked
against him. He won as far forward as the fore-brace-
bumpkins, just forward of the main-rigging screws. He had
steadied himself here when he felt what seemed to him un-
doubtedly a small shark rubbing against his legs. He kicked
out, and caught it fairly with his foot: it was only a floating
swab, but it made his heart beat the quicker for half a
minute, while he waited for a sea to run off. It was as black

as a pit: he could see nothing, except sometimes an oily
glimmer on a part of a wave, or an illusion of lightning on
a heaven too murky to let the light shine. He longed for
light. Oh, to be able to see, to know where one stood, to
see what was to be done, to be watching what was coming.
Now he was in the waist, in the danger part, about to launch
across the scene of all the wet work.

"Steady, my lads," he quoted. " 'Tis to windlass we steer."

He was nearly half-way there, now. The ship's side was
holding, but some of the deck staunchions were loose; his
probing feet told him this, and the discovery scared him,
for he could not imagine the side holding up against those
seas with the staunchions gone. He crawled on a few feet,
hand over hand, from pin to pin in the rail, up to his waist
in water. Then, suddenly, there came that indescribable
odd movement of warning that something big was coming
on board. He felt the ship give up the attempt: it was too
big and too sudden for her; it came on the wrong moment
of her roll, when she was committed to a movement and
could not change it to meet the new condition. He felt her
give up hope beneath his feet. He crouched into the rail,
got an arm over a pin and a hand onto another. Something
roared, shutting out the roaring of the wind, then a frightful
weight was on his back, and he was plucked from his pin
like a leaf taken into a mill-race. Away he went sailing, past
Javan and Gadire, Mombasa and Quiloa and Melind. He
went at great speed and hit several things which he could
not identify. He felt the rush relent, and fought till he came
into the air for a breath: he put down his feet. No; there
was deck there; he could not yet be overboard. Here his

feet went from under him, and away he went sailing again. He knew that he went one way, then another way, then bang into something hard, like a spare spar, then off round the compass, he knew not where, except that there were hard things into which he bumped. He knew from this that he was still in the ship. It was very cold, but apart from the bangs it was not so bad. He was a little stunned, to tell the truth, and in some danger of drowning. However, that was not to be his destiny, it seemed. That particular night was not to hold much pleasure nor any release for him. The current took him at very great speed in company with a big piece of wood. It dumped him down with the big piece of wood across his chest, and then rushed away leaving them together; then the piece of wood rolled off him; it seemed to have iron fittings on it; he could not recognize it. When it was gone he groped, and felt something hard: he knelt and found a hand-rail and pulled himself to his feet, quite out of breath and smarting from cuts and scratches. He was nearly at the end of his tether. Another time he would not be able to get up. Where on earth was he? He was holding onto a deck-house hand-rail. Which one? Was he at the fo'c's'le? He thought that it might be the fo'c's'le. He groped with a hand and felt a big teak handle-bar, which he recognized at once. It was the latch of the sail-locker. He was back under the break of the poop, back at the starting-post. It was like one of those race games which he had played as a little child. If your throw of the dice brought your horse onto certain jumps you had to go back to the starting-post and begin again. He had cast a dice which had brought him onto the dreaded wall at eighty-four, and here he was back again, winded and hurt.

He was so blown by his last adventure that he hung on for a long, long time without trying to do anything. The water came at his knees, sometimes at his thighs; he held on, quite stunned and very weary. He knew that he could not get to the windlass, no, not if the ship was sinking. Presently, he thought:

"I can at least see how Captain Cobb is and give him a drink."

He fumbled in his belt. His torch was there still. He pressed the button of the switch; nothing happened for two or three attempts, then on shaking the torch downwards gently and trying again the light shone out, on a deck full of water. Looking first to leeward he saw that the starboard poop-ladder had disappeared. Beyond its site he could see the crests of all manner of mad women dancing outside the ship; a lot of old witches, with white hair, or old devils with hooky fingers. They looked awful, whichever they were. Turning the beam aloft, he saw the mizen stay, with those forms of darkness still streaming and screaming across it.

"I wonder who made that gear," he thought, "and fitted it. Still, when the centre comes, she'll roll it out of her and nothing that we can do can stop it."

A succession of heavy seas checked his thought: he had to hang on for awhile; then, as the water cleared away somewhat, he waded across towards the alleyway doorway.

He had last seen it as a doorless gap in the poop structure. He saw that since he had been there someone had shipped a big weather-board above the coaming so as to keep out any sea likely to strike it. He wondered who could have done this: probably Okle, he thought. He saw that it was the weather-board usually fitted to that coaming in heavy weather. It fitted into clamps in the Steward's cabin when not in use; he had seen it there a score of times. With some trouble he clambered over it into the alleyway, steadied himself there, and at once realized that men had been busy there, getting the water away. The alleyway was not dry, but not enough water ran there to cover the soles of his boots. Men had been in Dudley Mac's cabin, too, he found, getting the water away, and the floating gear chocked, so that it could chase about no longer. A flash of the torch showed him that the cabin was occupied. In the upper bunk the cat, wide-eyed and open-mouthed, was lying, still terrified, uttering little yows of distress. Two men were in Dudley Mac's bunk, end for end, one pair of feet and one head on the pillow, one head and one pair of feet on a rolled coat at the foot. They were Okle and Cantlow, Carpenter and Sailmaker, both dead asleep in their heavy weather gear. Another man had wedged himself into Dudley Mac's settle by the help of a bunk-board. He was all crouched and hunched, but utterly asleep: it was Evesbatch. He woke at the flash of the torch.

"Remember the watch below," he growled; then, waking further, he asked: "Is it One Bell, yet?" Then, waking completely, he asked "if it had begun to moderate?"

"No," Dick said. "Where is everybody?"

"Waiting for it to moderate," Evesbatch said, dropping back, as a sailor often will, into deep sleep.

Dick left the cabin and pushed on quietly to the saloon.

There, too, men had done something to clear the wreck. At the moment, rain was streaming down the hole where the skylight had been. He thought:

"The rain may check the sea a little; beat it down a bit."

He very gently opened the Captain's cabin door and crept in. The lamp was still burning; there was about one poor candle's light in it, but it seemed the light of Heaven after so much darkness. Captain Cobb was lying still, asleep, breathing quietly. Dick muttered the sea-proverb that anyone asleep was well-off. He knew that sleep was the best thing in life: some say water, some say bread, others wisdom or women's love, but sleep seemed above them all. He could give nothing better to his patient. Very cautiously he groped for the door-ring behind him, opened the door, and backed himself out into the streaming saloon. There he decided to go up on deck to the shelter of the weathercloth for as long as it held. He could not bring himself to look into Mr. Duckswich's cabin, but hunger made him turn to the Steward's room for a handful of raisins. After all, he had had a hard time since coming on deck, and if the ship were to sink, as seemed certain, the raisins might as well sink inside him as in the case. He thought also that it might be a good thing to put a refill battery into his torch.

In the Steward's bunk, fast asleep, was the figure of Bill Guller, with his mouth open and his front upper teeth showing. He shook Bill awake.

"Rouse out," he said. "On deck, Bill."

"On deck, hell and blazes; what can a man do on deck? He can't see. He can't stand. You can't set sail. It would blow away if you could."

"You can set another weathercloth if this one goes, or when it goes. Come, out with you."

Bill turned out. There was a strong smell of whisky about him. There had been a splicing of the main brace down in the alleyway since Dick had gone on deck, and the neckless bottle had been hard to pour from.

"What's the time?" he asked stupidly.

"I don't know. Come on up. And get the others up. Sails and Chips and Evesbatch are in Dudley Mac's cabin."

"What? Aft here?"

"Yes."

"Of all the blasted necks." Bill hove himself to his feet and yawned.

"Come out, now," Dick repeated. "Out you get. Left turn for Dudley Mac's."

"Oh hell, I'm sleepy."

"You'll have plenty of sleep when the ship sinks."

"I'd forgotten the ship. Is it still like it was?"

"Worse."

He led the way into Dudley Mac's cabin, and shook the Carpenter's feet, so that they went into the Sailmaker's face and woke the pair of them. They started up, the Sailmaker saying something about rats, the Carpenter asking: "What's the matter?"

"Out you come. On deck with you," Dick said, turning to rouse up Evesbatch. "Come on, here," he called, "rouse and bitt. You've no business in here. Up on deck and away."

They were drowsed past power of protest, and turned out, perhaps not knowing where they were nor how they had come there, only knowing that an order had come and that all orders had to be obeyed. They all slouched up and out, blinking and clearing their throats.

"Not out by the alleyway," Dick called. "Through the companion. Up on the poop. Get another oil-bag over."

"We must go up the proper way," Evesbatch said.

Now that he was awake his old respect for the sacred part of the ship had returned. He had taken off his southwester.

"You can't go up the proper way," Dick answered. "The ladder's gone."

He shepherded them up the stairs to the poop, into the fury: in the blind gale they butted across to the mizen shrouds, to the shelter of the weathercloth. Dick, flashing his torch to guide them, showed up two figures sitting on the deck, lashed to the shroud-screws. He saw that they were Alfrick and Aylton. Thinking that they might be dead, since they looked it, he shook them. They were only dead asleep.

"Rouse out," he said. "Get another oil-bag over."

Alfrick shouted back: "We got her over."

"What?"

"Got her over. See?" He took Dick's torch and lit the place where the oil-tins had been lashed: only two tins were now there. "We got her over," Alfrick shouted. "Aylton and I."

"Good-oh," Dick shouted back.

He shouted to the others to lie down under the weathercloth, with lines from the gear about their chests to keep them from fetching away. They worked themselves down,

as close to the cloth as they could get, Dick aft between
Guller and Alfrick, the others forward from him. Some of
the mizen running gear secured them. There they were,
lashed on deck, to wait for what might happen. They were
all cold and wet through, but a warm breath from his neigh-
bours assured Dick that the neckless whisky-bottle had con-
soled all there, except himself, quite recently. Snuggling
himself down he shouted to Alfrick that now they were
ready for a call; having said this, he went over in his mind
what the call would be and how they could meet it.

He saw himself answering an Examiner, thus:—

Examiner. Mr. Pomfret, you are hove-to in a cyclone in
the Southern Ocean, shipping great quantities of water,
enough to threaten ship and crew. Tell me what steps
you will take to meet the situation.

Answer. Get oil-bags over, and keep the crew off the decks
as much as possible. But you would know, if you were
here, you silly ass, that in this sea not fifty oil-bags
would help. At any moment the weight of the water,
plus the weight of the masts on deck, may stave in a
hatch, or open her deck or break a transverse.

Examiner. Thank you, Mr. Pomfret; shall we suppose now
that the sea *has* staved in a hatch? Tell me what steps
you will take to save the ship.

Answer. Call all hands to rouse out a new topsail from
the sail-locker and get it over the staved hatch. But
you would know, if you were here, that we might
never know that the hatch was staved till the ship went
down beneath us. How would you expect us to know?

Would you expect us to have a sentry sitting on the hatch to sing out, or ring a bell, or light a bonfire, directly the covers are staved? And perhaps you will explain, while you're at it, how we're to call all hands? I'd be glad to know. At present, if I go five yards, everybody melts away, and it may be twenty minutes before I find him, or them, again.

Examiner. Thank you, Mr. Pomfret; you have answered me very properly. We will suppose that the hatches stand (we will only suppose, mind), but that in some very violent gust your weathercloth blows away. Will you tell me what steps you will take to prevent her falling off into the trough when this happens? Or do you suppose that the ship would be easier in that situation?

Answer. I do not suppose any such thing. If she gets into the trough she'll go down the well.

Examiner. Then, perhaps you will answer the first part of my question.

Answer. I might get another weathercloth set; but if one No. O weathercloth has gone, a second would probably go, too. And probably the gusts near the centre, coupled with the excessive strain which all the gear has undergone for many hours, will take not only the weathercloth but the mizen-mast, on the shrouds of which the cloth is set.

Examiner. Then you think that nothing can be done to save your ship?

Answer. Something might be tried. Since our lives would depend on it, something would be tried.

Examiner. You will recollect, Mr. Pomfret, that we are not now speaking generally, but particularly. I ask, what steps you yourself will take?

Answer. Possibly, if they stood, the mizen-mast and yards might keep her pointing up, but more probably these would go over the side; they should, therefore, not be counted on. In fact, we ought to consider them as gone. Without them little could be done or tried. If I were lucky enough to escape undrowned and unmaimed on the way, I might get forward and there, if I were very lucky, I might let run seventy fathoms chain; that might bring her up.

Examiner. Will you give me your reasons for thinking so?

Answer. I have no reasons, and I don't believe it would head her up. I say it *might,* but if it didn't nothing else would, and we'd be done for. Probably we'd be done for in trying to do it.

Examiner. But that is what you would try to do.

Answer. Yes. Authorities suggest it.

Examiner. Really? And you see no inconveniences in such a procedure?

Answer. Do you think that there is any convenience in the doing of anything in a gale like this? The windlass is in order of course; but it will be quite impossible to man the capstan, and, therefore, quite impossible to range the chain. The cable-ends will be stopped up down in the chain-lockers; how can I hope to get the ends up? Even if I do, how can I expect to be able to range the chain with the ship half under water and green seas going down the chain-lockers? If our cable were ranged, and all clear for running, which it isn't, the letting go would be worth trying. But how should we have time, or the physical strength, for that?

Examiner. It seems to me, Mr. Pomfret, that you incline to assume my office and to ask *me* questions, instead of answering mine with the frankness of a sailor. You will reflect that if you cannot answer my questions it will be my duty to withhold your Certificate till you are better qualified in your profession.

Dick went over this examination several times, until the figure of the Examiner became almost a real, and very unpleasant, person, with every faculty and character which he himself most loathed. He could see him with his insinuating, oily manner, his suggestion of sarcasm, his inexhaustible, faultless, theoretical knowledge, his superiority, his ease of life, his undisguised contempt, his hands that had done no work, his brain so critical that it had become a negation of all intellect. After some moments Dick lapsed into a stupor that was almost sleep. It did not last for ten minutes before the figure or figment of the Examiner was troubling him again.

Examiner. Mr. Pomfret, you said, just now, that if your weathercloth were to blow away, you might get another set. Of course, as a prudent officer, who has seen the storm approaching, you will have a second weathercloth in the shrouds, ready for setting?

Answer. No, I haven't.

Examiner. Oh, of course, if you haven't . . .

"Oh, my God," Dick moaned. "Why didn't we rouse out the second weathercloth while we were down there?"

As he thought over his talk with the Examiner, that smirking, yet contemptuous, creature was there again.

Examiner. Mr. Pomfret, I am somewhat surprised at your latest answer, because I gather from your manner that you are intolerant of lack of imagination in others. I should have thought that a spare weathercloth would have been the first thing to occur to you. I am yet more surprised that in your answers you have shown no indication that you have ever heard (still less considered the applications) of this implement known as a sea-anchor. But perhaps you will know this contrivance only as a drogue, or shall we say a sanguinary drogue? Come, now, Mr. Pomfret, perhaps you will tell me why you have made no mention of this article? Doubtless you have some very good reason, which may enlighten the men of your profession. Tell me, then, if you will be so kind, why you have not thought of rigging a drogue, or, having thought of it, have rejected the device as unsuitable?

Answer. Because our decks are full of wreck and awash. Because the officers are gone and the Boatswain drunk. Because it's black as pitch and blowing like blazes, and any man moving on deck will be washed from Hull to Hackney before he can cast a rope from a pin. If you and your kind had made it obligatory for a ship to carry a drogue, all ready bent, for letting go, I would have let one go. You haven't, and I haven't got one, and the time's long past for rigging one. If you believe in a drogue, or sea-anchor, up-hook, scratch-in, and rig one, then ride it out and ride with it and tell me when you sight London Bridge.

Examiner. I will make note of these expressions, Mr. Pomfret, which seem to me to be a part of that insolence which accompanies intolerance to veil incompetence. I reflect with pleasure that a sailor so little British (being by your own confession largely of Southern European extraction), will soon be beneath the waves which you have proved that you are unfit to dominate.

Dick was in a state between sleep and stupor. In that state the figure of the Examiner seemed present just in front of him.

"Lie down and sleep it off," he called.

He saw the creature, for a few seconds, in his mind's eye; then as one of the worst of the gusts blew over, he woke into the blackness in which he could see nothing. He cast off his lashings and roused up Alfrick.

"Pass the word to the others," he shouted. "These gusts are very bad. Get up new weathercloth, for when this blows away."

They roused up, stunned. Some of them had rigged a life-line to the companion; they groped along this, and so down the hatch and along the alleyway, to wade knee-deep to the sail-locker. They got the door opened and hooked back. They scrambled inside to stumble over what felt like the limbs of giants, the rolls of sails and of canvas. Sails shipped the weather-board, to keep out what he could of the sea. They turned to find the cloth.

"Where is she, Richard?" the Carpenter asked.

"Here, where we got the other," Cantlow said, groping for the familiar feel. "Give us the light a moment, Pomfret."

Dick flashed the light where the Sailmaker was groping. He saw the bulges of dirty-looking canvas, and the gleam on southwesters.

"For the love of Mike," Sails said, "what's gone with it? It's not here."

"Are you sure you stowed it there?"

"Am I sure Ireland's green?"

"When did you see it last?"

"Lend us the light over here a minute."

Dick lent the light over a good many places, but the weathercloth was not there: they could not find it. They groped in the stifling fugg, heaving at heavy bundles, but could not meet with any weathercloth; nor was this strange, for Lefty Morritz had, with great skill, stolen it the week before, being weary of having no mattress in his bunk, and it now lay sopped in the starboard fo'c's'le.

"Have you a hatch-cover handy?" Dick asked.

"A storm staysail would be better," Sails said.

"It wouldn't," Dick said. "For one thing, we'd have to bend it on top of the half-deck. Fifty to one we'd never get it set, even if we did bend it: it would blow to glory as we hoisted, and the stay is the main support of the mizen. It would be the last straw to the mizen."

"There's something in that," Alfrick said.

"There's everything in that," Dick said. "Rouse out the best hatch-cover you've got."

They dragged it out, hove it out on deck, got the locker door shut, and set forth to their pitch below the mizen-rigging. Chips had suggested that they should stay in the sail-locker, but Dick had persuaded them against it. Any extra big sea might come in there and drown the lot of them, he said; in fact, any real sea coming in there, might gut the place and leave them without sails. They stopped the hatch-cover to the foot of the mizen-rigging, ready to set.

When they had done this, all knew that the poop was no longer a safe place for any man. The wind was beyond all experience. They pierced another drum of oil and lashed it to the waterway, so that it dripped down a scupper-hole; then they filed off below into the alleyway. They went into the Steward's cabin and pantry at the foot of the stairs.

"We shall hear here when the mizen goes," Dick said.

They secured themselves with lines to the bunk stand-ards and hand-rails, and settled down, sitting or lying, to shift and roll and slither at each mad movement of the ship. Each had his past to think of and himself to feel for; but what was the use of feeling or thinking? This blind, appalling, raging madness, beyond all memory and experience, had them in its power now. It was beyond all strength and effort. It could out-fury strength just as it could out-howl order. No man could fight this: no gear could stand, nor ship swim this.

Dick, who was lashed to the Steward's bunk standard, as he sat on the deck next to Alfrick, asked:

"Alfrick, did you ever know anything like this?"

"No," Alfrick said, "nothing beginning to be like this. The worst, ever."

There came a crashing fall at the cabin door; the voice of Bill Guller rose in curses. Dick flashed his light and saw Bill on the floor with one of the doors which had been torn away by the big sea.

"What is the rally, Bill?" he asked.

"I'm bringing this in, to lie on, out of the wet," Bill said. "I caught my toe on the coaming. I've just about done for my knee. Hold the light a tick, will you?"

Dick held the light, while Bill got his uneasy mattress lashed, not very securely, so that he could stretch his legs on it without putting them in the puddle on the floor. The party settled themselves and talked about the weather.

"It is like great guns, like drum-fire."

"The thing I don't like is the scream. Hark at that one."

"Ah, and hark at that one."

"This will grow to a gale, boys, if it keeps on, you'll see."

Many, many times in the next half-hour those crouched there in the Steward's cabin told themselves that the worst was on them. Then, suddenly, the roaring to windward deepened to the thunder of a blast more awful than anything that had blown yet. Long before it struck them they heard it, and felt their bloods run cold. It was like an advancing explosion. They felt the water heaped before it strike the ship, much as though an enormous plank had smitten her along her length. The ship heaved over un-

der the blow, and shook herself like an animal cruelly
hurt, kicking in death. Then the gust struck.

It seemed impossible that the blow could be wind. It
could not be wind. Some explosion must be blasting the
planet. Yet it was wind. But what could have made it?
How far had it come? How far would it go? What
would check it, or nullify it? It was wind; air in motion;
nothing more. Birds had flown in it; men had breathed it;
perhaps some day it would be air again, but for this hour
it was breath of Death.

The gust lasted while Dick counted a hundred and
twenty-seven slowly. Then, plainly, it had passed on, hell-
hounds and hunters together. How far would it go, heap-
ing up its special waves? He knew that the paths of some
gusts of death in these cyclones had been traced for over
twelve hundred miles. What was the story of that gust?
What had made it, what would it do, how would it end?
If it were not blasted into being by some bursting open of
the earth, how could air become this devil?

"That was a bad one," he said, to Alfrick.

"Near the centre, now," Alfrick said.

Some three minutes passed with the usual roaring and
racketing and then, again, a gust blew its warning, and
shrieked and smote, pinning the ship down till they felt
that she would go over. She did not go over. The gust
passed on. What was it doing? Seventy miles, eighty
miles, a hundred miles an hour? Who could tell? Dick
thought that he had read that a wind gauge had blown
away after registering a hundred and twelve miles an hour.
If this were going a hundred miles an hour and had lasted

three minutes, it contained about five miles of air that was moving like a living destruction.

"They're like the little battles in a big war," Alfrick said; "but the sea's less than you'd expect."

It was only less than Dick expected because it was confused. The strain upon the ship was greater than it would have been in the formal seas of the Atlantic and Cape Horn.

"The mizen still stands," Dick said. He had been listening for the crash and none had come.

"She's a good spar," Alfrick said. "I hope she stands."

There was no more to be said, and nothing more to be done, but Alfrick's words remained in the mind as though they had been blown there. "Hope she stands." Hope did stand; one could always hope. Youth was strong in Dick. He had not had any experience of death or disaster; his knowledge of the sea was not profound. He had been scared by the red sky, and by the first furies of the storm, the big sea and the loss of so many; but all those things had been long, long ago, in another life; they had nothing to do with this. He was not scared now, exactly. He did not feel that the ship had much chance, yet did not think of death. Probably nobody there thought of death. He was thinking far more of being wet, cold, hungry, dog-tired and unable even to sit in comfort, than of going down with the ship forever. Presently, with the noise of the wind, its unending fury, the crash of the green seas coming on board and all the roaring, banging, groaning welter in which they existed, he was exhausted and numbed into a kind of deep sleep. Most of the others were asleep:

in a sleep like death, which death and the sea might at any
moment make eternal.

They were wakened constantly by the wild movements
of the ship, or by water splashing or dripping on them.
Sometimes in their sleep they felt the iron of their props,
or the hardness of the deck working into their bones; then
they shifted in their sleep again. The ship rolled them
hither and yon: often, but for their lines, they would have
been flung across the deck.

Dick woke refreshed after a time. He had fallen asleep
half-frozen, but woke with a kind of sticky warmth all
over him, thinking of his sister at home. She was a jolly
good sort of chap, he thought; he didn't know why he
should think of her now; but he did, with much approval.
She was a year and more older than he. She was very like
him in many ways, tall, straight, very dark, with almost
black eyes and thick smudges of eyebrows. She was fond
of riding, and deft at crafts, a neat carpenter and clever
silversmith: she made good beltclasps and rings: she had a
good voice and could sing: she danced well. In fact, she
did most things well. He called her Charles, from some
fancied suggestion in her face of the face of Charles the
Second. She called him Dog, or The Dog. They were
very good friends, and when together spoke a nursery language, which they had perfected in childhood, and now
spoke with ease and speed. It was made up of words of
their own invention, contractions and interchangements
agreed upon, and much slang twisted from its original
meaning. It was pronounced always "in the manner of
the governors"; the "governors" being the rustics of their

neighbourhood. He went over some of her remarks to him:—

"Where hast mut her cat, Dog? Her'llt be bun gobbed."

"Thoust a bison. Duck her tuddies and ging did a splodge."

They were incomprehensible to any but their two selves, no third in the world knew what they meant, yet to themselves the one meant:

"Where have you put your hat, Dick? You'll be sunstruck," and the other:

"You're a wise one. Chuck your lessons and come and bathe."

He thought of these things now with a great deal of pleasure. He liked her; she was a good chap. He did not know the depth of her love for him. He wondered vaguely if she were thinking of him in her bedroom at home in England. He tried to think of the difference of time, and what time it would be in England, but he did not know what time it was there in the heart of the storm and so could not do the sum. Where he was it might be any time, midnight or three in the morning. It might not be any time, but a part of rushing Eternity.

"Her'm didding some splodges," he muttered, with a grin, as water rushing along the alleyway flung a pint or so into his face.

He thought of his father, a very kind and good clergyman in the western midlands, with whom he did not get along, though they were fond of each other. He thought of his mother, a Spanish lady, who had eloped with his father while he was an undergraduate and she a girl of six-

teen: she was a lovely creature, his mother: they understood each other; but even so, a man had to get away from
his mother, to make his mark on the world. Would he
make a mark on the world? Why, at any moment, the
ship might go down into water a mile deep and leave no
mark whatever, except a few bubbles, all broken a minute
later.

He thought of his home, and then again of Dinkie, his
sister, with her two dogs, and her way with the rough lads
of "the governors." After this, he thought of a lot of
things which would be nice for breakfast, and so rambled
off to sleep again, for a few uneasy minutes, which yet
seemed long.

When he woke, it was with the thought that he must see
the Captain. In casting loose his lashings he woke Alfrick.

"What's wrong?" Alfrick asked.

"Nothing. Going to see Captain Cobb. Still blowing
very hard."

"Can't harder," Alfrick said. "This the limit."

It was blowing now steadily, almost as it had blown in
the gusts a few minutes before. If it could blow thus, why
shouldn't it blow harder? He had seen upper clouds cross-
ing heaven, oh, many times, and once had watched them
with an astronomer lying flat on his back among the grass-
hoppers on the top of Bredon Hill. The astronomer had
told him that the clouds were moving on a wind blowing
at least a hundred and fifty miles an hour. If such winds
could blow there, no further from Bredon than Gloucester
Tower, why should they not blow here, in the open ocean,

till they blew the ship away like somebody's blown straw hat?

"I must have a look at it," he muttered. "I must go up and look at it."

Look at it! How could you look at it? The sea and the air were mingled and coming at him together, like nothing that he had known.

"God, I'll be blown away," he thought. "I'll be blown clean out of the ship."

He caught the life-line with both hands and hove himself foot by foot against the pressure to the mizen-rigging. In all other nights he could have gone, even in the darkest hour of the darkest, to any rope in the ship, to cast it loose from its pin with certainty. Now, he could not see one yard. All was driving, roaring blackness.

"Oh, my God," he moaned. "If I could only see or hear myself speak. If it would only let up for a moment."

The withering of the wind struck icy-cold: it blew right through to his marrow. "Golly, it has all the attributes of Death," he muttered. He fumbled with the torch and cast the light down the wind. "My God," he cried, "the mizen stands, but the boom's gone."

The boom had gone. It was snapped at the gooseneck and gone, clean overboard, sheets and gear and all. It had gone silently. It had been blown away bodily. Something made him put out a hand; he could not feel the weathercloth. He turned the light on the shrouds, and saw that all the weathercloth was gone, and the hatch-cover which they had brought to replace it, that, too, was gone; one

little rag and two little trailing stops were all that remained
of the two of them.

"We're done, then," he cried.

But were they done? Even without the cloth she was
heading up to it. She had the wind on the port bow still;
she was bowing it. He knew that the *Hurrying Angel*
had the reputation of lying-to easily. Might it be that in
her present trim, with much water on her deck and the
helm lashed as it was, the mizen-mast was going to make
her lie-to?

Ah, no; even as he asked this he felt her fall off and ship
a thundering packet and then another and another and another. Then with a sickening stagger he felt her pick herself up and flounder and slowly point up again, coming
wearily back, to thrust her bow at it.

"Old girl," he said, "if ever a ship deserved a medal, you
do."

There came a crash from overhead, with a glare of
lightning. As he crouched from the blast, things struck
him on the back, and continued to strike and pelt him very
hard. By his torch, he saw hail-stones as big as grape-shot
leaping over the deck. He slithered down below to get out
of the way; and as he went, knew that she was falling off
again, floundering wearily back towards the trough. Down
went her head and rail to it, and wallop came a stunning
sea that checked her as she went.

He slithered down the stairs to the pantry. Once before
in that storm memory had helped him: she helped him
now. Something that he had read years before, of ships
speaking each other at sea, in the days before the Code of

Flags, came into his mind. They would sidle as near to each other as was safe, and write messages to each other in chalk on blackboards, which were then held up or set in the mizen-rigging. The Captains would read the messages with telescopes and dictate the replies:

"Our chronometer's gone to hell."

"So've ours."

"Can you spare some spuds?"

"Sure. Can you supply a hymn-book?"

This came into his mind in a flash, with a suggestion for something that would help the ship. If the mizen stood, their best hope was still something in the mizen shrouds.

"Away—hay—hay," he shouted. "On deck here, the lot of you. Rouse out of it. Come on, hay, Alfrick, Evesbatch; out you come here. Weathercloth's gone. Come on."

They roused up; he flashed the light in their faces and kicked their legs till they were up. He had noted a new log-line in Dudley Mac's cabin. It only took him a few seconds to fetch this.

"Come on," he cried, cutting the stops of Bill Guller's door. "Catch-a-hold of the light here, Bill. We'll sling this door, and lash her in the mizen-rigging. That'll bring her up."

"You're right," Alfrick said.

Bill held the light. They middled the log-line, and marline-hitched it round the door, so that it had three turns about it, and two ends for ear-rings at each end. They set it on edge, oxtered it up, and ran it up the hatch into the blast. The blast caught the door and knocked them all over.

"Keep it flat on deck and drag it," Cantlow shouted.

They got down on hands and knees and dragged it to the scuppers. It had been a door down below, and it was a wild horse possessed by seven devils when it reached the deck. The ship was floundering off towards the trough, but stopping on the way for drinks. Together they edged the door between the shroud-screws and the bulkhead. Cantlow and Evesbatch got into the shrouds to it and hove it up by the ear-rings, the others got under it and hove. It caught in everything that it could catch in; it jammed on everything that it could jam on, and the heaves of everyone always jammed it worse. Once the wind got on the wrong side of it and almost took it overboard, but it came back with a bat, and there it was in place at last, being stopped to the shrouds, while the ship slowly forgot that she was bound to the trough and wearily floundered back to bow it.

They lashed themselves again, near at hand, but away from the shrouds, to watch until the end.

"Was in the *Lodore Falls,*" Aylton shouted. "Falling off . . . Off the Horn. The Old Man put his coat in jigger-rigging. It brought her to. Fact."

"Blowing very hard," Bill Guller shouted.

"Must be near Centre," Dick shouted back. "I must look at Captain."

As he went, the hail beat down again, in blobs of ice like blackbirds' eggs. He crawled cautiously across the saloon, hanging onto the hand-rails, while the hail rattled all about him through the hole in the roof. Very quietly he turned the handle of the Captain's door and crept within. The Captain was still asleep, and the lamp still burning. Dick watched him for a moment, thinking that he would have rare trouble with him before the broken bones were joined. The Old Man suddenly opened his eyes, recognized him, and said:

"How's she heading?"

"Keeping up into it nicely, sir," Dick said.

"How's her head, boy?"

Dick thought that the head would be roughly E.-S.-E., and said so. Afterwards he thought that North-South-West, Easterly, would have been more accurate.

"What's she doing?" the Captain asked.

"Doing, sir?"

"Yes, boy. When did you heave the log?"

"We've been lying by, sir."

"Ah, yes," the Old Man murmured, lapsing into sleep again. "Don't take the masts out of her. Send my Second Mate to me."

He closed his eyes and was asleep on the last words.

Dick watched him for a moment, and then crept away to the pantry, where he found a closed tin half full of rice and another small tin with currants in it. He mixed rice and currants together and took them to the party on deck.

"Strike-me-blind," he shouted. "Have some strike-me-blind."

They roused and ate and talked of the weather, that is, they shouted that it was blowing very hard and that they must be near the centre now.

They were near the centre, but for some little time now the storm that held them had been itself held. It was turning on itself, with its way barred, though they could not know this.

It was too full of energy and evil not to suggest a mob. As a war or a revolution may begin from some flaw or falsehood in prosperity, so this perhaps had begun from a flaw or eddy at the edge of the Trades. Having once started, it had grown in size and violence. Like a revolution or a war, it had drawn into its madness all the sanity near it, and had proceeded raging and flaming across hundreds of miles of ocean. Now, somewhere far ahead of the *Hurrying Angel,* its avant-couriers were beating upon a system of weather too calm for fever and too strong for madness, and finding that it would not give way.

Spirits in the upper air would have beheld it, with their clear eyes, as a black, filthy roll or mill-stone revolving against a cleanness. They would have seen its monstrous horizontal wheel or disc rolling like a wall of night.

It had smitten on the crystalline wall of a fine-weather system much as a swell of the sea will smite a mole. Not bursting through, it rose, as a swell will rise against mole or cliff, flying high up and shattering out into a spray; only to the watching spirit the wall and wave may have been (each) miles high, and the spray shattered a wonder of tormented cloud.

As will happen at the base of mole or cliff, the wave thrown back had plowtered and joltered till, gathering from the impulse behind, it could lift and try again, to be again thrown back or scattered into spray aloft. For some time it had striven and been shattered thus, till at last the rolling fury had glid from the rounded calm as a rush of water will glide from a boulder in the riverbed. Very slowly it had adjusted itself to a new course.

It had heralded its coming with fire; now it preluded its greatest moment with fire. Those wet and weary ones, mumbling raw strike-me-blind beneath the bulkhead, were roused from soddenness and apathy by a flash of bluish, searing fire leaping down the mizen-mast, along the deck and into the sea. It seemed to burn a hole in the sea; all the water boiled (so they would have sworn) where the fire struck it. At the same instant a crash of thunder roared over their heads with a suddenness that nearly cracked their ear-drums. Dick's instant thought was:

"She's struck. That got her."

But instead of collapsing, the mizen-mast shone out conspicuously with balls or fuzzes of luminousness, which crowned the snapped cap, went down the lifts to the yard-arms, and stuck like globes there. Others clung to the shroud-screws in the top; others formed on the mizen bitts; one or two moved slowly and queerly on the deck. A big ball was on the stump of the main-mast. Why, they had not seen the stump of the main-mast for hours. One greenish globe flopped across the poop close to Dick: it was like a fish that he had caught in a night of phosphorescence.

"Corposants," Alfrick shouted. "It won't be much more now. Sleep."

About an hour after that, Dick woke in a deluge of rain. He went below to see the Captain, who was awake.

"Why in hell didn't you come when I called, boy?"

"I was on deck, sir, and didn't hear."

"Where's my Steward?"

"Dead, sir, we think. Taken overboard."

"In this pain," the Captain said, "I never know what's real and what's light-headed. Is it blowing?"

"Yes, sir; but nothing like it was. Can I do anything to make your head easier?"

"Damn my head and yours, too. Give me a drink of whisky."

Dick gave the Captain a weak drink.

"Hell," the Old Man said, "give me something that I can taste."

"No, sir," Dick said. "You've got bones broken and may get a fever."

"I'll give you a fever."

"No, sir," Dick said. "Weak drinks for the weak, everybody knows that."

The Captain glared at him.

"Where's my Boatswain?" he said. "You say my old eunuch's dead and my Second Mate overboard, where's my Boatswain?"

"He was drinking your whisky in the slop-room, sir, when I last saw him," Dick answered. "I turned him forward out of it. That was a long time ago. I haven't seen him since. I haven't been forward since."

"Well, get forward now and send him here to me."

"No, sir," Dick said. "It's not possible to get forward. The deck's awash fore and aft, with all kinds of gear adrift."

"My poor ship's all gone to hell," the Old Man said, "like her poor Captain. My God, my bones ache."

Dick was touched by this.

"I'll mix you a real night-cap, sir, to make you sleep."

He knew that in the pantry there were nutmegs and red pepper. With these he brewed a toddy which, though weak like the other, had the flavours of fire.

"Ah," the patient said, after the first fiery gulp, "that's better. That scratches as she goes. That's got a kick in it. God, I feel better after that. Cut to hell on deck, now, and don't let me see your grinning mug till I've had a sleep. I can sleep, now. I couldn't on your other brew. You're not a bad lad, Pomfret, only you're too dam conceited. You want that cockiness welted out of you. Now, cut on deck."

When he reached the deck he felt at once that there was a change for the better. The poop was streaming from a very heavy rain-squall which had passed over; the air, as though cleansed by it, had freshness and life. The oppression which had been so daunting to the soul, ever since the day before, had gone; there was a breath of healing blowing. It was blowing a romping, full gale still, but blowing true, without those gusts which had scared them.

"What d'you think of it, Alfrick?" he shouted.

"Moderating."

"How about centre?"

"No. Breaking now. Clearing."

"Centre's due."

"No. Centre's clear."

Dick was too dog-weary to argue the point; he snuggled down under the bulkhead, with a rope across his chest to keep him there. The ship was rolling herself sick and filling herself green. Every ten minutes there came the sighing of a pine-forest as a rain-squall struck them, but all there slept.

"Let her roll her silly soul out," Dick muttered, as he forgot ship and all things else.

Perhaps his sleep lasted for a quarter of an hour before an unusual rain-squall woke him. Looking up, he saw heaven as a smear of wild clouds smoking and rushing, "galloping" as he described it, and thinning as they sped. Then, to his joy unspeakable, they thinned away, leaving a rift of the deep blue of heaven, with a star in it, then another, then another, till the rift was all bright with them, bright as in frost, bright as in a moonless midnight, dazzlingly bright, with none of the smudging and fuzziness of the storm. They were the Sons of God with their spears, truth from of old, beauty, blessing, and wisdom. No wonder the Wise Men followed such.

They shone there in the gap like the lights of cities in the mountains of heaven. Dick gazed and gazed at them. Surely those dark heights were mountains, and the brightness the burning of their watch-towers. Old Wallers had once said to him that the real delights of life cost nothing. He remembered that now, thinking that that colour of almost black blue, and that brightness spangling it, were joys without price, beyond price.

Then he remembered that the centre of a storm comes with a clearing of the sky, so that one may see stars or sun for perhaps half an hour. This clearing might be the coming of the centre. If that were so the worst would be still to come. He gazed and gazed, thinking that if the worst were still to come their lot would be hard indeed. The rift grew larger, but the wind did not abate: it was blowing a full gale, dead true.

"This cannot be the centre," Dick said. "The centre is always calm, without wind. This is clearing weather."

The rift suddenly dimmed at its edges and smudged out rapidly, so that no colour nor star appeared, then, with a washing hiss, and a spatter as of ten thousand horses fording a shallow at a gallop, a rain-squall rushed down upon them. When it cleared there were more stars in a paler heaven; the light was coming.

In the course of time the light grew, so that they could see the sea and marvel at it. Though a little lulled by the beating of the rain-squalls, it was the most frightful sea which they had ever known. It drove from to windward and toppled from to leeward, tossing the ship both ways and flooding her doubly. Being dim still, it was dark, as though dirty and trodden. All the dirty surface was made filthier by scufflings and smearings of tattered foam, cruddled like old wool. All the rags of newspapers, that a mob will scatter, seemed to have been scattered on the sea and then danced and trodden on till mess was everywhere. In such a mess in a town the lighter fragments blow about: the main squalor is on the ground. Here the whole filthy floor was alive and lifting with menace. It was raggedness linked with raving and ruin, such as none there had looked at nor dreamed of. All there had seen big seas in many a roaring storm:

"By many a tempest had their beards ben shake." In their experience they had known the power of storms to be associated with order. They had seen the march of the big seas coming like ranges of downland, greyback after greyback, sometimes two miles long, well-aligned, moving to the wind, curling in one direction, slipping under the curlings in one direction, and following each other in succession with an arranged space between them, and something like an arrangement in the space between one really big set and another. Now they looked upon a water that was not only defiled but had gone mad.

There was no kind of order in it, but every kind of devilry. It was (as Dick judged) not so big as the ordered "greyback" sea of the Western Ocean or Cape Horn. It did not give him any sensation or impression of majesty, nor of power, but it seemed to him to be evil cast loose to do what it would; not big, determined evil, but limitless hordes of selfish evils, "little devils that fight for themselves," too devilish to agree even about evil, but determined each to rend his neighbour, even if it rent himself.

The thing which impressed Dick most was that it was a shapeless sea. It looked like a revolution. It was a succession of points, teeth and pyramids, coming up confusedly in jags and tatters, butting and boiling into each other, collapsing and spouting. It was as though some devilry had kept all these jags of water under the surface till they had gone mad, and that then they had burst out, choking, to bite their neighbour and die. Although the seas were not high as seas run, they were high enough to be wicked and dangerous. Those that struck the *Hurrying Angel* did so with venom. As he watched, he saw continually, in all quarters, what he had never before seen in open water, two great cones or jags of water smiting into each other, and flying up into a kind of geyser blast perhaps a hundred feet high, which collapsed and fell, or seemed to fall, almost into the space from which it rose. When this happened, as it often did, near to the ship, the effect was terrifying.

In this sea gone mad, the *Hurrying Angel* bowed, rocked, rolled and staggered, with cataracts spouting along and across her. Big, uneasy seas would thud under her bows and explode into columns of flying white: peaks of crazy water would leap up and fall across her weather side. She would lie down a little, then wallow and take three toppling spouts together in the lee waist. She was making sad weather of it; her deck was full to the rails.

Slowly the daylight came onto that frenzy of sea gone mad. There was as yet no sunlight. What rifts of sky appeared were soon blotted out by rain-squalls. Whenever they cleared away there was still that heaving, jagged, spouting sea, dark grey, like slate, all littered with the scum of her boiling. The *Hurrying Angel* loitered in the midst of it, like an old cow tormented by the gadfly. She would feel the bite and settle herself down against it, to endure and endure. Then, at last, driven past all endurance, she seemed to throw up her head and start forward, as though to run, with the flies lifting in a cloud about her, to find some moment of ease, or half ease, before the pricks drove her on again.

"A bad sea, that," Alfrick said.

"I read somewhere," Dick said, "that long ago the crew of a French man-of-war went mad from the sight of a cyclone sea."

"It wouldn't be the sight of the sea," Alfrick answered.
"Very few of them would have seen it. They'd have been
battened down, with the ports shut. No, it was being in
despair, dismasted, in the trough, pumping spell and spell,
that made them mad, if it was mad. But foreigners scream
very easy. We shouldn't call it mad, what they got into.
It was nerves, as they call them."

It grew slowly lighter, though all the northern and some
of the eastern heaven was billowed black with the involving
smoke of the cyclone. There was something red in the
blackness at one point; glimmers of lightning shot through
it; perhaps that was where the Devil lived. Now and then
a blasting glimmer seemed to shoot upwards from it towards the zenith, as though he flung his bolts at heaven.

Dick and some of the others were watching the eastern
heaven for the coming of the sun, though it still seemed
impossible that the sun could shine again. They stared
ahead, into the blast, over the toppling and the tumbling,
at a distance now dark with squall, now angry with storm.
Presently they saw the darkness there become greenish and
diffuse upwards a vaporous faint fan of green.

"That's the green flash," Alfrick said. "You'll see it in
Ireland. I saw it in Sligo, when I was there in the *Moydart*.
They say that those who see it will be happy for life."

The fan deepened in colour to what Dick called "old-
glass green," and then to the darker "bottle-green." But
it was not green for more than a minute, it changed to yellow and then, as the rain-squall cleared from it, showed
orange to the water's edge, with the sun's bright crown
emerging from the jags of the sea. A way of brightness

spilled from him along the water to glitter to those weary ones. As he rose, the jags and spoutings became beautiful. The sea was again blue in her hollows, green in her crests and like snow in her bursts. And now, looking to the storm, they saw it like an island, hull down, with swathes of smoke upon it. The topmost rolls of smoke were like the cumulus clouds which promise thunder. They were coppery and glaring and came slowly, heaving up as bubbles blown from below. As the sun rose, these flushed to pink, then chilled to a dazzling whiteness, so that they stood above the sea like the Cordilleras, in new snow. A few dead birds and patches of dead fish drifted past. A stream of smoke blew away from the galley funnel; the Cook had contrived to start a fire.

Light had come to them, life had been given back to them, but the ship had to be remade. Nothing in her decks or within her living quarters but had suffered a sea-change. Something of the smash wrought below, in the Captain's quarters, has been described. Daylight now showed what had been done on deck. Presently, under the rain-squalls and the falling wind, the sea abated, so that men could move on deck and take stock. She was a miserable sight to a sailor's eye. Dick, who had to make a list of the damages done, found these, among others, as he began·aft and walked forward.

Her flagstaff was snapped off short at the rail; her starboard poop-bulkheads for three yards on her quarter were bent in towards the deck. Her wheel-gratings, the top of her wheel-box and half her wheel were gone, with the patent log and the hand log-reel, which had once been stowed near them. The brass binnacle had stood it out. The big skylight, a solid structure, which had made in its foundations a solid teak seat for three on a side, and had been heavy with glass, screened by brass rods, was gone, cut clean to the deck. The Captain's charthouse and all within it was gone. About one half of her poop-rail, with the fresh-water bucket-rack, which had once stood beneath it, was gone, with both the poop ladders and their railings. The railings to the standard compass had gone; but the compass, like the other, had stood it out. Her mizen top-gallant-mast had gone at the cap, with both its yards. Her gaff was gone. Her boom had been blown away out of the gooseneck, with all its gear and the foot of the spanker. Of the missing mizen spars nothing remained on board: they were gone. A few splintered dents and dips in the teak top of the buckled starboard bulkhead showed where boom (or gaff) had struck in passing.

Of the rest of the gear of the mizen-mast, some toll had been taken. All the sails had been blown to little rags, and all that remained of the spanker, crojick and topsails were a few flogging trailers. All the chafing gear on the stays had been blown away. Most of the running gear, blown loose when the sails went, had flapped and flogged itself to ruin. One chain topsail sheet, in falling, had splintered the standard of the mizen bitts and driven a link of itself one inch deep into the deck.

So much for the poop. Its glory was the mizen-mast. That still stood, to the credit of the man who made and set up its standing-rigging. That the lower yards still stood was due to Dudley Mac's interest in the old ways of leading braces and to the Old Man's hatred of the Mate. If the braces had been led, as usual, to the mainmast doublings, the mizen yards would have had no braces, and would have flung themselves about till they broke clear.

The two ship's boats, which had once stowed on the skids, between the poop and the mainmast, were gone, with their chocks and davits. The starboard forward skid was badly bent by falling wreck. The little skiff, the pram, and the two scows, the ship's lesser boats, used in port for pleasure or the scrubbing of the ship's side, which had once stowed on the top of the half-deck, were gone, with all their gear. The skylight on the top of the half-deck had been cut off clean and carried away. Every rag of the mizen staysail, a new Number O storm sail, had gone. Its hanks had worn themselves and the stay to brightness of silver by jangling there.

On the main-deck, starting from aft, there was abundant ruin and loss. The alleyway door and the poop-ladders have been mentioned. The harness-cask, containing salt meat in pickle, and the scuttle-butt containing drinking water, both handsome works of teak, with brass hoops which the boys had kept like gold, were gone from their stands under the break of the poop.

The big hen-coop, which had stood on the booby hatch, had gone with its inmates, a Buff Orpington cock and seven white Leghorn hens.

The half-deck, Dick's home, was in a sad state. It had been flooded from above and below. Its door had been wrenched away and sent sailing. The chests of Newbarn, Rue and Pillows had been taken away and overboard.

The other two chests (Dick's and Bill's) were flooded and staved. All the bunks had been washed out, and the bunk-boards floated away. On the floor, when Dick took stock, a foot of water was washing the broken tables, the smashed lockers, chests and other gear, with bedding, clothes, boots, oilskins, bits of pantile, parts of lamp, pipes, the tin kettle, and some tin dishes and pannikins. Dick had looked for corpses in the half-deck, thinking that the big sea might have swept them there. But, as Evesbatch said, "A corpse is a helpless thing and goes where the sea wants; anything that could float has floated." The sea had "wanted" the corpses elsewhere, and had taken them.

Near the half-deck was more ruin. Of the two small deck capstans (known as Hadfields) one on each side of the main bitts, the one to starboard had been broken in the whelps by the falling foremast; the one to port, apart from a singular deep dent on the top of the drum, was un-harmed. The mainmast in going had smashed the bitts below it, with the winch for working the main hatch; all the gear on the bitts had floated or blown away into confusion beyond all telling.

When the mast fell, the ship had been moving wildly on some staggering 'scend which had plucked the back-stays away and perhaps searched out some flaw in the iron. It had come down with a blow upon the rail which had flung the main yard fore and aft, snapping its truss and slings. The lower topsail yard had had something the same fate. It had been snapped from its truss and flung fore and aft, but so that it cocked up at the forward end and jammed the port fo'c's'le door. The upper topsail yard had gone overboard, to thump the side till cut away by Barty Berrow. The main topgallant-mast and yards (also overboard), had been cut clear before this.

All the port deck on which the ruin lay was cut, dinted, splintered and gouged: jags of iron, of wood and of chain were stuck in it here and there. It was all strown, matted, tangled and confused with crumpled, kinked and trailing gear, bent iron, knotted chain, splintered wood, some of it afloat, some of it thumping and collapsing, lying across it at all angles and in all disorder. From every little point of vantage, shroud-batten, wrenched-out jackstay, bit of wire or flying pendant a flag of canvas blew. It seemed to Dick that all these little flags of torn sail had been bleached by the night of terror to something whiter than sailcloth.

The port rail in the waist had suffered. The main and fore fife-rails had been torn off by falling yards; about a third of the bulwark staunchions were loose; five swinging ports had been wrenched off. The main hatch was unharmed; but a spare topmast, once in chain-grips alongside it, was now poised athwart it, having no doubt had some sails about decks before coming to her moorings there.

Just forward of the main hatch there was that after extension of the fo'c's'le known as the roundhouse, where the Idlers, Cook, Boatswain, Sailmaker and Carpenter lived. The door of their compartment opened aft, facing the main hatch: it was a strong sea-door of teak. Driven into this was the heavy iron pan, or dipper, which had once hung on the scuttle-butt for the use of anyone who wanted a drink of water while on deck. It held about a quart: it had once been part of a foot-soldier's kit, and was strong enough to serve as a shrapnel helmet. The edge of its lip had been driven into the door two inches deep.

"The wind did that," Evesbatch said. "One of the worst of those gusts did that. I was in the Havana once, in one of these storms. I saw a corrugated-iron roof driven edgewise into a malobo tree nine inches deep. It would have split a man in two if it had met a man. That was the wind. You can't beat the wind. There's nothing wind can't do, when it gets going."

The roundhouse had been flooded, like everything else on board, but, as its door had held, it had suffered much less than the half-deck. The skylight had been taken away. All the skylights of that big house's different compartments had gone, the one over the Carpenter's shop, the one over the galley and the two over the fo'c's'les. The two big boats, which had once stood on chocks, one on each side of the skylights, had gone with the chocks into sudden matchwood and Davy Jones. The Carpenter's shop had been flooded, and some small wood and quarterings washed from it. His tool-chest was unharmed.

The galley-funnel had gone; both the galley doors had gone and the sea had taken all but the range. Every pan and kid was gone. Only the Cook's private kettle remained to him. At a very early hour that dauntless soul found means to rig a spare funnel, to find firing and start a fire. There he stood, or hopped, in a place full of smoke, while splashings hissed on the range and raised steam. Twice he was washed out of his galley, but he hopped back both times, "to get something hot for all hands." He was a very

hot and wrathful little man; when he was not swearing he
sang there:—

"Who travels by Hoxton, to breathe the sweet air,
But meets with my Phyllis, the charming and fair."

The starboard forward end of the fo'c's'le had been
grievously buckled by the fall of the foremast. The fore
bitts were smashed, and had been floated away. The funnel of the donkey-engine was gone, but the donkey-house
itself was unhurt. The pigsty, with its two pigs, had gone.
The forehatch was unharmed. All the fo'c's'le rails were
gone. The bowsprit had snapped off at the knightheads
and had gone with its iron bobstays and all its gear. The
port wing of the figurehead, the *Hurrying Angel,* had been
clipped at the base, so that she could hurry no more.

Lying along the starboard side of the main-deck was the
wreck of the foremast, foretopmast, and the three lower
fore yards. The topgallant-mast and yards having snapped
athwart had at some time in the night been wrenched away
and floated overboard. The remaining wreck looked like a
giant hand with its fingers spread. From the cocked upper
yard a streamer of sail six feet long was flying out like a
pennon. The rest of the wreck, after rolling and smashing
in ways not to be described, harrowing the plank, ripping
off the fife-rail, and battering side and fo'c's'le to the bright
steel, had jammed itself so that it could roll no further.
The deck was gouged, ploughed and planed in all directions on this side, more than half the deck-staunchions were
gone, and all the freeing-ports, save one, had been torn off.

But this, in the main, was only the account of loss and ruin. What impressed Dick far more was the condition of the decks and paintwork. On the decks, when the seas cleared off them, was a sort of slippery green scum difficult to broom away. In two or three places on deck were little dead fish, or strange black things, still alive, which the men said were "suckers." Certainly for most of the night, the deck must have seemed like a part of the sea to many little sea-creatures. In a big patch under the break of the poop was a gleaming mass stuck to the deck. It looked whitish, like paste, and no doubt had once been alive. They got it away with a scraper, but the place where it had been shone faintly after dark for some nights.

Some of the paintwork of the ship, the day before the storm, was new: all of it had been spotlessly clean. Now it was all defaced, dirty, rubbed and scratched. Most of it had been exposed to the assault of floating wreck or the grinding of moving wood, wire or iron. Great tracks of paint were gouged away. In many places things had beaten and flogged upon it till it had fallen, leaving the bare iron, which was now red with rust, in all sorts of splashes, sprays and tetters, as though the plate had skin disease. On the port side, which had been the weather side, the ship was crusted white with salt to the rail. Her deckhouses and stumps of masts were also white with salt. It glistened in the sun, and was slimy to the touch.

There was no yard in all the ship's visible structure that was not fouled, marked, chipped, dented, splintered, gouged, starred or fractured. The damage visible was terrible enough, but it was not likely to be all. The worst wounds would be the hidden ones, the butt started (to give way at the next strain), the deck-planks opened, a plate holed, or the rudder-pintles bent. From her lumpish movements in the sea it was plain that she had a couple of feet of water in her. This might have come down the hole of the foremast before Chips plugged it, but who could tell? It might have come from a dozen other wounds. She might well have a death-wound somewhere. The loss of her masts might prove to be a death-wound. She was at least fifteen hundred miles from any port, and unable, at present, to move. Until she could move she might wallow and roll herself down the well.

"I don't know what you call it," Bill Guller said. "I call it hell and high water. And all because the Battler crooked his elbow. He went over the Bay and got mottled, and we've got all hell to pay and no pitch hot."

Early in the forenoon in the moderating weather the Captain, full of fight and knowing that his Mates were dead, sent Dick to fetch the Boatswain to him. Beyond all doubt his intent was to make William Purple an acting Mate.

The Boatswain had drunken heavily in the slop-room and since being turned thence had drunken from a stolen bottle in his bunk. Dick found him in his bunk, purple as his name, snoring heavily. He had long had a proverb about himself:

> "First glass, after none at all,
> Indicates Will Purple's fall."

"The first bottle always puts me under," he used to say. "I can carry the next three at a Royal Inspection and no one notice it." However, this was the first bottle.

"Here, a sheer hulk, lies poor Bill Purple," Dick quoted, "the darling of our crew (I don't think). Come on, now, Boatswain, hey; the Captain wants you."

He shook the man's foot. Bill Purple gurgled and growled.

"Wazzarmarrer?"

"Captain Cobb wants you."

"Wat say?"

"Captain wants you."

"Captain?"

"Yes, the Captain."

"What Captain?"

"Captain Cobb."

"Wazzywommefor?"

"To give you hell for pinching his whisky, probably."

"Ah, hell."

"Yes; hell."

"Hell."

Bill Purple rolled over into sleep, puffing out his lungs and stretching. Dick took him by the shoulder and shook him.

"Out you come, Boatswain. Lay aft with you. The Captain wants you."

This time Bill Purple roused, raised himself on an elbow and stared at Dick; he had a fierce, purple face with a swollen nose; and a sullen temper that relished battle.

"You say the Captain wants me? D'ye mean Captain Cobb wants me?"

"Yes."

"Well, tell him from me, will you, please, that he can go and chase himself: d'ye hear? Yes, and sell himself for what he'll fetch, and give the girls a drink with the proceeds."

"Come on, now, Boatswain: out you come," Dick said. "You must go to the Captain. Pull yourself together and lay aft."

"You can tell him I said so," the Boatswain shouted. "If the Captain wants me, he can come for me himself. Them's my last words to Obadiah Battler. I'll come when I've made me toilet. James ain't brought me shaving water yet, nor the butler me hot towel."

With these words the old drunkard plucked his wet blanket over his shoulders and fell asleep again.

"He's as drunk as an owl," Evesbatch said. "Now the Old Man will break him, and a good job, too. A damned old purple hyena is all the Boatswain is."

Dick had many things to see to during the next hour; presently he was summoned to the Captain's cabin.

"Why haven't you sent the Boatswain to me?" the Old Man began.

"He's drunk, sir, and refused to come."

"Why didn't you bring him, when I told you?"

"You didn't tell me to bring him, sir, but to send him."

"If you couldn't send, why didn't you bring him?"

"He's a warrant officer, sir: I'm nothing."

"You're right," the Captain growled. "What did he say?"

Dick repeated the Boatswain's remarks, adding that the man was drunk and would be all right after a sleep.

"Will he?" the Captain growled. "We'll see."

Dick did not answer this, but waited for orders.

"What are you going to do now?" the Captain asked. "Have a nice turn-in, I suppose, and sleep the round of the clock, after a good scoff of cabin-food?"

"I'm here for your orders, Captain Cobb."

"Ah, yes, my orders. You've been thinking, I don't doubt, that now you're as good as in command. You're not, let me tell you. I'm in command."

"Certainly, sir."

"You're a boy here; a sort of ship's boy."

"Certainly, sir."

"And I'll see you keep your place."

"Certainly, sir."

"And your place is nothing. You're a kid. I could spit a better seaman than you at new moon. You know nothing; you do nothing, and you're going to be nothing."

"Certainly, sir."

"Don't say 'Certainly, sir,' again, like my aunt's parrot . . . What do you think you are?"

Dick felt that the truth was due and spoke it.

"The only Navigator left on board, sir."

"The only Navigator," the Captain cried, "God's one and only. You, The Navigator; God save my soul. Our Navigator; a kid in his third year, without a ticket. Touch your hat when you speak to me, my man: I'm the Navigator."

"I am, sir," Dick answered. "The only one, till you are better."

"There won't be much navigation here, till the ship's rigged," the Captain said, "and is the only Navigator going to rig her, may I ask?"

"I shall do my best, sir."

"Gottseck, boy, you assume command then. Gottseck, if I'd my leg I'd boot you forward."

"My place is aft, and I'm your officer, sir," Dick said. "As your officer, I will not be talked to like that."

"You'll not be what?"

"Bullied, sir, by you."

"By God, boy, am I the Captain of this ship?"

"Yes, sir, you are, and you've got her into a fine mess. You drove her across a cyclone's track when you were too drunk to know what you were doing. You caused the deaths of two Mates, two helmsmen, your Steward and a boy, and ripped the masts out of her. You, by some miracle, are alive: the ship's a wreck and will be a wreck for a week, even if she lives: she may not live: we're not out of the wood yet, by a long way. Some of us have been up all night, trying to save her, and when I come to you for orders you tell me that I'm a ship's boy. I am a ship's boy, and one that would blush to handle any ship the way you handled this one yesterday. There's hardly a man on board that doesn't think of you as a sot and a murderer; and if it comes to a Court of Enquiry, as it will, there won't be much talk of your being Captain of this ship,

but of your being prosecuted for the deaths of six, one of
whom was only a boy, and another one of the finest seamen I ever knew, or who ever sailed for that matter."

He was overstrained by the night, and his deliverance
from death; he said far more than he had meant to say;
when he spoke of Ed Newbarn and of Mr. MacLerrinnan
he nearly wept. It was the kind of speech which goes from
soul to soul. He saw the Old Man blaze up and struggle
forward to smite him; then flush crimson to the point of
apoplexy; then suddenly change, and turn pale, with all
the fury, and indeed all the life, gone from it. He thought
at the moment that he had pierced the Old Man through
the heart: it was really simpler than that; he had pricked
him through the gas-bag, and the collapse was immediate.

"No, no, Pomfret," the Old Man stammered. "Come,
boy, you didn't ought to talk like that; about murder and
that. I was seizing the fair wind when it came. I didn't
cause the deaths. The Act of God took those men . . .
The Act of God, no man can prevent. I've had a touch
of it, too, Pomfret, in all these broken bones. No, no, boy
. . . you and me, we was always good friends . . . and
you've got your chance, now. . . . I'll stand by you and
you'll stand by me. What was it you wanted to talk
about?"

Dick felt that for the moment the hatchet could be set
aside.

"Sir," he said, "there's a world to talk about. The ship's
a wreck and a scarecrow, but Chips thinks she's sound,
apart from what she's made. The crowd's dead beat

and starved, sir; all their whacks have gone over the side. Would you sanction an issue of stores, sir?"

"Yes," the Captain said, "you could issue a week's whack."

"Thank you, sir. Then, about poor Mr. Duckswich, sir; may Sails prepare him for burial?"

"Yes."

"Would you bury him at sunset, sir?"

"Who would take the service?"

"You, sir, the Captain."

The Captain turned white and took a quick, scared look at Dick. Dick knew from it that his words about murder had gone home. Plainly the Captain was scared at the thought of coming near to the body lest the blood should flow and denounce him as the murderer.

"No, no, boy," he said. "I'm not able for the service. Perhaps you would take the service."

"I'll take the service, sir, if you order me."

"I do order you, boy. That would be best. Me and Mr. Duckswich . . . he wouldn't have liked me burying him."

There were other matters to arrange, such as the saving of the dead men's things, the appointment of Pillows as sick nurse, and then, the main question, of how the watchers were to be re-arranged, and who was to have charge of them. Dick, who had clear views about all these things, carried his will in all of them, after some dispute and much abuse. However, the heart was out of the Captain now; he was thinking of what Dick had said about the Court of Enquiry.

"Then I'll call all hands aft for you to speak to them," Dick said.

"Yes, that would be a good thing; quite the best thing," the Old Man said.

Had that mood been on him a day earlier, how different things would have been.

The men came aft, and hung about the break of the poop till they were summoned. Dick hooked open the Captain's door, and told them to range themselves against the saloon's after bulkhead, where the Captain could see them from his cot.

They came in, with the shame-faced awe which long sea-custom had imposed on them. No others than those taken by the big sea were gone; but there were minor casualties. Old, white-haired Nab Wallers had wrenched his right arm, while hanging on, so that he could not now use it. The cheery Cradley had had a fall on to one knee, so that he limped, leaning on a batten. Botloe had had his head cut open against a deck-staunchion, and had mended the seam with tar, not very neatly. Suckley looked white and sick, and had a badly-swollen head. All the rest were haggard and strained, dark under the eyes, and the worse for wear. They had been banged about, rolled over decks, cut, bruised, half-drowned, half-starved, cold and exhausted; but they were alive still. They ranked themselves silently, peering to see how the Captain looked. They swayed there, to the motion of the ship, all the twenty of them, for even Tom Coggins had come aft, in their old oilskins, torn by jags of wire and showing whitish where a new coat of oil was needed. They stared at the Captain, who stared back, not speaking. He was in a good deal of pain and much confusion. Dick's words had scared him, and some reaction had set in from his voyage over the Bay. At the moment he was trying to decide whether some of his memories of rolling about decks in the water had been real or imaginary.

"Well, men," he said at last. "We've had a knock. The sea's taken some good men from us. It was very severe weather."

The men were silent. They were sorry for him, knowing that no light injury would have laid him up; at the same time, it was not for them to speak.

"Those the sea took," the Captain went on, "were good men and good officers. It was very severe weather; I've known none worse.

"I hope to be on deck to-night." As this seemed to be a giving way to weakness, he added, "I'll be on deck this afternoon. There's much to do on deck. If we all bear a hand we'll soon be clear. It's the old English saying, 'One and all.' Till we get sail on her, it'll be all hands on deck as long as it's light, and at night an anchor watch, to keep the lamps trimmed.

"I'm the Captain of this ship. Don't let any of you think you can work Tom Cox on me just because I'm sick a little.

"No Captain can run a ship without officers. I need two. It's for me to choose the first, so I take Mr. Pomfret here, with me. He's *Mr.* Pomfret now, remember. Mr. Pomfret, you will please move your things to Mr. Duckswich's cabin."

"Thank you, sir," Dick said.

"Mr. Pomfret is your officer," the Captain went on. "I'm

sure we all wish him success. Don't think to fool him because he's young. You'll obey him as you'd obey me.

"You've a right to choose your Second Mate, if you wish."

He glared at them in a way which plainly said, "I'll shoot the first man who tries it, for mutiny." He went on at once, before any man could speak.

"I see you're afraid to choose your Second Mate. I choose for you. I choose Mr. James Alfrick as your Second Mate. Mr. Alfrick, you will please send your things aft to Mr. MacLerrinnan's cabin."

"Very good, Captain Cobb; thank you, sir," Alfrick said.

"That's that, then," the Captain said.

The men looked at each other, wondering if they were to be dismissed. The Captain checked them.

"You've lost your whacks of food. If you'll bring your whack-pots aft you'll receive new whacks."

There was a murmur of thanks.

"No noise, there," the Captain said. "Where are Purple and Loach?"

"Here, sir," the two answered.

"Let me see you." The two lurched forward.

"You broached stores last night, and drank whisky in the slop-room. You, Purple, were drunk and refused duty this morning."

"No, sir; never, Captain Cobb."

"Where were you two last night, if not in the slop-room?"

They looked at each other; Purple, being the readier, said:

"We were under the fo'c's'le head together, sir, trying to chinse up a plate where it was coming in."

"Did anybody see you there?"

"It was black as a pocket, sir; nobody could have seen us."

"Did anyone here see the Boatswain and Loach forward there?" the Captain asked.

The men looked at each other: nobody had seen either of them, but nobody wished to speak: there was silence.

"Did you see anybody there while you were there?"

"Yes, sir," William Purple said. "I'm sorry to have to say it, Captain Cobb, I did. I seen the one you say is to be Mr. Pomfret hiding in the locker and told him to get on deck out of it."

"And what did he say?"

"He said the storm was too bad."

"You hear that, Mr. Pomfret?" the Captain asked.

"Yes, sir."

"What do you say to it?"

"Which locker was it, Purple?" Dick asked.

"My locker: the starboard locker."

"You say you saw me?"

"Yes."

"I seen you, too," Loach said.

"Although it was so black that nobody could have seen you?" Dick answered.

There was a general laugn from the men.

"I knew you by your voice: you were crying," the Boatswain said. "You were mammy-sick."

"Come here, Purple," the Captain said. "Just come into my cabin a moment and reach me the mug there."

Purple lurched across, peered for the mug, found it, and handed it to the Captain.

"Gottseck, Purple," the Captain said, "what have you done to your face? Turn it here a moment. Bend this way a moment. Gottseck, I thought you'd had a dose of Asiatic Crabs: all little yellow devils."

"No, Captain Cobb, not me," Purple said.

"You blind mutt," Captain Cobb began, "you stink of whisky now like my Aunt Jane's vaults. I asked you to bend your face to me so's I might smell your breath. It was a trick a kid would have seen through: only you're drunk now, drunk and blinking. And you try to put it off on the boy here. You and Loach were caught in the slop-room by him, necking my whisky. And this morning you told the lad to tell me to chase myself. Gottseck, you . . . don't you dare to answer back. One word of lip and I'll smash your faces in, both of you.

"I break you as Boatswain of this ship. Out you get into the fo'c's'le.

"D'you hear, you, men, this dirt here is no longer Boatswain; he's Purple, A.B. And as soon as we reach London River I'll charge you two with barratry and get you two years, good. You'll shift your gear forward right now."

The old Boatswain's face had paled under his purple; he bowed his head to the blast, fumbled with his southwester, touched his forelock, and turned to go forward. Drunk as he still was, he knew enough not to answer back; his world was all fallen about him, this was not the time to try to better matters.

"Come back there, you drunken scum," the Captain shouted. "What d'ye mean by turning your back on me before I tell you you may? Fall in there, with your mates, while I speak to you."

The old man shuffled back into the line of men and stood there bent and blinking, waiting for the storm to pass. A good many officers had sworn at him, first and last; it meant nothing; it was just their way of carrying-on, so much powder to drive the bullet of the order forward; but this was more than a swearing, this was a breaking; and he knew that the hands forward would not welcome him as a brother; his methods as Boatswain had not endeared him to them. The Captain went on with his speech.

"The man, Will Aylton, is Boatswain of this ship."

"Thank you, sir," Aylton said. "And we all hope, Captain Cobb, that you'll soon be well and about again."

"Thank you, Boatswain; I shall be," the Captain answered. "Wait one moment, men; then get your whacks. You know the rules; see you keep them. You know me. I'll see you do. Get forward."

As the men shuffled away, the Captain called the Sailmaker.

"Get Mr. Duckswich ready for burial," he said. "And you, Mr. Pomfret, get him buried when Sails is ready."

"Very good, sir."

"You'll not forget the sun?"

"No, sir."

"Get him buried as soon as you've got the sun, and made Eight Bells. It'll only keep all hands five minutes."

"Very good, sir."

Dick found that the men had waited in the alleyway to speak to him before going forward. Many of them (all his old watch and some of the other) congratulated him on his promotion.

"Mr. Pomfret, sir, I wish you good luck, I'm sure, sir."

"Mr. Pomfret, all the watch is delighted, sir."

"Mr. Pomfret, that's just what we would all have wished for you, sir."

"I'm sure, Mr. Pomfret, sir, that there's nobody we would rather have over us. We hope you'll have every success, sir."

But the real reason of their lingering aft, was to ask to be permitted to take a last look at Mr. Duckswich before the Sailmaker shrouded him. Dick opened the cabin door to them, and told them to pass in, but not to linger long. They passed in, one after the other, with a crackle and rustle of oilskins, to have a look at their dead officer. Some said nothing: some said that they hoped he had a quick death; others, that God wouldn't be hard on him, since he'd not had much of a picnic here in life: others, that it was sad for him not to have any friends there. It did not seem to Dick likely that Mr. Duckswich had any friends anywhere: he was a lonely little island of a man in an ocean of life, and now was going off the map. Dick was wondering how he could bury him, for there was no Prayer-Book nor any Bible on board. As the Old Man had told him "he would have to make up something," and that in less than an hour, all weary as he was. Even the Nonconformist Sermons in the "library" had been spoiled by the sea. The melancholy Pencome said that he had a Moody and Sankey's hymn-book, but on being pressed to produce it found that the sea had taken it.

At noon, Dick and the other boys went below to the Mate's cabin, where the Sailmaker had shrouded Mr. Duckswich for burial. He had found a new Red Ensign in the slop-room, as a covering for the shroud. Getting lines underneath the body, so as to sling it between them, four of the boys, Sails and Chips, carried it on deck to the poop's lee side. Aloysius Rue stood aside from the ceremony, thinking that he might do the wrong things. He had heard the Captain saying that he wasn't going to have any foreign religion aboard the *Hurrying Angel*. Dick did not like to see Aloysius out of it, so went to him and asked him to toll the bell, which Aloysius did, to call the men to gather aft, near the body.

It then fell to Dick, who had not before spoken in public, to invent a burial service. He was very deeply moved. He had been in the Mate's watch for the greater part of a year. Many little acts of kindness came into his mind. Often the Mate had given him bits of cabin cake, or cups of hot coffee in the morning watch. They had talked together in countless night watches. He had been a sad and weary old man, but endlessly patient in explaining, and with a varied life's experience to illustrate the points. One thing Dick remembered vividly; how years before, when still young, Mr. Duckswich had signed as Second Mate in a coaster taking cattle up the African coast. "They told me to go down among the cattle and sling them round the horns, so down

I went; and the first thing I knew, one of these beasts with horns a yard long was after me; so down I went into the lighter and ashore. I let another man take that job. I said I'd signed as Second Mate, not as a matador."

As Dick moved across the deck, he crossed the spot where the Mate had stood when he told that story. Just over the way was where he had stood when he had called to Mr. MacLerrinnan. "There'll be a big push behind yon packet, by my way of it." That was less than a day ago. There had been a push behind the packet: it had pushed speaker and hearer away into the unknown.

All hands (except the Captain) had gathered there. They stood all bare-headed, battered and unconquered, with great rings round their eyes, and that high look of having been pushed to the limit. They were all in oilskins ragged from moving over the wreck: they would have looked like scarecrows but for that high look. As it was, they looked like the unconquered.

The bell clanged irregularly, for Aloysius had a poor sense of time; the ship laboured and spouted, making the lines of seamen sway, as they leaned to the movements; the wind which was blowing hard made their hair stream out. Dick tried to begin the burial service, though the words mixed in his mind and stuck in his throat, or passed out of memory. At last he said what he could remember:

"Man that is born of woman has but a short time to live.

"He cometh up as a flower and goeth down like the beast that perishes."

As this did not sound right, here he stopped; some of the men said "Amen."

He did not know how to go on. He wanted to put the verse as his hearers knew it:

> "Man that is born of woman has but a short time to live.
> "He goes up like a main upper topsail and down like a flying-jib,"

but that did not sound fitting. He wanted to say something about all the others who had gone. Some words floated into his mind: he uttered them as they came.

"We here in this ship, in this Act of Burial, remember our shipmates, Mr. Dudley MacLerrinnan, Niagara Torrent, Able Seaman, Lefty Moritz, Ordinary Seaman, Edward Newbarn, Apprentice, and Enoch Mince, Steward, taken overboard from us last night, and drowned in the great sea. In the midst of life we are in death."

He stopped again, wondering what to say next; some of the men helped him out by saying "Amen."

Aylton was standing beside him. He turned to Aylton, who had a good voice, and asked him if he could sing something. Aylton said he would sing a little of "Shall we gather," and did so, all that he could remember, four lines in all, and the men joined in the chorus and then repeated it. After this he sang a chorus from a Salvation Army hymn, which the men repeated twice. After this there was a pause.

Dick seemed to remember something more:

"Forasmuch as it has pleased God to take unto himself our shipmate, Lionel Duckswich, we now come to commit his body to the deep . . ."

He paused, deeply moved, while the bearers, with tears running down their faces, lifted the body to the rail. Dick could not think of other words to say. Forcing himself to say something, he added, with some memory of an English funeral:

"We, therefore, commit his body to the deep, in the hope of a blessed resurrection, earth to earth, dust to dust, ashes to ashes. Amen."

At a sign from him they hove the body to the rail and held it there. He drew away the Red Ensign, which flapped out free before he smothered it. Then they launched the little bundle of seaman into the sea, which took him away into its depths.

With the Captain's leave, Dick had mixed the contents of two bottles of whisky and a bottle of lime juice with a pound of sugar in a bucket of water. As the body faded from sight he called to all hands "to splice the main brace." Kit Pillows at the alleyway door served a tot of the mixture to each man.

"So they ordered the funerals of Duckswich, tamer of top-
    sails."

When the dead had been cared for, the living had the ship to remake, "all hell to pay," as Guller put it, "and no pitch hot." It was the usual lot of the sailing-ship sailor, to have much to do, with insufficient means. Usually there was the Will, that conquers difficulty. Pitch, of a sort, was improvised and heated, and hell was payed. Even in the lamed and broken-winged *Angel* something was done.

First, as she had made a great drift off her course in the storm, and was still drifting dead to leeward, they rigged a drogue for her to ride to with less drift. When this was done, as the sea moderated, they did what they could to make the ship safe. Chips and Alfrick together got the donkey-engine to work, and pumped out the eighteen inches of water which had got into her, mainly no doubt through the hole of the foremast, and the rest through strainings in the deck-seams. They thought themselves lucky to have got off with eighteen inches, and luckier still to find that the ship was tight; for no more came in after the pumps had sucked. After this, Chips and three others made a more thorough job of the plugging of the foremast hole, while all hands worked on deck till after dark, securing what could be secured, cleaning up what could be readily cleaned, getting life-lines across danger points, lashing spare hatch- and boat-covers over the holes where skylights had once been, rousing home (where they could) the bolts of loose bulwark-staunchions, lashing and bowsing and making fast all over the deck.

Dick knew that the Old Man would not agree to any extra allowance to the men, but by an arrangement with Kit Pillows he got up potatoes and a few onions, as well as some flour and raisins, and caused Tom Coggins to make not only a stew, but a duff for supper, which was taken after dark, when the anchor watch had been set. After supper there was all night in, save for two at a time on

anchor watch. Before dawn Dick roused them out to coffee
and then to work.

"Your first job, Mister," the Battler said, "will be to have
me up on deck where I can see you don't play hell with
her."

They bore his cot on deck, and lashed it to the weather
side of the poop, so raised at the head that he could see the
deck and most of what took place on it. They rigged a
little awning for him, and put his speaking-trumpet handy.
Dick was then free, as he thought, to begin the job of clearing the decks. The Old Man lifted his trumpet and called:
"Lay aft, all hands."

They laid aft, wondering what the trouble might be.

"Now, men," the Battler began, "you may think that
because gear's broken it can be dumped. Don't let me see
you dump one rope-yarn. You'll need all the gear you can
salve, and more. Even a rag of canvas is worth salving.
You can clean paint with it, you can parcel rope with it.
You'll find that with all that's gone overboard you'll not
have too much when you come to re-rig. Now there's
nothing to growl at in the job you've got. You can be all
clear to re-rig to-night if you heave round. It's a good
straight sailor's job, a farmer's job, with all night in. I'll
know the man I see slacking and he'll know me. Now, let
me see all clear for rigging sheers to-morrow."

The men listened respectfully and then, finding that that
was all, went to the work. The Port Watch was to clear
the foremast; the Starboard Watch the main. The Old
Man had told them that it could be done in the day, if they
hove round. Well, they had had a good supper and all

night in: it was fine, clear, sunny weather; calm but for a bit of a swell still; and they were ready to heave round for all that they were worth. Dick, going forward with his watch, heard someone behind him say (generally) that talk was an Old Man's perk, and then add (particularly) that he had known an old goat talk more sense than some Old Men. The voice sounded like Botloe's, but he could not be sure.

Dick reached the port fore-rigging with his men.

"Come on," he said. "Turn-to, here. Let's see if we can't get our mast clear before Mr. Alfrick clears his."

He had thought, good easy lad, that to clear the rigging would not be difficult. Where the shrouds had not been broken by weight falling on them, or snapped by sudden overwhelming shock, they lay kinked, bent and prone. He had thought that with the shroud-keys he could unscrew the boxes and free them. He had his shroud-keys all ready, and set-to.

Alas, all those bent and kinked lengths of iron had been smitten by strains too great. The screws inside the boxes had sometimes drawn, sometimes stripped, but in all cases had jammed. The boxes were so bent that the threads would not work: they were stuck fast.

He had learned to be patient with threads of screws. He got his watch to try all the dodges of the trade with them; squirtings of paraffin, soakings in paraffin, gentle persuasion after paraffin. This had no effect whatever on those screws which could be got at. He remembered that heat applied outwardly would sometimes expand a nut or shackle, so that the fitting might be freed. He got an iron pan from

the Boatswain's locker, lit a fire of oakum in it, and set the
fire beneath a box-screw. The pan was not big enough,
the screw did not budge; the Old Man saw him and hailed
him through the trumpet.

"Pomfret, there, Pomfret; what in hell are you playing
at?"

Dick went aft to the break of the poop.

"What in hell are you doing? Trying to set the ship on
fire?"

"Trying to start a box-screw, sir."

"That's not the way to do it. If it won't start, it's
stripped. You'll have to cut it. You'll be all day and all
week starting screws in that way. Why, my Aunt Jane
would know that."

Dick nearly said, "I thought you said we were to salve all
gear," but remembered, just in time, that that would bring
the Old Man's unfailing snub of, "You're not paid to
think." (Poor lad, he wasn't paid at all for anything.) He
answered, "Yes, sir. What would you like done, sir?"

"I told you. Cut it."

"Very good, sir."

"Cut it, and get on with it."

"Cut it, and get on with it: ay, ay, sir."

In the Carpenter's shop he found Chips making sick-
room appliances.

"Chips," he said, "I've got to cut through the rigging-
screws. What tools can you spare me?"

"You can't cut through the rigging-screws. What do you
expect to cut them with?"

"I don't know: an axe maybe, or some cold chisels."

"You'll never cut through the screws."

"Have you an axe?"

"Mr. Alfrick's got the one axe. There's a chopper which the Doc brought, and I've some cold chisels left."

Dick pocketed some cold chisels, and took the chopper. The chopper had been used by the Cook for the splitting of fire-wood, and the cracking up of blocks of coal. It had also been used as a hammer. It had been so misused in the night of the storm that there were flattened blobs on the edge more than a quarter of an inch across. Dick found a top-maul in the Boatswain's locker and prepared to cut through the screws as he had been told.

He had a couple of good iron wedges, which he thrust underneath the first screw. Pencome held a cold chisel to the screw, and Barty Berrow smote on it with the maul. The screw was dinted, certainly, but the cold chisel's edge was turned. They tried for a good long while; and presently learned how to hold the cold chisels with improvised grips of pliant wire. They also learned that the cold chisels were mostly made of lead.

"We'll never cut through the screws at this rate," Dick said, with a sinking heart; for with all their work they had not half cut one. "Come on. Leave the screws. Get what hammers you can find in the locker; we'll try cutting through the shrouds."

There were several hammers in the locker: they set to work to cut through the thick wire rope of the shrouds.

The shrouds lay tossed at all angles in every kind of kink and bend. Here and there, they lay against iron, over the moulding of the rail, on the fallen mainmast or one of the lower yards: some lay stretched over the shell of the fo'c's'le. In these cases they could set the chisel on the wire and smite. In other cases they had to contrive to slip a wedge under the wire to get an iron backing for the blow. In the one case the wire usually slipped at the blow, and the chisel, after marking the wire, dinted the backing and was blunted by it. In the other case the wedge went flying and chisel and wire bruised or cut the deck. They learned, too, how good, strong wire rope, which always has a heart of soft stuff, will flatten out on being smitten, rather than give to the cut. The mauls smote, the chisels bent, the wire dented, but did not give. The crew gave the Old Man the image of absorbed, energetic industry, but the results were deplorable. Dick had the feeling that they might well be a month cutting away the rigging. If they were a month cutting through the rigging, how many years would they be in cutting through the masts?

He moved over to the Carpenter's shop, seeing, as he went, that the men of Alfrick's watch were as worried and angry as his own.

"Chips," he said, "will you lend me that old firmer chisel you have, for a moment?"

He had seen an old, big, firmer chisel in the shop that morning. It was in a much-battered handle, but was still a useful tool. Chips lent it, without any suspicion. Dick took it, and tried it on the wire, striking an angled blow against a wooden backing. It was not good for the chisel, but it worked much better than anything they had tried so far.

Unfortunately, Chips was rightly jealous of his tools;

he came out a minute later to see what was being done with it.

"No, no, for God's sake, Mr. Pomfret," he said. "Oh, no, sir; you mustn't think of doing that. I've only the two firmer chisels in the ship, and I've all these spars to set off and trim. I may be lost for want of a chisel, as it is. You mustn't think of a good tool for a job of that sort. I gave you all those cold chisels for this job."

Dick saw that the firmer chisel had better be kept for the spars; he gave it back.

"Your cold chisels are just about as much good as lead," he said.

"They're not my cold chisels," Chips said, with dignity. "They're the ship's. Have you tried taking them down on the grindstone?"

The grindstone had been in use all the day with men "taking them down" in the hope of better things further down. They had described it as like sharpening pencils, the same lead all the way. Grinding was not any good: the things were useless; and the men were hot, angry and disappointed at the little progress made.

During the afternoon, Dick thought it wise to give his watch a change. He put them to unreeving, and stopping up, all the running gear of rope and chain that could be salved. This was pleasanter work, with results which could be seen. They salved all the running gear that was left, with all the blocks that could be got at. Dick had begun to feel, with the Captain, that they might not have too much left, even if all were salved. How long would they be there? How long would it take them to clear the decks?

Here was the second day nearly gone and nothing vital done; nothing really begun. Why, they might be weeks at this game, out of the world, helpless and beyond help, till they died of want of food and water.

Late in the afternoon, as he was hacking at a shroud, he was aware of some disturbance aft. William Purple, the ex-Boatswain, was standing below the break of the poop speaking with the Captain. Dick told his men to carry on, while he slipped aft, in case of trouble. The work in the ship ceased on the instant, though all hands showed an intent eagerness about something on the deck beneath their noses.

"What ails you, Purple?" the Old Man was asking. "Why've you left your work?"

"I've got my feelings, Captain Cobb," Purple replied. "Any man would have feelings."

"What feelings?" the Old Man asked. "Are you in love or have you a belly-ache?"

"I've got feelings of pride, Captain Cobb," he answered, "at not being done right to."

"You get to your work, what you're rightly put at," the Old Man answered. "If you've a complaint to make, come aft in the proper way, at the proper time, when you're off duty."

"Very well, Captain Cobb," he muttered.

He turned irresolutely to find Aylton, Alfrick and Dick standing at his elbow.

"Get to your work there, Purple," Dick said.

The Old Man bent his head to the blast and shambled away to the starboard side.

"You want to keep at it, Purple," Alfrick said, warningly. "Don't leave your work another time."

"Come on, now, Will," Aylton, the new Boatswain, said. "Heave round. You won't make a wrong better by doing another."

The ex-Boatswain picked up his maul, and tapped on the deck with it.

"What in hell are you playing at there, Purple?" the Old Man called. "If you dent that deck, I'll make you kiss it smooth on your bare knees. Get on with your work."

"My heart's broke, Captain Cobb."

There was a general burst of laughter from all hands, who had, in some strange way, by this time all contrived to be intently busy within earshot.

"Get on with your work, there," Dick called to the men, who bowed at once to their tasks.

"Your head'll be broke, too," the Captain said, "if you give me any of your nonsense here. I've got bones broke, like dogs gnawing in me, a damn sight worse than your heart. Heave round on your job."

"No, Captain Cobb," he said, "I'm not going to heave round on any job. When you've done me right, I'll work my fingers to the bone for you; but until then there's my job." (He flung down his maul.) "I've got pride, though I may be only a seaman."

He started to walk forward, knowing very well that everybody in the fo'c's'le loathed him, yet at the moment sympathized with him, partly for being, in his small way, greatness fallen, partly for his defiance of authority.

"None of this, Purple," Alfrick said. "Pick up that maul."

"I can't."

"Pick it up."

Purple did not answer; he tottered about uncertainly and then sat down on the booby hatch and mopped his eyes with a blue handkerchief. Alfrick and Aylton got him up onto his feet and thrust the maul into his hand.

"Pick up that maul and heave round, when you're told," they said. "You'll only make it worse for yourself."

The ex-Boatswain shook his head and wept.

"Put that man in irons," the Captain called. "Get the irons you, boy, there; they're in the top locker in my room."

Pillows soon brought the irons.

"Come on, now, Purple," Alfrick said. "You've done yourself no good. You'll have to go into these, now, unless you turn-to. What about it, now?"

"Put me into irons," he said. "I'll live to spit poison on some of you, yet."

Alfrick snapped the handcuffs on him.

"You see," he said, "now you've done it: now you'll be logged. That's all the good you've got by being so silly."

"Get over to looard," the Captain ordered. "Fall in there to looard by the break of the poop. Give him a bucket to weep into. Him and his heart. Get to your work, there, you others."

It was not a well-chosen moment, since his leader was now in irons, but Obbie Loach chose it for his protest. He had been working, or pretending to work, at the box-screw of one of the starboard main swifters; he now pitched down the iron rod with which he had been trying the screw, and crossed the deck to the break of the poop. They had nailed a temporary ladder to the poop; he hopped up it, and there he was, alongside the Captain. He was wearing a soft cloth working-cap, stolen during the War from a French sailor; with this he struck the Captain over the face. He received an instant counter over the nose from the Captain's speaking-trumpet, which drew blood. A little blood was all that Obbie needed.

"You dirty little swine," he called. "Putting an old man like that in irons. You think because you got poor men at sea you can play hell with them. You might once, perhaps; not now you can't. No, not now you can't. Not after the War, you can't. Your day's over. Now you've got men to deal with; not a lot of curs. Don't think to order me any more, for I've done with you; a little red-eyed tup; a little reach-me-down poop ornament . . ."

But by this time Dick, Alfrick, Aylton, Bill Guller and the Sailmaker were surging up the ladder after him: they were almost on him. He flung his cap into the Captain's face, upset his pannikin of lime juice, and darted aft as they stretched hands to collar him. There was only one place of safety; the companionway; he made a running jump of it and was down in the alleyway with the hounds close at heel. Blood was running into his mouth. He spat it onto the deck as he reached the deck.

"That's what I think of you," he called to the world in general.

Dick collared him at this instant, but he shook off Dick,

and contrived to pluck Botloe by the collar so that he collided with Dick as he returned to the tackle.

"Come on, you paltry wage-slaves," Obbie called to the crew. "Dividend-makers. Come and make a stand for once."

They were making a stand: they were looking on at the fun: all work was at an end. They stood, watched and grinned. They had no intention of joining in a mutiny; the ship was in trouble enough without that. They were not going to help the officers: the officers could help themselves. What with old Purple being broken-hearted, and Obbie in mutiny they felt that life was being good.

"Ah, you parasites," Obbie cried to them. "You won't help one of yourselves. You haven't got the blood of a midge."

By this time he was near the main hatch, where Alfrick had laid a strip of sail on which he had piled a great many salved blocks of different kinds, with smaller matters such as hanks, cringles, thimbles and hard-wood fair leads. Obbie darted upon these and at once opened fire with them on his pursuers. He had the advantage, because he was by this time in a frenzy and cared for nothing. If he killed a few of them he would jump overboard. He flung wildly, but with great speed. More than once in the War he had been up dangerous saps bombing the enemy. He got Alfrick a beauty in the chest with a jewel-block. What with laughter and surprise the attack here was not pressed home; Obbie held them for an instant. He struck Aylton in the shoulder.

"That's what you'll get if you come after me," he shouted.

"Taking the bread out of an old man's mouth. Yah, you, wage-slave; you let yourself be bribed by the blood-suckers. Come on, you, Starboard Watch, are you going to let your shipmate be outed by these penny-grubbing bourgeois? Be men and end them. Heave the lot overboard, and take the grain for your reward. You're workers, you've earned it: not these slave-drivers. Take this ship's cargo, it's yours. Take this ship, she belongs to you. We'll go to some island in the tropics and get wives and live with Nature. Take that, and that, and that."

The small-shot of hanks and cringles flew aft. He was swift with his shots, and being now drunk with the joy of defiance he flung at everyone, and struck Evesbatch with a hank on the right ear. Evesbatch had been knocked on the ear too often, in the way of business, to mind the blow, but he felt that in this matter he was audience, not a party in the fight.

"Here, Obbie," he said. "Chuck it."

"Yes, I'll chuck it," Obbie cried. "Since you ask me to you shall have it. It's men like you deserve it most. Fighters. You won't fight for your own class. But you fight the men of your own class for a rich man's purse . . ."

Evesbatch received a well-aimed volley.

Suddenly, Obbie's flank was turned; Dick, Bill Guller and Alfrick were at him from over the hatch. Bill hove a running bowline at him and almost caught him with it. It hit his head and glanced off it.

"Gorblimey," Obbie said, "it's you, is it, me lad," and laid Bill out with a cringle on the temple.

He was collared on the instant, but some he ducked from,

some he shook off. It was his moment. It had been working towards this in him for many months. All his loathing of authority, which had simmered within him in hatreds and bitternesses suppressed through years of War and disappointment now flamed out in action. He still had a few shots, which he turned suddenly to fling; then he was off before they could close. He heard the crew laughing at him, not cheering him, and longed to smash their silly heads in.

The hounds were at his heels, but there was the open galley door at hand; he nipped into it, and flung Tom Coggins aside.

"Here, my lad," Tom Coggins said, "none of that, now, in here. Get out of it."

"To hell with out of it," Obbie answered.

He had no instant for the preparation of a plan of campaign. He was an instinctive fighter, like Cæsar or Nelson. He had two seconds in which to think and do. He dug the old shovel into the galley fire and flung the shovelful of red-hot coals at his pursuers. As they ducked he gave them a second shovelful, and was at once out on deck through the port door, carrying the shovel with him.

Here he felt nearly at the end of his tether. He was being boxed up in the bows. There on the deck at his feet among the port-fore-rigging was a two-pronged iron crow, which he seized.

"Now, I'll smash in that Battler's Cobby crumpet," he shouted. "Come on, you, Battler, you're for it. Long you've ground poor sailors down, now you're going to ride to hell on the end of a Dutchman's poker."

He charged aft. His way was clear. The crew were over to port; his chasers were picking up red-hot coals from the galley.

"Battler," he cried, "make up your sins, brother. Your doom's coming."

The Battler was sitting up in bed, with a pistol in his right hand, waiting for him. As Obbie's head came in sight, as he ran up the ladder, a bullet came at it, very near to it; then another.

The Battler was not speaking, save very quietly to Kit Pillows, who was standing near him.

"Stand aside as he comes in, and then smash him one."

He fired a third shot, which went through Obbie's sleeve and just burned the skin of his arm. Obbie felt the sting, and thought that he was hit. He stopped in his career, and dropped down to the deck.

"Ho," he said, "pistols is it? Your doom must wait, then, Battler."

His own doom seemed closing-in on him; he could not hope for much more success. His one thought was to get back forward. He cast a glance at the crew over on the starboard side there.

"Ah, you curs," he said. "You'll stand by and see a mate shot like a dog. Well, I'll kill someone before they lay hands on me."

He drew a deep breath, and faced his pursuers now coming aft on the port side from the galley.

"Away—hay—hay—hay," he shouted, charging them.

As he passed the half-deck, Evesbatch, who was waiting for him, drenched him with a bucket of water, which gave

him, if anything, new strength. He lashed out with crow
and shovel, meaning to kill if he hit; his attackers dodged
his blows and let him pass, but turned and chased him.

Now there was nothing for him but the triangular
fo'c's'le-head. If he went onto the top of it there were two
ladders up, and he could not hope to hold more than one.
There was no retreat from it, save over the knightheads to
the figure-head, and beyond that to the sea. For an instant
the thought of getting down the hawser to the drogue ap-
pealed to him; but sharks? There would be sharks, no
doubt. Yet, if he got under the fo'c's'le-head, he would be
boxed.

"Got you," Aylton said, tackling him.

He tripped Aylton, and they fell together. He shook
himself clear of Aylton and got up. He had only one port
of escape, the port lavatory: he darted into it, slammed the
door and drew the bolt. Aylton picked himself up; lashed
the handle of the door securely with a bit of chain; and
then said:

"That's got him for the present."

He picked up the crow and shovel which had been
dropped in the tussle. "Bit of a fracas," he said. "If he'd
got us with one of these boys the going would have been
rough."

Dick went aft to the Old Man and reported the quarry
"gone to earth."

"Pump him out of it," the Old Man said. "Rig the head
pump. Bore a hole in the door for the hoze-nozzle, and
then pump the devil out of him. Nothing like cold water

for a lunatic. Bring him to me when he surrenders. I want to speak to him."

"There's others wants to speak with him," Tom Coggins muttered. "He's made a mess in my galley and burned a hole in my best pants. I'd a pair of pants drying there was worth a good half-quid. They've had a coal clean through the seat. When a man calls on his girl, he don't want a pair of pants like that. They're burned through, right fore and aft."

Dick called Chips to bring a brace and bit to the bolted door.

"Now, Loach," he said. "You'd better give in and come out."

"Not for any sea-scout, I won't; nor naval volunteer," Obbie answered. "Go and tell some more tales to the Old Man about poor chaps finding a drop of comfort; yes, and be made a Mate for it, do; you brass-bound puppy."

"As you are, then," Dick said. "Heave round, then, Chips."

Obbie thought that Chips was going to break open the door; then, as the bit began to move, he thought that the lock was being taken off. He heard the noise of a tool, and wondered what to do, whether to charge out or to wait. After unbolting and very carefully feeling the door, he knew that he was secured there. He wondered what the next move would be. He re-bolted and waited. Dick's watch moved up the head pump; Dick screwed a good nozzle to the hose.

"Heave round, there," he said.

The water jetted out onto the deck and gushed away.

"That's the way, my men," Obbie called. "Wash the decks down for tea when the sea-scout calls you. I wouldn't obey a school-kid, if I was you; but it's no good trying to put soul into slaves, that's sure."

The Carpenter's bit went through the door here, and sent the last disc or biscuit of wood flying into Obbie. It fell with a clatter. Obbie saw at once that a hole had been cut, and at once clapped his eye to it to see what was happening. He chose his moment ill, for he received the full blast of the jet in his eye. He was knocked down by it. Before he could get to his feet the nozzle was lashed to the hole and the water spouting in upon him. Several of the pumpers had been hit by Obbie's missiles: they sang as they pumped:—

> "*Only one more wash for Obbie,*
>   *One more wash,*
> *Oh, rock and roll me over,*
>   *Only one more wash.*
> *Only one more drink for Obbie,*
>   *One more drink.*
> *Oh, rock and roll me over,*
>   *Only one more drink.*"

Obbie tried beating back the nozzle; but it was secure, and he had only his hands and sheath-knife. He tried putting his fingers up the spout of the nozzle, but a few twitches on the nozzle which nearly broke his fingers made him give up this. He then tried to ram a fillet of his shirt up the nozzle, but this failed, too, for the same reason.

There was no escape from the blast. He was soon standing up to the knees in water and only dodging the full jet by crouching in a cramped position against the door. Suddenly he was driven from this point by another blast. The enemy had rigged another pump, and were heaving round through another hole, singing a cheery song:—

"*Cheer, boys, cheer,*
Our Obbie keeps a mangle.
Cheer, boys, cheer,
It's made of wood and stone.
Cheer, boys, cheer,
He turns it with a handle,
Cheer, boys, cheer.
It's all our Obbie's own."

"Yah, you think you're funny dogs," Obbie said.

Unfortunately, they did. They were enjoying themselves.

"That's the style, sons," came the voice of Tom Coggins. "Give him plenty of cold water. He may not be so free with his coals another time. He burned the seat of my pants, off, right fore and aft; worth half a quid."

"I wish your seat had been in them," Obbie said.

The streams of cold water continued to spout. Obbie was soon cold and very wretched. If he dodged one spout, he was certain to be hit by the other: there was no escape and nothing that he could do made his lot easier. The men preferred pumping in the shade to cutting wire shrouds in the sun: they could sing: and in the spells after pumping they did nothing. They did not like Obbie. They had no moral qualms about his taking the Captain's whisky, but they had honest indignation at his not bringing them a bottle; they pumped with a very good will, singing song after song.

After an hour, Obbie thought that if they pumped much longer they would be so sick of pumping that they would break in the door and ride him on a rail. It would be wiser not to keep them pumping too long: as it was, his credit was strained. The cries of the men to him, to "Duck down, Ob, old son, and lap the cream of it," or to "Cheer up, Ob; nothing like a shower to make the skin bright," had changed now to cheers to themselves to "Heave round and drown the swine."

"Come along, now, Loach," Alfrick said. "If we come in for you, God help you."

"All right," Obbie said, pulling back the bolt, "you can come in now."

Aylton opened the door, and caught Obbie by the scruff of the neck. "Aft with you, son. The Captain wants you," he said.

"Here," Obbie said, shaking him off, "there's no need for hands on me: not your hands, anyway. What are you rossing about?"

"I'm rossing about you," Aylton said, getting a good grip of him, "and now you'll come aft."

"I'll come aft when I please," Obbie said, sitting down.

He was roused up by a kick and a blow and dragged aft. At the main hatch he showed fight, and rose up tamed, with a black eye. He was dragged to the break of the poop, where Captain Cobb sat up in bed waiting for him.

"You dirt," the Battler said. "Don't think you can play hell with me and get away with it. I'll make you a sicker man than I am. Chain him up, there."

They had chains and padlocks at a ringbolt on the deck there. They handcuffed Obbie and then chained his ankles to the ringbolt; they took his knife away and left him there. Presently, as it was sunset, they cleaned up the decks, all that they could, and then knocked off work for the night. Neither Obbie nor Purple had any supper. Purple was released from irons and allowed to sleep forward: Obbie had to spend the night where he was, with Purple for his steward. Obbie did not get much sleep. After work was over he had to listen to some bitter reproaches from Bill Guller, who had been knocked out by the cringle on the brow; from Evesbatch, who was going to give him change presently for the thick ear; from Tom Coggins, whose pants cried for blood-money, five shillings and five plugs of tobacco, which seemed to Obbie excessive; and from all hands, who had had to pump for an hour because he had played the silly goat.

The mutiny had been in many ways a godsend to the ship. It had come as a variety, after two dreadful days, but it had broken the day's work. Very little had been accomplished on deck. Hardly any standing rigging had been cut: the main mess of the wreck was still untouched. To Dick, thinking of the work done, the results seemed beneath contempt. He thought:

"This is all that we have done, while we are fresh and

the tools remain with us, and with the working conditions perfect. We haven't started on the shrouds yet, really, and when we've cleared those, we've got the masts to clear. How in God's name are we to clear them?"

He was dispirited by the day's events. The Old Man had talked of being under sail in a week. Why, even if the fine weather held, it might take them a week to clear the ruin away. What if the fine weather did not hold? What if the crowd wearied of the jobs on deck, and insisted on abandoning ship upon a raft? They had been against Obbie, but supposing they had been on Obbie's side? There would have been a rough house, if they had been, and how would it have ended? One other thing dispirited him. The excitement of the mutiny had been too much for Captain Cobb. When they carried him below for the night he was a very tired, sick man, from whom all the energy had gone.

Alfrick at supper talked of a marvellous tool called Dendy's Patent Bolt-cutter, warranted to cut through any bolt or bar by pressure of the hand alone. Aloysius said that there was another thing, he could not remember its name, which brought revolving blades down upon a bolt or wire-rope, much as the knives come down on the hay in a chaff-cutter. Bill Guller, who looked very sick, with a pigeon's egg bump on his brow, said that in the War the troops had had secateurs on their rifles, which would cut through any wire; and that each man in the Army had had one, "more than four million all told." They thought of these things and talked of them as Lucifer and his mates, cast out, may have talked of Paradise, where the will to beauty made beauty. Ah, with Dendy's Bolt-cutters and the Army's cast-off secateurs, now under the mud near the Somme, and Rue's revolving blades coming snip in succession, how happy they would be.

Early the next morning, Dick woke with a happy thought. Since they could not cut through the wire shrouds, why should they not draw the splices? It seemed to him that the problem of the rigging was now solved. Nothing would be easier than to turn all hands to the drawing of the splices. There were dozens of marline-spikes: they would have the splices ripped out in no time. He was so filled with cheer at the thought that he went forward, before turn-to-time, to rout out the marlers and lay them ready under the pin-rails. He found the Captain not so well; not wanting food, and complaining of pain and being unable to sleep.

"But I'll be better on deck," he said, "where I can drill a hole through that dirt, if he gets uppish again."

They carried him up to his post on the weather-poop. Dick told all hands that he wanted the splices drawn; so they turned-to at it. Alfrick and Aylton had a few words with Obbie and Purple, who turned-to a little sulkily, but still, did work. They were mocked a bit by the crowd. Obbie had a black eye, and Purple plainly felt the disgrace of being broken.

The men found that drawing the splices was infinitely quicker and much easier work than the cutting of the shrouds had been. Even so, it was not in itself easy work. The splices had been well put in by master-riggers, who had known their job. Since then the splices had been slowly

squeezed and jammed by the straining of the strands onto
the tucks in the years of hard service of holding up the
masts. The tucked strands were now almost merged into
the lay. Then, in nearly every case, it was difficult to get
at the splice. Men had to work stooping or cramped down:
and they were not used to drawing splices: most of them
had never done it before. Still, there they were, pitted
watch against watch, heaving round hard, sometimes with
two men holding a shroud while two unpicked the splice,
sometimes working alone, but all markedly more cheer-
ful than they had been the night before.

Unfortunately, as the day wore by, the pace of the work
slackened. They did well all through the forenoon, but
by that time every finger in every hand on board was sore.
The jagged ends of wire scratched and pricked them on
what was already pricked and scratched. Often, too, as
they stooped and hove upon the wire, they pricked themselves with the marlers. Their finger-ends were not
toughened and hardened like the palms of their hands.
Presently, every man on board had fingers so sore that he
shrank from working with them. Every wire in every
strand had been sharpened at the end, by the act of cutting,
into something, like a jagged little chisel. These were the
things that now cut and scratched them. In addition to
these, there were many broken wires in every shroud. The
work became more painful every moment. Dick had no
remedy for the scratches, except the slush, or melted fat,
in the slush-pot.

"Sails," he said at last, "all hands will be laid up with

sore fingers. You must turn-to and make us some mitts to work in."

There were many rags of sail that could be spared for this. Six of the best of the sail-makers knocked off from splice-drawing, took needles and palms and began to make mitts. These were little better than rough bags with an added bag to take the thumb. Crude though the bags were, they took a long time to cut out and make. Dick, Alfrick, Cantlow, Guller, Kempley and Berrow were the six best sail-makers on board. To these, as they went along, Dick added Purple and then Wallers, whose wrenched arm was mending. After they had made a bag apiece, they went on gaily, man-fashion, making duplicates, and realized, too late, that the thumb on the left hand calls for a bag on the left side.

The day wore by in growing disappointment to Dick. All hands had started the day full of confidence and were now disheartened and unable to do the job in hand. He knew very well from old experience that even a tiny scratch from the wire of rigging may fester and be painful for days. When they knocked off for the night he knew that little had been done, and that less would be done on the morrow, when the scratches which were now sore would be inflamed. He went below much out of spirits, to be distressed further by the sight of the Captain, who had been growing worse all day and was now coughing.

"I thought it was a bad sign," Alfrick said, "when he didn't give Loach hell this morning. I'd expected he'd let him have it. Still, I didn't like to discourage you about him. If he'd been himself he'd have ridden Obbie down like a fore-tack. But, poor old man, he's as you see. That'll be the rib-end, working into his lung, that makes him cough."

"If that's so," Dick thought, "it will be hitting Loach that swipe with the trumpet that has started the bone."

He was as terrified of loose ribs working about inside him as Adam would have been, had Adam known the future; still there was nothing to do but stick it. He looked after the Old Man as tenderly as he could, and told him that the work was going forward well. Towards the end of his talk he was sure that the Old Man was either not paying much attention, or wandering in his wits. He left him, told Kit Pillows to sleep in the Old Man's cabin, with one eye open; and then himself turned-in, to pass a bad night of anxiety, sore fingers, worry and dread. The figure of Death was hovering near. What if the Old Man were to die? It would be weeks before they could reach any port. Would the Old Man last for weeks?

Two or three times in the night he turned out into the alleyway, to listen to the dry hack of the Captain's cough, and to creep to his door to see if there were anything that he could do. He blamed the Captain for much, and hated him for many things, but now in this crisis, with the ship all smashed, he knew that he longed for him on deck, in charge. After all, he was the ship's father; and all on board were as helpless children. Supposing the Old Man were to die: supposing he himself were to be knocked out before the ship were re-rigged? Who, of all these grown-up children, would be able to bring the ship to port? At the moment, with the Old Man ill, he was the man responsible:

they all depended on him. If he were to go, they would have no one competent to navigate.

At about two in the morning, knowing that Bill Guller was on anchor-watch, he went on deck and found him asleep there. He roused him up and made him walk the deck awhile.

"Bill," he said, "if I were to get knocked out, how would you navigate her to port?"

"Why," Bill said, "I know that if I sail west, I shall come to Africa. That's good enough for me. Long before I reach the coast, I shall speak some ship or other, and probably they'll have wireless and I'll get them to wireless for a tug."

"That's a bright idea," Dick said.

"I suppose there's no doubt that Africa's west from this?"

"None; she's there all right."

"That's all right then," Bill said. "It's simply a matter of keeping a good look-out."

The night passed over slowly, with worry and dread. He kept thinking of the Captain's good points, and wondering how he could hurry on the clearing and re-rigging, so as to bring him to port, in time to save his life. He thought that it might be done, but, then, when he considered all those sore, festering fingers, and the steel masts and yards not yet touched, but waiting to be cut by leaden cold chisels and the cook's chopper, his heart sank. He now thought that it might well be a fortnight before the ship was on her course. After that she would be at least three weeks upon her voyage: five weeks in all. Long

before then the bone would be through the lung into the
heart, or wherever it was bone got to. Death would come
on board and take the Battler away West, where he would
not see the well-stowed grain discharged.

Presently, Kit Pillows brought him his coffee; he turned-
to upon another day.

As he went on deck, Suckley came past him trundling
aft a wash-deck tub, in order that he might swab the poop.

"Old Purple's coming aft to speak to you, Mr. Pomfret,"
Suckley said. "It's a try-on, but I thought I'd warn you."

"Thank you, Suckley," Dick said. "I'm obliged to you."
To himself he thought, "Now here is mutiny to add to my
other troubles. That old devil knows that the Old Man is
out of action, so now he's going to spring a surprise on
me."

He still had a moment; he slipped below, got the Captain's revolver from Pillows (there were still three car-
tridges in it), passed the word to the after-guard, including
Alfrick, and went to the break of the poop, where the
broken rail had been replaced by life-lines. Purple was
coming aft followed by all hands. The after-guard stood
handy, at the foot of the ladder. Alfrick stood beside Dick,
above them.

Purple took post, not far from the foot of the ladder. It
was still not fully day, but light enough. Following the
custom of the sea Dick paid no heed for a while, then
sharply asked:

"What's the matter with you?"

"We've come to speak to Captain Cobb, Mr. Pomfret,"
old Purple began.

"You can't speak with him. Speak to me."

"Perhaps you would take a message from us, Mr. Pomfret."

"I'm not your messenger," Dick said.

He turned aft with Alfrick, and walked twice along the poop with him, while the men waited. Then, he faced them again and said:

"Either speak to me or go forward and turn-to."

"It's like this, Mr. Pomfret," old Purple began. "All hands have toiled themselves sick and sore trying to clear this rigging. We know we can't clear the decks; you've not got the gear. We say we're not going to toil on, like wage-slaves, when for half the toil and in half the time we could build a raft and abandon ship and come safe to port."

"Who's going to build your raft?" Dick asked.

"We can do that, Mr. Pomfret."

"And who is to navigate her?"

"We suppose you, Mr. Pomfret, if Captain Cobb is too ill. But we know there's land in every direction but south of us. We've only to keep on to come to it."

"I didn't think an old man like you would speak so like a fool," Dick said; "at any rate, not in public.

"Hear you, men, once for all. We're in charge of this ship to bring her from port to port, and we're going to do it. We can clear her, re-rig her, and salve her; and we'll do it or bust. What are you growling at? You've been through the worst weather ever made, and you're all alive and the ship's sound as a bell. You growl because you've all night in and sore fingers. You talk about a raft.

It will take you a fortnight to build and rig a raft big enough to take twenty men and their stores. How do you propose to launch a raft that size? I'd like to know. And if you launched a raft she wouldn't sail ten miles a day. It would take you five months to reach anywhere; even if you could reach anywhere, but you wouldn't; you'd all be dead first; long before.

"But there isn't going to be any raft. Take that from us, right now. We're here to work the ship and we're going to do it; and you're going to do it. I know your fingers are sore; so are mine; but don't let sore fingers make you think of any such tomfoolery as a raft. As for you, Purple, I thought it was your heart that was sore, not your fingers."

There was a general laugh at this.

"My fingers are sore, too, Mr. Pomfret," Purple said.

"Let's have a look at them," Dick said. Purple spread his fingers for all to see. "I see what's happened," Dick said. "You're like the landsman who went to sea for the first time, and heard them call 'All hands on deck,' so he put his hands on deck and somebody trod on them."

There was a cheer of laughter at this.

"Get forward and turn-to," Dick said.

To his intense relief, they broke up, cheering, laughing and dancing about old Purple, booing him.

"Ah, Mr. Pomfret," Alfrick said, "you got all hands then, sir. You'll have no more trouble from those fellows. Not a threat in all your speech; just good, sound sense; and then a laugh at the end. That old fool of a Purple will eat out of your hand, you'll see."

Dick felt no triumph, but deep relief that the "laying aft" had come to an end without mutiny. His heart was heavy enough, as he splashed the water for his watch in the washing-down of decks. He had no doubt now that the Battler would die, without regaining consciousness. More than ever he longed for him to live.

"An ass, of course," he thought, "or rather, a pig-headed, obstinate, abusive mule; but a first-rate practical bear-a-hand seaman when he hasn't gone over the Bay. This is just the situation he'd have been good at."

After washing-down, they put on mitts and again tackled the clearing of the rigging, by drawing the splices of the shroud-eyes: they had learned a few dodges now, but it was weary work.

At about Six Bells in the forenoon, Pencome, who had very good sight, reported a steamer to the eastward. She was little more than a smudge of smoke on the horizon. She was the first ship sighted by them for more than three weeks. Dick glanced at the smudge and went on with his work, judging that she must be coming his way, but that five minutes more would make that certain. He knew that his ship was so like a wreck that any steamer sighting her would close her.

He thought, "In a few minutes I'll hoist a signal of distress and make a smoke-smudge to make sure; but a half-blind man would see that we are dismasted."

The men in the steamship were not half-blind. High up in her bridge they had seen the *Hurrying Angel* long before Pencome had seen their smoke. They now had glasses bent upon her. A minute or two later, at a word from her Captain, her helmsman altered course a little, just as Dick ran up a weft (or Red Ensign knotted in the middle) to the spreaders of the mizen cross-trees. At another word from her Captain, the helmsman altered course again, so as to close her. Dick, fetching his telescope, watched her carefully.

There was soon no doubt of what she was. She was one of the big ships, of nearly 30,000 tons, then running Winter Cruises in the Southern Hemisphere, and now bound to the African coast, on her way home by way of some of the Brazilian and West Indian ports. Alfrick, who had come to Dick's side, named her as either the *Pororoca* or the *Parramatta*. He had seen both at odd times; they were sister ships, he said, both built on the Clyde.

She came up very fast, with a big bone in her mouth. Soon Dick could see that she was crammed with passengers who were flocking up to see what looked so like a wreck. Little bright flashes showed where binoculars were being focused.

"This'll be the time of their lives, Mister," Alfrick said. "They'll talk of this till they die, how they came down on the wreck and 'took away the poor seamen.'"

"There go her signals," Dick said, as four coloured flags flapped clear from her signal yard. He could neither read them, nor answer, as the big sea, which had taken the charthouse had taken with it the signal-book. He had improvised semaphore flags out of battens and old bunk-curtains. With these Bill Guller was able to make it clear that they wanted a doctor, and other matters. The ship drew nearer, so that Dick could read the name *P O R O R O C A* on her bow; she stopped her engines and lay by.

She stayed there, bowing easily into the swell, while all the hundreds of her pleasure-seekers flocked to her rail to stare. They did not understand what had happened to this little, shabby, battered ship, so salt-caked and rusty. They did not know the kind of ship, nor that sort of experience. They felt, somehow, that at last they were looking at the sea, about which they had so often read. Questions floated from all those hundreds of mouths: answers to some of them filtered down from the bridge or along from some of the seamen; and this main answer, that she needed a doctor.

A motor-launch on the liner's port side suddenly filled up with her crew; the falls joggled her down; an officer, the doctor and the nurse scrambled into her, and away she sped, watched by the hundreds of eyes. Dick in the meantime had rigged over the side ladder and got a good tackle onto the crossjack yard.

The men in the *Hurrying Angel* watched the steamer with interest. Indeed, the noble ship, with her sheer and height, was an image of power and beauty. Even so, they did not knock-off their work to watch: they lifted their eyes to her and talked as they drew the splices.

"You can't beat the Clyde Yards."

"No, she's a fine ship. Say what you like about these big ships, they'll move by their own strength, while this sort would be helpless."

"Them little trotties don't seem to have much on."

"Them stewards bring them soup every hour; that or ice-cream soda."

"I'd a brother in one of them things. He said, 'They dance until pretty near midnight: then they go to the bar and have cocktails.'"

"I would, too, if I'd their luck."

"She's got all those decks to keep clean, and all that brass and glass to brighten. All those decks have to be gone over two or three times a day. The stewards sometimes don't finish serving dinner till half-past nine or ten; then there's the washing-up. Then up next morning to do out the saloon and lay the breakfast; and berthed down in the glory-hole all the time, down on F Deck or G Deck in the tropics or in the Red Sea: I'd rather be where I am."

"Some of them little trotties look good in the leg."

"Yes, they got good legs all right, and like to show them."

"It's all those ships are, if you ask me; Leg Parades."

But by this time the launch was alongside, hooked-on, and the officer was hopping up the ladder. Dick knew him at once; he was "Tom Sock," Captain of the Fo'c's'le in his first term on the *Conway*.

"Hallo, Sock," he said, "you won't remember Pomfret. I was only a new chum."

"Hallo, anybody who knows my name," Sock said. "What has happened to you?"

"We got dismasted. Our Old Man's ill."

"Anything infectious?"

"No; it's broken bones; they're not doing well."

"What's his temperature?" the doctor asked.

"I don't know," Dick said. "Our thermometers are gone. He's very ill, I'm afraid. Perhaps you'll come this way."

He led down the alleyway to the sick-room. Dick, who was used to the scene, thought nothing of it, but the wrecked saloon impressed the doctor and nurse. The hole where the skylight had been, the broken panels, the stumps of the chairs, and all the other scars of battle were evidences of a power which they had not yet seen. Dick led the way into the cabin.

The Captain's cabin was not unlike a sick-room. It smelt of disinfectant, and had an air of cruel cleanness. The port was open, yet screened from the sun. Chips had made a sick-bed-table, with compartments for the two necessaries, the mug of lime juice and water, and the hand-bell (made from half a bully-beef tin, with a cringle for clapper). "In the midst, the sick man on his bed" was away from all these things, muttering and coughing a little. The doctor and nurse ceased to have any eyes for the scene: there in that prone, unconscious figure was their enemy.

"Let's have a look now," the doctor said.

He had a look, a prolonged and very thorough look, then talked for a moment with the Sister, then turned to Dick.

"Your Captain ought to have proper medical treatment," he said. "We can deal with him in the hospital on board, and have him in hospital ashore within five days."

"The trouble is that he's my Captain," Dick said, "and I know that he would rather die ten thousand deaths than leave the ship."

"You're *his* Captain," the doctor said, "when he's in this

state. Even if he lives, he won't be your Captain again before you reach port. You know what that cough means, don't you?"

"No, I don't," Dick said. "But you'll understand that it's a strong step for me to send my Captain out of the ship. Will you give me a chit, to justify me?"

"Certainly," the doctor said, writing and signing one on a leaf of his prescription-book. "You'd better make an entry in your log-book and let me sign that, too."

When Dick had entered in the Remarks Column of Mr. Duckswich's Log-Book that he was sending the Captain away in the *Pororoca,* on the advice of the doctor that without proper treatment he would die, he asked the doctor to sign it.

"I know you sailors," the doctor said, as he signed. "In another two days you'll not ask doctors to sign an entry in the log. Far from it. You'll be making entries like, '8 A.M. Sacked Admiral for incompetence and towed him ashore on a grating. Fine, cool day. Some cirrus.'"

"I'm not quite used to command, it is true," Dick said. "I'll get some hands along and have the Old Man's things packed."

"However did you get your fingers into that state?" the Sister asked.

"Ends of wire," Dick said. "If you could spare some ointments, it would be kind."

Most of the Captain's personal belongings had gone over the side with the chart-house. Pillows, who was acting Steward, found a black tail-coat, some check trousers and a pair of go-ashore boots in a locker in the slop-room. He packed these in a bag which he found, with some pyjamas, shirts and small wares from the slop-chest. Rummaging about, he found an old hard hat or "felt topper" and an umbrella. He brought these down with the bag to the launch, so that the Old Man should not be without a kit. Dick knew the Old Man's London address. He could find no money anywhere. The money, whether the ship's or the Captain's, had gone over the side with the big sea.

Having seen the things packed, Dick called some hands aft to carry them down and to bring the Battler out. Only a few hours before the Battler would have brained anybody who tried to send him out of the ship; now, poor man, he knew nothing about it; he was weak, muttering and coughing. Dick helped to carry him out, and stood beside him, screening him from the sun, and talking to Tom Sock, while the cot was being slung, and the yard tackle overhauled.

"The sea's made a pretty general average of you," Tom Sock said, "but I've got the general hang of what you need; and if you'll add a word to our Old Man I don't doubt we'll be able to fit you. I've had your bunting-tosser giving him a general idea so as not to delay us. You see, we carry mails. You'll find a whole shop of stores waiting for you, when you get aboard."

But now the yard tackle was manned; the poor old Battler was hoisted over the side and tended gently down into the launch.

Dick spoke a word aside to Alfrick and to Tom Sock. "The thing I'm afraid of," he said, "is that when they see the Captain going all hands will want to abandon ship, too. I won't abandon ship, and I won't let them. I hope you'll back me up in that."

"We'll back you all right," they said.

Dick went down into the launch, which shoved off. The crew of the *Hurrying Angel* did not like to cheer. They were all moved at the thought of the Old Man's going. After all, he had been a Battler, who had kept a smart ship and made them toe the line. Now a sheer hulk lay poor Bob Battler, going over the side in a sling like a cask of dry goods, who could tell to what; to a hospital bed and a workhouse ward very likely, with a parish grave at the end; a poor finish to one who had fought in Q ships and sailed crack ships round the world. Dick also thought of these things, as he sat by the unconscious man, screening him from the sun with a big, floppy African straw hat.

The vast bulk of the *Pororoca* loomed and towered bigger and bigger as they drew nearer. Dick, glancing up at her, saw her as a sort of cliff of a ship, with heads craned over every rail. Near half the heads something bright was being pointed, as glasses and cameras were focused. Dick hoped that he might be spared the ordeal of going through all those multitudes.

The big side doors on one of the lower decks were open, and the gangway lowered below it. As he went up the ladder to the Captain who was waiting there, he heard two remarks: "Don't look, my dear; he may be frightfully hurt," and, "I suppose that boy is the sick man's son." Seamen already had the Battler's stretcher in hand. They had it up the ladder and then at once away past Dick to the hospital, with stewards clearing a passage before them, saying, "Make way there, please."

Dick found himself shaking hands with the Captain of the liner, a tall, grave, one-armed man, with a beautiful face, made somewhat set and rigid by a wound in the jaw. Dick knew the man at once; during the War, for a time, the face had been famous. This was Captain Fletcher-Beaumont, V.C., of the Q ships.

"Well, sir, what can I do for you?" the Captain asked. "Come on up to my cabin, where we can talk."

As the *Pororoca* carried mails, Dick made his story as short as possible. He wanted Captain Cobb cared for and taken to hospital; he wanted cutters and wrenches, some stuff for sore fingers, any food that could be spared, because he was not sure when he would reach port, and a wireless message sent to his owners in London.

A wireless officer took his message:—

"Ship *Hurrying Angel* lost fore and mainmasts in cyclone. Mate Duckswich, Second Mate MacLerrinnan, Steward Mince, Seamen Torrent and Morritz and boy Newbarn drowned. Captain badly hurt, transhipped to *Pororoca*. Rigging jury-masts. Making for Port Francis. Send new spars to meet us. Will re-rig there. Ship's structure sound. All well. Pomfret."

"It would be awfully kind, sir, if you would send that," Dick said, "but we can't pay for it. We haven't any money. The sea's got all we had."

"I daresay we can manage to send this. I'll add the position," the Captain said. "May I ask if you know your position?"

"Oh yes, sir; thank you."

The message was sent off.

"May I ask what certificates you hold?"

"Only the *Conway* one, sir."

"You feel able for Port Francis?"

"Oh yes, sir; thanks."

"I rather gather that the people are sending you some contributions," the Captain said, "but perhaps you'd better see the Tiffies' things yourself, and see what will serve your turn. What you want is a safe-blower's outfit; acetylene drills and the rest of it. I doubt if there's anything made that will help you to cut through those two lower masts of yours."

As Dick went with the Captain to the Engineers, he passed several casks prominently displayed as Collection-Boxes for the Crew of the Wreck. "Meaning you," the Captain explained.

"Wreck," Dick said. "We're not a wreck. We're a fine clipper ship in the rigger's hands."

"When do you expect to get sail on her?" the Captain asked.

"I hope in a week," Dick said.

"Good," the Captain said. "It will be fine to feel her under way again."

He said afterwards that he had tried not to discourage a zealous officer, but had thought that the week would be a long one.

"Now, sir," he said to Dick, "while the Engineers complete their gifts to you, do you write a brief account of your dismasting, which I will post, by air mail, to your owners.

I'll get busy on the air, meanwhile, to find out your owners' agents in South Africa, so that they will see to your Captain on his arrival there."

"Sir, I don't know how to thank you."

When the letter had been written, Dick asked to have a last look at his Captain.

There he was in the white and shiny hospital, newly washed, newly bandaged, ready for inspection, still unconscious of what was happening, and with a dreadful moment soon to come when he would wake up, to find himself out of his ship in the command of a capable young woman who would stand no nonsense from any man. It smote Dick's heart to leave him there.

"Poor old Battler," he thought. "His next war will be with an Amazon."

To the Amazon it was quite clear that the Battler was not a sea-captain, nor a potential mate, nor a vicarious child for mothering, nor a male for possible desire, but something quite inhuman, though long longed for, "a fracture case, with complications." A competent, happy gleam was in the Amazon's eye; poor old Battler was for it.

Dick was about to hurry down to the boat, where various casks had now been stored for him, when two young men who had been waiting for him near the gangway asked if they might speak to him for a moment. They were first-class cabin passengers, aged about twenty-one or twenty-two; one rather tall, the other of middle height, both broad, well-fed, and dressed alike in cricketing flannels; both had the modest good manners of the University. They explained that they wanted to join the *Hurrying Angel* as

amateur seamen, that they had no experience of that kind
of thing, but felt that they would soon pick it up. Their
names were Gwin Breinton and Thomas Tugg Mordiford.

"I'm afraid you don't know what you may be letting
yourselves in for," Dick said. "May I see the palms of your
hands?"

They showed their palms, unmarked by any work, not
even hardened by the deck-quoit-grummets.

"I've tried to tell them what they'll let themselves in
for," Tom Sock said. "What I can't explain they'll soon
learn."

"That's true," Dick said. "But I can't bind the company
to pay you wages."

"We don't want wages," they said, "only the experience."

"I don't know what the unions will say about that,"
Dick said. "I could only take you at a shilling a month
each, on the understanding that you will be treated exactly
as other members of the crew, and discharged at the first
port."

"That is all that we ask," they said.

"It won't be any picnic," Dick said.

They replied that they were seeing the world a little,
before settling down to a profession, and that this was the
thing they had longed for.

"You'll find it rough and ready," Dick said. "We shall
make you stamp and go."

"We long to stamp and go."

Dick thought that they would be another set of hands
on the jobs to be done, and two fresh points of view in the

fo'c's'le. These were things well worth having; he knew that two new men would be welcome.

"Come along, then," Dick said. "I'll sign you on when we get on board. You may be separated, remember; you may be in different watches when we get sail on her."

"We shan't mind that," they said. "We've got our things all ready."

"Shove ahead, then," Dick said.

They thanked him. One of them asked:

"Will you please tell us how we ought to address you?"

"Mister Pomfret, sir, and touch your hat," Dick said.

"Very good, Mister Pomfret, sir," they said.

When they had been signed on, and the casks had been hoisted inboard, Dick watched the launch speed back to the liner, hook on and run lightly up the side. As her crew secured her or scrambled inboard, the water whitened suddenly at the steamer's stern; she trembled a little and lurched forward; they heard her bell; they saw a white leaf at her bow broaden and roll out and shatter. She drew ahead of them while all those hundreds of passengers seemed to shoot out and shatter; they were cheering, waving hats and handkerchiefs, morsing with arms, semaphoring with legs. The siren blew and blew again to them and the great ship's colours dipped, to which Dick and Kit Pillows replied by dipping theirs. In a moment, the liner was on her course, driving full speed ahead. She was soon hull down and out of sight.

She had left behind her in Dick's heart a deep cheer and comfort. She had been a change: she had taken the Captain; she had given new strength after taking the old weakness; and now there were all the gifts to see to.

The liner had been generous to them. The tools were such as they had dreamed of for days. There were ointments and finger-stalls for the sore fingers. There were joints of beef and mutton and some excellent potatoes. There was a cask half full of tins of preserved meats, jams and pickles, and then topped up with oranges and apples. There were two other casks containing a tarpaulin muster of gear from the passengers. This was an odd mixture of matters. There were eighty-nine books, mostly stories about murders and their detection, with some few reminiscences of big-game shooting, some guides to bridge, "A Rush Through India," "Italy Skimmed," "On a 'Plane to Greenland," and a First Handbook in Palladian Architecture. There were many articles of clothing, coats, trousers, some caps, shirts, socks; some ladies' underwear; two pairs of corsets; half a dozen towels and mats belonging to the liner, all these last put there by some would-be wit. There were also some shoes, some tins and boxes of sweetmeats, chocolates and cigarettes. There were many cakes and cartons of scented soap, several bottles of scent, some safety-razors of different makes, a lady's handbag containing mirrors, rouge, and a manicure set (somebody in malice to the owner had picked it from a chair and dropped it into the collection), thirty magazines, mostly containing short stories, some private bottles of intoxicants, all partly drunken, a suit of beach pyjamas, one bath-robe, a pair of dumb-bells, one lady's glove, four packs of cards, three garters and a pair of sock-suspenders, a solitaire-board, two skeins of wool, a bridge-marker, a pair of gilded high-heeled slippers, three combs, one hair-brush and one bottle of hair-oil.

Dick and Alfrick sorted out these things and divided them with the fairness of the sea, as the fo'c's'le will divide meat. The assortment of things puzzled Alfrick.

"Odd people, passengers, if you can call them people," he said; "and they've sent an odd lot of junk. But there's one thing they've sent, which I'll ask to keep; I've been wanting one a long time, and that's a new shaving-brush."

Unfortunately, what had looked like a shaving-brush turned out to be a powder-puff from the lady's handbag. Alfrick tried it when he went below, and brought it to ruin.

"The damned thing is no more good than a sick head-ache," he said, and consigned it to the deep.

From the "Port Francis News and East African
Intelligencer." Saturday, 22nd April, 1922

"Readers of our issue of March 4th will remember the sensation caused by the report from the s.s. *Pororoca* of her meeting with the dismasted sailing ship, *Hurrying Angel*, at sea, towards the end of February. Yesterday afternoon, Friday, the 21st of April, a furore was caused on the water front by the arrival of the *Hurrying Angel* at Port Francis. She was escorted into the harbour by the tug, *Voorlieper*, and moored off Smidt's warehouses, where she has attracted much attention. It will be remembered that in the cyclone which dismasted his ship her Captain received injuries which necessitated his removal in the *Pororoca* to Cape Town, where he has sufficiently recovered to be able to return to England. By a strange coincidence he learned of his ship's safe arrival just before he went on board the mail ship which will convey him home. The *Hurrying Angel* narrowly escaped destruction. All her survivors are agreed that it was the worst weather they had ever experienced. A striking feature of her voyage is that the clearing of the wreck and the rigging of her jury-masts was undertaken by her senior apprentice, Mr. Richard Pomfret, on whom the command devolved when the Captain was incapacitated. Some idea of the magnitude of his task may be gathered from the fact that it was three weeks from the ending of the storm before the deck was cleared of wreck, the jury-masts in place and sail set. Since then, the *Hurrying Angel* has had an uneventful and rather slow passage with light and baffling winds of exactly five weeks. As her new masts have arrived from England, she will proceed alongside the Riggers' Wharf this afternoon, so that the work of remasting may begin on Monday. It is hoped that she may proceed upon her voyage early in May.

"Mr. Richard Pomfret, to whose seamanship the ship's arrival is due, is a young man in his eighteenth year, now in his third year at sea. Several members of his crew have expressed the liveliest admiration of him as a commander. Overleaf will be found photographs of Mr. Pomfret and his ship."

A letter from Dick Pomfret to his friend, Frank Tereu.

"Port Francis, April, 1922.

"My dear Poss,

"This will catch the mail to-night and should reach Calcutta before you sail.

"We have had a most interesting voyage so far, but a very sad one. We lost bowsprit, foremast, mainmast, and mizen topgallant-mast in a cyclone, with both Mates, two men, the Steward, and poor Ed Newbarn, whom you'll remember. A big sea took them all. The same sea laid out the Old Man, with three broken bones.

"The mainmast fell forward, port side; the foremast aft to starboard. You never saw such a mess. It made one sick to look at. One did not know where to begin to clear, nor how. We'd no tools to speak of. We tried cutting the rigging next day and found that it would take us about a year. Then (the next day), we tried drawing the splices (my idea). It wasn't so bad. We got on famously at first, but by evening our fingers were so sore we could hardly bear to use them. I got Sails to make a sort of hedger's gloves out of canvas.

"On top of this, the Old Man became light-headed, and began to have a cough. I was in despair and didn't know what to do.

"Well, just in the blackest, the *Pororoca,* pleasure ship, bore down, with all her thousands staring at us. She awayed her launches and there we were, Saved.

"I can't tell you what fun it was. The *Pororoca's* Capt.

is Fletcher-Beaumont, the V.C., a simply topping chap.
He was most awfully decent, sent off wireless for us, gave
us all sorts of medical comforts, took off the Old Man, and
got his Tiffies to give us some simply heavenly bolt-cutters
and shears and things. It was huge fun going on board
a ship like that. You may not remember Tom Sock
(C.S.F.); he was fourth on board, and in charge of the
launch they sent to us (all our boats went in the gale).
He told me that Fletcher-Beaumont is simply adored by
all hands. I would simply love to be under an Old Man
like that. He was easily the finest chap I've ever seen.
Well, he gave us all these things and then filled his main
yard, but he had made all the difference to us.

"I'd been scared lest all hands should insist on abandoning ship in the *Pororoca,* for we'd had the sort of rudi-
ments of a mutiny in the two days before. I was prepared
to play the part of a bucko to stop them going, but didn't
have to; they never even hinted that they wanted to.

"That was our first good fortune. We were able to heave
round on the rigging with what the *Pororoca* gave us, but
I still didn't see how we were to shift the lower masts and
yards; and Fletcher-Beaumont had as good as said we
couldn't, without an acetylene drill. When we got the rigging cleared, and faced all those broken steel tubes, it looked
pretty hopeless. As old B—— used to say, 'We were in a
clove-hitch. One foot in the grave and the other on a bar
of yellow soap.'

"You remember Kit Pillows? He brought our next good
fortune. You wouldn't think it, would you? It seems that

Destiny doesn't always choose the kind of agent we should choose.

"I'd made Kit Pillows make an inventory of all the stores in the lazareet, for I did not know how long we were going to be delayed, and I wanted to know what we could count on.

"As you know, our ship used to carry passengers in the Australian trade, in the boom years: lots of ships of her stamp did. She hadn't carried any, oh, for ten or fifteen years, of course.

"When she had carried passengers all her 'tween-decks was fitted with cabins, and all sorts of rain-water tanks and other gear. She had had a Carpenter and two Carpenter's mates who had done nothing but all this extra work of fitting cabins and tanks and things. As a matter of fact our Chips had been in her then, and often talked of how the carpenters had to heave round. She had carried a great kit of tools for these fellows; they were the ship's gear, not theirs. Our great good fortune was that Kit found them all laid up in the lazareet out of the damp, not suspected by anybody. Among them were some very fine braces and drills, with any number of twists, bits, wedges, cold chisels and cutters. They were all in apple-pie order, laid away in oil, in a kind of woolleny serge, and tin boxes over all. When I showed them to Chips, his eyes gleamed. 'Ah,' he said, 'them's the real sort; pre-war. You can't get tools like that in England now.'

"I asked Chips if they would make any difference to the job of clearing away the steel spars. He said, 'Why, yes, now we can do it; but it'll be a slow job.'

"It was all that.

"First, we drilled holes in the fallen masts, so as to make a kind of girdle of holes all round, or nearly all round, within two chalk-marks. Then, with cold chisels and wedges we beat and banged and cut and wrenched the holes into each other, and pried them apart with crows.

"All the last part (the underneath part) took twice as long as the rest. We had to cut and cut to get at it at all; and the stuff is just as tough as tough can be.

"Still, in time, it worked; we did cut off a great roll of the foot of the foremast. There it was; cut off. They must have heard our cheers at the South Pole.

"We built up an inclined plane of scantlings from the deck to the rail, rigged up some tackles, took them to the capstans and parbuckled the relic, up the inclined plane to the rail and over the side, ker-plonk, amid loud cheers. We had to watch the roll, of course. Every bit of mast that we buried thus was a deadly enemy. We buried the lot in time. The yards were less of a nuisance: they were nothing, after the masts.

"I thought at first that we would be under sail in about a week from the dismasting. Well, you'd have thought so, too. As a matter of fact, it took us over two weeks to clear the decks, working all hands on deck from daylight to dark. When we had the decks cleared we could start to re-rig.

"We were very lucky, for we had a man called Alfrick in charge of the other watch, who was a first-class seaman, with some knowledge of rigging sheers. He had been a rigger for a time in one of these Newfoundland places where they built and rigged soft-wood schooners. He said that sometimes there they wouldn't have a crane and had to use sheers. The mainmast had left a stump, which was a great help. We got up a spare topmast as a mainmast and bowsed it well into the stump. The heel set into a shoe on deck and we got four tackles, two to a side, and bowsed the foot of the mast absolutely plunk. We crossed a spare upper topsail yard for a mainyard, and bent an upper topsail for sail.

"The foremast was much more of a problem as it had gone at the deck, in between the fo'c's'le and the donkey-house, an awkward place to get at. When we got our sheers forward we had the very devil of a time trying to get the heel of our new foremast (the other spare topmast), into the hole. The sheers had to come down, and be re-lashed, so as to give us more hoist; then, when we had done that they didn't seem to me too safe; so, when we were beginning to sway away, sure enough, they began to dodder; so we had to avast heaving, and we had to have them down again. We relashed them and reguyed them, and this time, with endless bother, and swayings away and 'vast heavings till we were just about sick, we got the foot into the hole, eased by about a stone of slush; and there we were with a foremast.

"We were very short of spars; so much had gone overboard. We had only just enough to rig the sheers and re-rig with.

"I had always been scared of sheers, but when I had to rig them and got the hang of them, I found them fascinating. You have enormous power and yet can do very delicate work with them.

"We were very lucky to have four absolutely first-rate seamen in the crowd. An old tough of an ex-Boatswain, a drunken old knave, turned out to be one of the best.

"We crossed a spare upper topsail yard for a foreyard, and rigged out some of a spare topgallant-mast for a jib-boom, and there we were.

"Two passengers (men) from the *Pororoca* volunteered as O.Ss. They were university men, and didn't know anything about it, but were good fellows and workers.

"In all, we were twenty-three hands. When we really got the decks clear and could buckle to, it only took us a week to step and secure the masts, cross the yards, reeve off the gear, and make sail. When we did make sail, with two jibs, two staysails, two courses and spanker, and felt her really moving again, we all danced for joy and spliced the main brace. I was never so happy in all my life.

"Of course, we were watching all the gear all the time, especially the heel-tackles on the mainmast, but we'd no trouble at all. After the first day I thought that we could risk a sort of topsail on the two jury-masts, but Alfrick said we'd better let well alone. I'm sorry now I didn't try it, but it's better to be sure than sorry, and if we had carried a mast away we should have been very sick men.

"We had light airs and a fair slant all the way. We just slipped along: a sort of one degree westing a day. Seventy-two miles was our best day's work.

"When we reached here we found the masts which had been wirelessed for by the *Pororoca;* they'd been cleaned and shipped and there they were waiting for us: quick work. We've been getting them in, under the crane. They were not new, of course, but the masts of the *Colding Falls*.

"We found that our Old Man had been saved, and shipped for England. He sailed just after we reached here and sent us a telegram, and we sent him one.

"We shall be sailing from here as soon as we get our topsail yards across. We shall ship a new Old Man and Mate, but I'm to be continued Second, they tell me: it is jolly decent of them, really.

"Well, cheerio; I do wish you'd been with us. If we could get together for a yarn before I sail again it would be A1; but I suppose no such luck.

"Yours ever,
"Pom."

A letter from Dick Pomfret to his sister.

"July 24th, 1922.

"My Dinkie,

"You'll see me tomor by the 4.45. We'd a good passage home: the new masts were all right. I did not write y'day as I'd rather a rush: the newspapers made a silly fuss, photographing everything. Then I had to go to Lloyd's and then on to see the owners.

"A word in your ear: Lloyd's gave me a cheque for fifty guineas.

"Fifty (50) guineas: (£52 10s.).

"Golly, my Dinkie, we are going absolutely halves in this (£26 5s. each, or do I dream? Is visions about?). I expect you'll bank your half, but with mine we'll have a simply topping hol.

"They said they'd much admired my work in re-rigging the ship and bringing her to port. Then the Board of Trade officials came along and said they had much pleasure in presenting me with my Mate's Certificate, all made out and everything.

"My Mate's Certificate (about eighteen months at sea time given to me as a present . . . You could have knocked me down with a feather. I didn't know what to say or do).

"Then on to the owners. One of them, old Sir Theopompous Harker, is a director of the Southern Cruises. He said that he'd been talking to Fletcher-Beaumont about me. It seems that F.-B. said he would like to see more of me, and I'm to go fourth in the new Southern Cruiser, the *Parakakau,* under F.-B. if I like.

If I like,
IF I LIKE,

joining her in dock about mid-August and sailing the 1st of Septr., on one of their cruises, Panama, Sydney, N.Z., the Australian and African ports, and home by S. America and W. Indies.

"However, all I can think of now is coming home and spending my £26 5s. with you. We'll have such a hol. as never was. It will be nearly three weeks.

"I would come to-night, only the owners are giving the ship's company a Dinner, at which *I've got to make a speech!!* Brethren, pray for me (and for the audience).

"I hope to see you and the two dogs at 4.45 tomor. I'll

tell you all the rest of the news, then, and hear all yours.
Love to the Ps.

"Dog."

From the "Merchant Seamen's Shipmate," for Tuesday,
July 25th, 1922.

"A pleasant gathering was held last night at Bolter's
Hotel, City, when Sir Theopompous Harker, Chairman
and General Manager of Harker and Harker, the well-
known shipping firm, sometimes called the Blue Stripe
Line, entertained the crew of the *Hurrying Angel,* the full-
rigged ship whose adventurous voyage was described in a
recent issue of the *Shipmate.* The guest of honour was
Mr. Richard Pomfret, now famous throughout the English-
speaking world as the Boy-Captain. There were present
(beside Sir Theopompous and the other partners of the
firm, Sir Cantrip Siskin and Mr. Aston Tirrold Harker)
the Captain of the *Hurrying Angel,* Captain R. B. Cobb,
now, we are glad to say, fully recovered from his recent
injuries, together with Mrs. Cobb, Mr. R. Pomfret, Mr.
James Alfrick and all the members of the ship's company.
By a happy thought of the management, the visitors in-
cluded Mrs. Duckswich, mother of the ship's late Mate,
Mrs. Mince, the widow of the ship's late Steward, and Miss
Jeanie MacWhirter, the fiancée of the ship's late Second
Mate, unfortunately lost in the storm.

"After the loyal toasts had been honoured, Sir Theopompous addressed the company. He said that he had
been brought up in the old school of British Industry,

which was in some respects a hard school. In some respects
it was as difficult for a leopard to change his spots as for
their house-flag to change its stripes (loud cheers and cries
of 'Good old blue and white'.) Some had said hard words
about British Industry. But two great things could be said
about it:

"One. It had weathered the storm. (Cheers.)

"Two. It was not so hard-boiled but it could adapt itself
to meet new conditions. (Loud applause.)

"He flattered himself that this gathering, in this historic
hotel, in this historic City, was a sign that a new spirit had
come into at least the shipping branch of it. He hoped
that all there would join him in welcoming the spirit, and
seeing that the seed sown there in that gathering came to
a noble harvest in the future. (Tumultuous applause.)

"He would not dwell on the achievements of the gentle-
men before him, but was sure that whenever the British
Merchant Service was mentioned the deeds of the crew of
the *Hurrying Angel* would flash into memory and bring a
throb to the heart. (Cries of 'Spare our blushes.')

"Continuing, Sir Theopompous said that in the old bad
days, now, he hoped, gone for ever, it had been too often
the custom of firms to use seamen as chattels that could be
thrown aside, perhaps after a life of faithful service. He
was glad to be able to say that Harker and Harker had
determined to put into force a new system from which
everybody present would, he hoped, benefit in the future.

"They had determined to move with the times, and to
part with their sailing-ships (cries of 'Shame'); but would
continue in their employment, or in the affiliated venture

of the Southern Cruises, all those officers and men who
had served them in the past and wished to continue with
them. With the help of his son, Aston, he had worked out
a scheme by which every member of either staff or crew
who remained in their service for five years, would become
entitled to a bonus, while all long-service men, such as he
hoped all present might become, would qualify for a pen-
sion. (Cheers.)

"Though the *Hurrying Angel* would soon pass from
under the Red Ensign, he hoped that all present would
continue under the Blue and White Stripes of Harker and
Harker. Berths waited for them in their new ships, the
Piddington and the *Plimsoll,* now nearly ready to sail.
(Loud cheers.)

"Continuing, Sir Theopompous said that he was sure
that all present had read in the papers how the shipping
world had taken Mr. Pomfret to its heart; a hard heart,
some might say, but then it was a heart of oak. (Applause.) He wished Mr. Pomfret all success in the profession he had so startlingly begun upon.

"In the words of the poet most familiar to all of them:

> "*'First Rise after very low,*
> *Indicates a stronger blow.'*

They looked forward with lively anticipation and every
confidence to the 'stronger blow' by which Mr. Pomfret
would continue and consolidate his triumphant career.
He had the greatest pleasure in giving them the toast of
Mr. Pomfret.

"Mr. Pomfret, in reply, said that he thanked all there, and especially Sir Theopompous, for the kind way in which they had welcomed him that evening. They had been through some hard times together, but like British Industry they had weathered the storm, and he was sure that he was speaking for all hands when he said that like British Industry they would all gladly and gratefully adapt themselves to the new conditions so generously provided by the firm. (Loud applause.) He said that a lot of tosh had been written about him ('No, no'); well, if not tosh, tripe. (Cheers.) He had been lucky in all sorts of ways, but especially in being shipmate with some of the finest seamen in the world. He hoped that he would often sail with them again.

"Captain Cobb, in proposing the toast of the Firm, said that Sir Theopompous had tempted him to swallow the anchor and to come ashore for good to a shore-billet. He had sailed with many crowds in many ships, but could truthfully say that the *Hurrying Angel's* crowd was the best he had ever known. In fact, if they hadn't been, they would not be there that night. He had never known such weather, nor such men. He wished the Firm long prosperity, and said that while it employed such men it would be sure to have it.

"After Mr. Coggins (Cook), Mr. Cradley and Mr. Botloe had obliged with songs, Sir Cantrip Siskin, replying for the Firm, said that the old English motto was 'One and All,' and that while they remembered that, then the long pull and the strong pull would be a pull all together. (Applause.)

"At this point in the proceedings much amusement was caused by the performance of a nautical farce,

'The Limping Devil,' or
'Hell Afloat,'

written and performed by Messrs. Breinton, Mordiford, Rue, Pillows, Guller, Coggins, Okle (Carpenter), Cantlow (Sailmaker), Pencome and Staplow, with the assistance of Loach, whose singing of the song, 'Pump, boys, pump,' brought down the house.

"Mr. James Alfrick paid a well-deserved tribute to the Firm. He then asked all hands to stand for a minute in silence in memory of the much-loved shipmates whom the storm had taken.

"When this touching homage had been paid, the Angel Glee Quintet, Messrs. Aylton, Berrow, Evesbatch, Wallers and Suckley, gave spirited renderings of some old English songs, including such old favourites as 'Rocked in the Cradle of the Deep'; the accompanist throughout being Mr. Bert Kempley.

"Mr. William Purple, on being called on for a speech, gave the ballad, 'We'll go no more a-roving' (Byron), and said that he, too, like Captain Cobb, was going to swallow the anchor. He had got a job as caretaker on the water-waggon. (Cheers.)

"The proceedings terminated at a late hour with a brief speech from Mr. Aston Tirrold Harker, and the singing of " 'God Save the King.' "

When the last captives left the Skaian Gate,
And, looking back, beheld the fallen towers,
Crushing the young men's bodies in the flowers,
And heard the curses bidding them not wait,

And felt the spear-butts in the hands of hate
Strike as the stick falls on the beast that cowers,
They knew that they had done with happy hours,
Not even God could remedy their Fate.

No hope for them; but other Troys have risen,
And fallen, since, whose broken hearts have found
Comfort among the blackest nights that are,

Water in babble from the desert ground,
The Cock in carol for the Morning Star,
And Hope the living Key unlocking prison.

GLOSSARY

A.B.—An "able-bodied" seaman; formerly one who had served five or seven years at sea.

Alleyway.—A passage.

Amberline.—A light line or cord.

Backstays.—Wire ropes which support the masts against lateral and after strains.

Bald-headed.—Rigged without royal masts and yards.

Beam sea.—A sea breaking at right angles to a ship's course.

Bells.—Two bells (one forward, one aft), which are struck every half-hour in a certain manner to mark the passage of the watches.

Binnacle.—The case in which the compass is held.

Bitts.—Strong wooden structures (built round each mast) upon which running rigging is secured.

Block.—A sheaved pulley.

Boatswain.—A supernumerary or idler, in charge of much of the ship's smaller gear and holding considerable authority over the crew.

Bollard.—A strong upright projection of wood or iron to which vital gear may be secured.

Booms.—The space filled with the ship's spare spars. The spare spars themselves.

Bows.—The forward extremity of a ship.

297

Braces.—Running rigging by which the yards are trimmed to one side or the other.

Brace-blocks.—Pulleys through which the braces travel.

Breaker.—A wooden cask or small barrel.

Break of the poop.—The forward end of a ship's after superstructure.

Broaching-to.—Suddenly shifting course so that the ship's head points into the direction from which the wind is coming.

Brought aback.—In such a position that the sails are pressed by the wind against the masts.

Bulkhead.—A ship's partition or wall.

Bulwarks.—The ship's sides, especially those parts of them which fence the upper deck.

Bumpkin.—A small iron boom projecting from the ship's side.

Bunt.—Those cloths of a square sail which are nearest to the mast when the sail is set. The central portion of a furled square sail. The human abdomen (figuratively).

Buntlines.—Ropes which help to confine square sails to the yards in the operation of furling.

Caught by the Lee.—Taken unawares by a dangerous sudden shift of wind, as in a revolving storm.

Chocked.—Secured against rolling about.

Chocks.—Wooden stands on which the boats rest.

Cleats.—Iron or wooden contrivances to which ropes may be secured.

Clew-lines.—Ropes by which the lower corners of square sails are lifted.

Clews.—The lower corners of square sails: often spelled "clues."

Clipper.—A title of honour given to ships of more than usual speed and beauty.

Clove hitch.—A simple fastening.

Clues.—See "Clews."

Coach-work-mat.—A plaited cover.

Coaming, or Combing.—The raised rim of a hatchway; a barrier at a doorway to keep water from entering.

Cockbilled.—Pulled askew.

Coir.—Cocoanut fibre.

Companion.—A hatchway, or opening to a cabin. A staircase in the same.

Courses.—The large square sails set upon the lower yards of sailing ships. The mizen course is called the "crojick."

Cringle.—A round, flanged ring of metal sewn into sails at particular points.

Cringled.—Fitted with iron rings or cringles, many of which are let into sails or sail-roping for various purposes.

Crojick or Cross-jack.—The lowest yard upon the mizen-mast of a full-rigged ship; also the sail set upon this yard.

Crowd.—A crew.

Crutch.—A movable rowlock.

Davits.—Curved iron appliances to which ship's boats may be hoisted.

Day's work or Dead Reckoning.—A means of computing

a ship's position from her course and the distance traversed.

Dead Reckoning.—See "Day's work."

Dogwatch.—A short evening watch, from 4–6 or 6–8.

Donkey-house.—The structure containing the ship's steam engine.

Doublings.—The part of a masthead doubled by the foot of the spar above it.

Downhaul.—A contrivance of ropes and pulleys by which sails such as jibs, staysails, and upper topsails and topgallant sails can be hauled down before furling.

Drogue.—A floating sea-anchor, to which a ship or boat may ride in foul weather.

Dungaree.—A thin stuff like coarse cotton.

Fairleads.—Rings of wood or iron by means of which running rigging is led in any direction.

Fall.—A stretch of running rigging, especially that part handled in hauling.

Fenders.—Mats, wads, or pieces of wood used to protect the sides of ships or boats when lying alongside anything.

Fid.—A wooden marline-spike. An iron bar.

Fife-rail.—A teak ledge stuck about with belaying pins for the securing of rigging.

First watch.—From 8 P.M.–midnight.

Flog the clock.—Advance the hands.

Fo'c's'le or Forecastle.—A deck-house or other living space allotted to seamen. The men living in such space.

Fo'c's'le-head.—The forward superstructure.

Foot-ropes.—Ropes on which men stand when working aloft.

Foremast.—The most forward of the three masts of a ship.

Forenoon watch.—From 8 A.M.–noon.

Foresail.—The lowest square sail set upon the foremast.

Fore-tack.—A contrivance by which a lower corner of the foresail is secured.

Foxes.—Strands, yards, or arrangements of yards of rope.

Frap.—To wrap round with rope.

Frapped.—Wrapped and tied round.

Freeing-ports.—Iron doors in the ship's side which open outwards to free the decks of water.

Full-rigged ship.—A three-masted vessel with square sails on all three masts.

Futtock-shrouds.—Iron bars to which the topmast rigging is secured. As they project outward and upward from the masts they are difficult to clamber over.

Gaff.—A forked spar by which the head of the spanker is extended when set.

Galley.—The ship's kitchen.

Gantline or Girtline.—A rope used for the sending of sails up and down from aloft.

Gaskets.—Ropes by which the sails are secured in furling.

Gear.—Things proper to the work in hand, such as running rigging.

Gimbals.—A contrivance of rings upon pivots used at sea for lamps and barometers to keep them upright when the ship is in motion.

Griping.—The tendency of a running ship to turn her head to the wind.

Grummet.—A ring or garland of rope.

Gudgeon.—A metal socket.

Half-deck.—A cabin or apartment in which the apprentices are berthed. Its situation is usually the ship's waist; but it is sometimes further aft, and occasionally it is under the poop or even right forward under the topgallant forecastle.

Halliards.—Ropes by which sails are hoisted.

Handy billy.—A portable tackle or pulley for obtaining greater power.

Hank.—A twist or roll of light line or twine. A kind of metal ring.

Harness cask.—A tub containing salt meat.

Hawse.—The bows or forward end of a ship.

Hawser.—A strong rope, usually made of coconut fibre, laid in a peculiar manner.

Head.—The forward part of a ship. That upper edge of a square sail which is attached to the yard.

House-flag.—The special flag of the firm to which the ship belongs.

Idlers.—The members of the round-house mess, generally consisting of the Carpenter, Cook, Sailmaker, Boatswain, Painter, etc., are known as the idlers.

Jack or Jackstay.—An iron bar (fitted along all yards in sailing ships) to which the head of a square sail is secured when bent.

Jibboom.—A spar secured to the extremity of the bowsprit. In modern use, the bowsprit itself.

Lazarete.—A strong-room in which provisions are stored.

Leeches.—The outer edges of square sails. In furling some

square sails the leech is dragged inwards till it lies level with the head upon the surface of the yard. This is done by the first man who gets upon the yard, beginning at the weather side.

Lifts.—Ropes which help to support the yards.

Log.—A record of a ship's voyage kept by her Master or Mate, containing an account of the courses sailed, distances traversed and other remarks of interest connected with the voyage. Adverse comment on members of the crew in a Captain's log may lead to action by the Police on arrival in port.

Log ship.—A quadrant of hard wood used in estimating a ship's speed.

Lower Topsail.—The second sail from the deck on square-rigged masts. It is a very strong, important sail.

Main bitts.—A strong wooden frame, surrounding the main mast, to which much gear is secured.

Main-deck.—The open deck between the forward and after structures.

Main mast.—The midmost of the three masts of a ship.

Mainyards aback.—An arrangement by which the wind presses the sails of the main mast against the mast and stops the ship.

Marler or Marline-spike.—A steel spike, about 15 inches long, used in splicing ropes, etc.

Marline.—Tarry line or coarse string made of rope-yarns twisted together.

Mate.—The First, or Chief Mate is generally called the Mate.

Middle watch.—From midnight–4 A.M.

Mizen-mast.—The aftermost of a ship's three masts.

Mizen-topmast-head.—The summit of the second of the three spars which make the complete mizen-mast.

Mizen topsails (lower and upper).—The second and third square sails from the deck on the mizen-masts of ships.

Morning watch.—From 4–8 A.M.

Mudhooks.—Anchors.

Nettles or Knittles.—Light cords such as are used to spread and support hammocks.

One Bell.—A warning struck fifteen minutes before the end of a watch as a signal for the calling of the relieving watch.

O.S.—An Ordinary Seaman, not yet able to qualify as A.B.

Painter.—A line by which a boat may be secured to anything.

Pannikin.—A tin cup containing nearly half a pint.

Pantile.—A ship's biscuit, usually a round hard object, weighing four ounces.

Pin or Belaying Pin.—An iron or wooden bar to which ropes may be secured.

Poop.—A ship's after superstructure.

Poop-break.—The forward end of the after superstructure.

Port.—The left side of a ship, looking forward. A ship's window.

Quarter.—A little to one side of the after end of a ship.

Ratlines.—The rope steps placed across the shrouds to enable the seamen to go aloft.

Reef-points.—Ropes by which the area of some sails may be reduced in the operation of reefing.

Reel.—A part of the machinery used with a log ship.

Roaches.—The curved feet of "square" sails.

Round-house.—A part of a deck-house set aside for the berthing place of a ship's warrant officers.

Royals.—Light upper square sails; the fourth, fifth, or sixth sails from the deck according to mast's rig.

Sail-room or Sail-locker.—A large room or compartment in which the ship's sails are stored.

"Sails."—The Sailmaker is meant.

Scupper.—A channel at the ship's side for the carrying off of water.

Scuttle butt.—A tub containing drinking water.

Sennits.—Fancy plaits of several kinds, flat, round and square.

Shackles.—Rope handles for a sea-chest.

Sheer.—The line, curved or straight, of a ship's rail.

Sheet-blocks.—Iron blocks, by means of which sails are sheeted home. In any violent wind they beat upon the mast with great rapidity and force.

Sheets.—Ropes or chains which extend the lower corners of square sails in the operation of sheeting home.

Shrouds.—Wire ropes of great strength, which support lateral strains on masts.

Shroud-screws.—Iron contrivances by which shrouds are hove taut.

Sidelights.—A sailing ship carries two of these between sunset and sunrise: one green, to starboard; one red, to port.

Sight.—Observation of sun, moon or star, for determining the ship's position.

Skids.—Supports on which a ship's boats stand.

Skysail.—A little sail set above the royals in lofty, square-rigged ships.

Slatting.—The noise made by sails flogging in the wind.

Slops.—Clothes, kit, tobacco, knives, etc., etc., issued to sailors during a voyage and charged against their wages.

Slush.—Melted fat.

Southwester.—A kind of oilskin hat. A gale from the south-west.

Spanker Gaff.—A spar by which the head of the spanker, a fore and aft sail set upon the aftermost mast of a ship, may be extended.

Splice the main brace.—Drink and be merry.

Spreader.—A mast-head fitting of iron or hard wood; a light spar fixed to masts in certain positions so as to spread the standing rigging.

Spunyarn.—A light tarry line spun from rope-yarns.

Starboard.—The right side of a ship, looking forward.

Staunchions.—Supports or props.

Stays.—Powerful forward supports to masts.

Staysails.—Fore and aft sails set upon the stays between the masts.

Steerage way.—Motion sufficient to enable the ship to be steered.

Stern sheets.—A clear space at the after end of a boat.

Stow.—To furl.

Straik.—A streak or line of planking.

Swing ports.—Iron doors in the ship's side which open outwards to free the decks from water.

Tack block.—A purchase pulley used at the corners of certain sails.

Tackle.—(Pronounced "taykel"). Blocks, ropes, pulleys, etc.

Take a Caulk.—To sleep upon the deck.

Thimbles.—Small metal rounds or eyes spliced into ropes, or sewn into sails for various purposes.

Tom Cox.—To work Tom Cox is to loaf or cheat or idle.

Tomm.—Hit or hammer.

Topgallant fo'c's'le.—A raised forward superstructure.

Topgallant-mast.—Upper spar.

Topgallantsails (Lower and Upper).—The fourth and fifth sails from the deck in square-rigged ships.

Top-rim.—The edge of a small platform on each mast.

Topsails.—The second and third sails from the deck on the masts of a modern square-rigged ship are known as the lower and upper topsails.

Trick.—The two-hour period of steering.

Trough.—The hollow between waves.

Trucks.—The summits of the masts.

Truss.—An iron crutch or hinge supporting a yard upon a mast.

Upper Topsail.—The third square sail from the deck on the masts of square-rigged ships.

Watch.—A division (usually one half) of a ship's company. The space of duty kept by such division at one time.

Weft.—A flag knotted in the middle as a signal of distress.

Whack.—An allowance.

Yards.—The steel or wooden spars (placed across masts) from which square sails are set.